Rosaleen Love was born in S
and grew up in sub-tropical
lives in Melbourne, where sh
Philosophy at Swinburne Un
Her previous extraordinary collection, *The Total Devotion Machine*, was published by The Women's Press in 1989.

Also by Rosaleen Love from The Women's Press:
The Total Devotion Machine (1989)

EVOLUTION ANNIE
AND OTHER STORIES

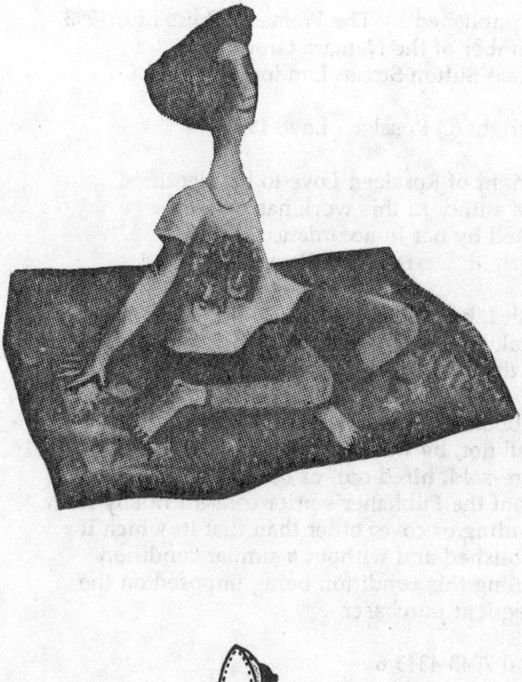

ROSALEEN LOVE

First published by The Women's Press Ltd, 1993
A member of the Namara Group
34 Great Sutton Street, London EC1V 0DX

British Library Cataloguing-in-Publication Data
A catalogue record for this book is available
from the British Library

ISBN 0 7043 4343 6

Typeset in 10 on 12 Palatino Roman by
The Electronic Book Factory Ltd, Fife, Scotland
Printed and bound in Great Britain by
BPCC Hazells Ltd
Member of BPCC Ltd

Acknowledgements

Some of the stories in this collection have been published previously. 'Evolution Annie' was published in Dale Spender (ed.) *Heroines*, Penguin, 1991; 'Cosmic Dusting' appeared in Helen Daniels (ed.), *Millenium*, Penguin, 1991; 'The Palace of the Soul' in *Overland*, Winter, 1991; 'Strange Things Grow at Chernobyl' in *Westerly*, June 1991; 'Blue Venom' in *Eidolon*, September 1991; 'The Heavenly City, Perhaps' in *Arena*, 92, 1990; 'Turtle Soup' in *Eidolon*, 1990; 'Hovering Rock' in *Aurealis*, issue 2, 1990; and 'Holiness' in Bill Congreve (ed.), *Intimate Armageddons*, 1992.

This book is for Nora

Contents

Evolution Annie

For Roy Lewis who nearly got the story right, but not quite[1]

You know all those stories of origins, those myths of our beginnings. 'A group of animals lived in the trees,' they'd start, and continue with the saga of how one day, down we came, we discovered the plains and the joys of upright posture. We stood up, looked around, and decided to stay.

I have to tell you something. That story is a myth. That wasn't how it happened, not how it happened at all.

I suppose you've read all about the importance of the dominant male in this early group, the primeval Father, and how civilisation began one day when a group of his sons got together and co-operated for the first time in rejecting their Father's authority. They killed him and ate him, or so the story goes, and that was the beginning of it all – guilt (naturally) and civilisation as the o-so-thin veneer covering the beast within, and since incest had something to do with this version of what we did to Father, this dark deed of our early days led (allegedly) to bonding outside the family group. For the greater good of the gene pool, some say, though I think that is stretching the evidence too far, imagining we knew all that back there in the Pleistocene, when of course we were just doing what came naturally. We had the trick of moving on to higher things. We had other reasons for doing the old man in.

Another story has it that we suppressed all knowledge of this dirty deed, sublimating it instead into the act of going to church on Sunday.

I ask you, does that sound a likely story? Just because it's complicated, and inherently improbable, doesn't mean it has to be true. Take hold of your own common sense in these matters. It sounds improbable because it is.

Call me Annie. Evolution Annie. Come listen to my tale. Let me tell you the story of our beginnings.

We didn't decide to come down from the trees as an act of free choice. We fell out of the trees and had to make the best of our new circumstances. It wasn't Father whom the boys killed and ate one day in the (alleged) first act of ritual communion. It was Mother who decided someone had to go, so she . . . but that is getting ahead of my story.

I am Annie, a diminutive prosimian, or so they will later describe me. I can tell you I am neither ape nor monkey, but something with the edge on both, as far as brains go, and their use in the skilful manipulation of what brawn I possess. Diminutive I may be, prosimian I am, but never underestimate the sheer animal cunning, the near-human intellect of the humble small prosimian. Look at the merry dance our bones have led you all, look at the clever way we've let fall a hint here, a hint there, that we were far more than we seemed.

Call me names, I can take it. Come on, 'Ape-like ancestor'! Ya, heard it all before. 'Primitive' – ouch, that hurts, that really hurts. I am what I am, and proud of it. 'Primitive' is a relative not an absolute term.

We know it now, though we didn't know it then – that we didn't need to progress much further along the line we were taking when we first fell out of the trees, but nobody could predict it, back then. Least of all Mother. If only she'd known she'd have made us climb back at once. Her death was to be a triumph of the simians, her rebirth a source of inspiration to us all. What we learned from Mother was that the bigger brain has not been worth the effort.

When we first fell out of the trees there was great consternation.

'This is it,' said Father. 'This is a sign from above that we must embark on a long and dangerous journey. Clearly the moment has come to get up on our two feet and take a long walk. We shall meet danger, and suffer discomfort, and we shall be sorely tried along the way, but we must go on, upwards and ever onwards.'

'That's a good idea, Edward,' Mother agreed. 'Why don't you and the boys go off and do all that, and we'll stay here in the long grass under this shady tree, and wait for you to return?' So the boys went off with Father, and some of them returned, after tests of fortitude and endurance which Mother agreed would surely have been too much for me, Annie, and my various aunts and cousins and sisters and their babies. While the boys battled raging torrents and the common cold from the icy blasts from the north, and sandy blight from the hot desert winds from the south, and lions, tigers, killer ants one way, the woolly mammoth in the opposite direction, Mother just sat underneath the tree. She taught us all she knew: sewing, rope-making, splicing, basketwork, the practical things of life, though she did not neglect our higher natures. Along the way she also devised the first alphabet, a fairly primitive affair in the light of what came later, but the little ones picked it up quickly. She baked a few clay tablets, for the cuneiform, she said vaguely, though she never did much with them, being busy at the time with plans for her funeral. Not for her the old ways, where we chewed the deceased around for a bit, and threw the bones out of the trees. She wanted something more for herself, a small burial chamber inside a largish pyramid, to keep out the hyenas, and our father, for eternity. (Though this was a passing phase. Later Mother decided the pyramid was not really her.)

Mother stayed at home and developed tools and the skills of reason. Father and the boys went out into the world and got cold and wet and suffered broken bones and fell into chasms and some of them survived frostbite, crocodiles, tigers, giant leeches that fell from the trees, snakes that rose up from the earth, poisonous berries (soon to be so labelled by my mother, the experimental botanist), killer crabs with giant pincers, elephants, and worse. So many ways for a primitive prosimian to die out there, but we were protected from it all through Mother's care and foresight. The male of the species, we knew it even back then, is more prone to accidental death. Staying home under the trees made excellent sense to us girls.

Fire, now, I'm sure you've heard their version of events. How Man the Hunter strode to the edge of the spitting volcano, bravely dodging the hissing dragons, the smoking sulphurous fumaroles, the lions, and bears that stood between him and the precious new discovery. Man the Brave strode to the edge of the bubbling lava, thrust a stick into the fire from below, and took it back, overcoming all the trials and tribulations of keeping it alight. Man harnessing an unruly Nature to his own ends. Man bringing Woman the tools of cooking. Man pointing the way to the Division of Labour, with Man the Hunter of Fire, and Woman the Grateful Recipient.

No. These are stories they tell, but they are truly myths of our beginnings. They are the yarns men spin around the camp fire to make them feel good about things.

Father didn't bring fire from the volcano. Fire just happened. One day there was a great storm, and a lightning strike, and fire came to the grassy plains of the veldt, and we ran before it, until it veered away from us. It left behind a few burning logs, which we kept alight out of scientific interest in manipulating and controlling our environment. Father was away doing something else at the time.

I don't want to make too much of it. Fire happened,

that's all. It was an event in our lives. Fire, from which, when we lived in the trees, we frequently had to flee, but now we lived on the ground, we could discover the value of the firebreak. Properly under control, fire could become a hearth, and with the hearth came the possibilities of a true home, in the sense we now know it. We couldn't do that when we lived in the trees. The forest would burn, taking us with it.

When Father first saw the hearth on his return home from what he and the boys liked to call hunting, but I call mucking around in the bush, the first thing he said was, 'Why did you have to ruin a perfectly good camp site by messing around with fire?'

Mother said, 'OK, you take it back to where it came from then. You and the boys, see that volcano over there? Kilimanjaro? Why don't you take this burning brand – mind you keep it alight all the way – and run up to the smoking crater at the top, and throw it in. Propitiate a fire god or two, and you'll feel a lot more comfortable.'

Father and the boys took some of the fire back to heaven, and they felt all the better for it, while Mother and me and the rest of us girls just got on with learning the finer techniques of cooking. Meat with the inside quite raw, and the outside thoroughly blackened, the way we liked it best.

Then Mother figured out a way to divert some water from the river down a channel and across the savannah, so that we had reticulated water and the beginning of a sewerage system.

'What are you doing, ruining a perfectly good camp site by bringing running water to it?' asked Father on his return, minus one or two of the boys. 'Dirt is perfectly natural, and we should all be rolling in more of it, such is nature's way.'

So Mother gave Father a goatskin full of water and told him to go off and find the source of the Nile, and return it to the Earth our Mother and then everything would be all right.

Before he left this time, Father called us all round him and gave us a lecture on the division of labour. 'It works like this. You women stay home, now we've got this hearth, not that I approve of fire in the home, the proper place for fire is in the volcano, but be that as it may, you girls stay here and make this place as nice as you can, in preparation for our return, and we'll go off and become the specialists in our field.' Father waved regally at us as he prepared to leave. 'You may, if you like, gather a few berries while we are gone.'

Mother saw it differently. She was developing the hearth-based multi-skilled workforce. Like Leonardo da Vinci who was to follow her so much later, Mother kept churning out the ideas, and some of them worked, and some of them were years before their time.

'Running round after wild animals will mark a dead end in evolutionary development,' said Mother, as she fed grass seed to what she called her chicks, small feathered creatures she encouraged round the camp site for their eggs. They had to be good for something, Mother reckoned. Burnt feathers tasted quite revolting.

'Without effort there can be no improvement,' said Father, kicking a chicken out of the way.

'I agree,' said Mother. 'After the Nile, you could try Mt Everest, and after you've done that once, you could try it a second time, without oxygen.' She was careful to remind him as she rescued a couple of eggs from in front of his feet, that if he was going to try Everest, he had better remember to take long strips of gazelle hide to wrap around his feet as moccasins.

Father's trips gave Mother the peace she required to get on with the work of her gravesite. She was quietly persistent on the topic of the afterlife. 'It will be a time of peace and quiet. Calm after the storm. Rest after work.'

'What about the boys, Mother?'

'There will be boys,' said Mother, 'but they will be changed. They will be more like us.'

Naturally we scoffed.

'The savannah will bloom, and the lion will gambol with the dove . . .'

My sister, Sukie, fell about laughing.

'And if you don't believe me, you can go down there and help with the digging.'

We said we believed her all right.

For the afterlife, Mother knew she would need a new kind of dwelling place, but she never could work out in her own mind what it should be. She moved on from the pyramid to the barrow, a pre-dug affair, basically a hollow chamber under a mound of dirt. 'Get cracking,' she'd say to the boys, first thing in the morning on one of their increasingly shorter sojourns in the camp. 'Hollow out those shelves there for the sacred relics.'

'Sacred relics?' Father would snarl and stamp off, but we noticed he used to slink back and listen when Mother explained what she meant. 'I'll need food,' she said, 'if I'm to set out on a long voyage into the afterlife. And I'll need a few of the comforts of home, a vase or two, and a pot for the unguents.'

'Unguents are unnatural,' said Father. 'We were born to eat pulverised cockroaches, not smear them on our bodies.'

'Take no notice of your Father. You'll all miss me, when I'm gone.' The little ones burst into tears, and Father and the boys could stand it no more, and went off to explore the ancient continent of Gondwana.

The invention of alcohol took all our female skills. Who else but Mother could take the grated root of one cassava, a few juniper berries and a handful of banana skins, and make something drinkable from it? Father would have us all dead from using the wrong cassava, the poisonous variety. Mother was the one who was rock solid reliable in all botanical matters.

The problems really began when the boys came back again. They returned from the life of action and started sitting round the fire drinking gin and causing trouble.

This time they proved more than usually resistant to Mother's plans to send them to China across the overland route. 'The Himalayas and the Gobi Desert. You know, over there.' She waved her hand in a direction in which they hadn't yet gone off. 'Spices, tea, trade. That's where the future lies. The Orient and its mysteries. Why not give it a go?'

'No,' said Father firmly. 'Pour me another gin, Giselle.'

Though Giselle spiked his gin with a deadly nightshade berry or two, Father survived, while crying feebly, 'Pour me another gin, Giselle. That last one packed a wallop.'

Mother called us girls together. 'Those boys will be the death of me,' she said, staring into her half-completed barrow.

How could we all combine to keep Mother out of her grave that little bit longer? Especially when some of the boys were getting rebellious. 'If she wants to go on a trip to the afterlife, why stop her?' they said. 'It's time she started going on one of those long trips she's so fond of sending us on. Let her see what it's like. And while we're about it, why not give her a shove along the way?'

Of course the girls told Mother, and she kept the boys on short rations for a week.

'I'd like a nice grave, facing the sunrise,' said Mother. 'Or perhaps the sunset. The sunset over that part of the savannah I always find particularly entrancing. Perhaps some idols in my grave, images of frogs, fish and snake, to ensure regeneration after death, and propitiate the Archetypal Feminine?' She kept the girls busy inventing sculpture.

*

It marked the turning point in the evolution of the prosimians, the way we were tried and tested again and again, whenever the boys came home with Father. Back they'd come and settle into the joys of hearth and home, and though Mother said she was listening to the travellers' tales, she often had that faraway look in her eyes, as if she was preparing a speech to which one day they would all have to sit up and listen.

The boys came home, some of them, and rolled around the rush floor wrestling, and they took the mickey out of Mother for her funeral plans, and Father sat down in the least windy corner and expected to be waited on, and that was the first time in human civilisation that women realised how much better off they were when the men were off and away doing their own thing.

The first act of human co-operation was when we got together, Mother and the rest of the women, and worked on plans to send the men away. We held what was probably the first Council of War about it. (This was before we came to the conclusion that peace was the way to go.)

'Annie,' said Mother, 'see that tribe of *Homo habilis* over the hill?'

'What, that lot that eat giraffe?'

'They're gross,' said my sister Sukie. 'Giraffe!'

'The eating habits of *Homo habilis* may not be our own, but that is purely because they have developed the stone axe, while we are specialising in the refinements of civilisation.' Mother recognised that the stone axe gave them an edge on us with respect to carving a haunch of giraffe, but she could see further than this. She could see the potential uses to which a pre-chewed thighbone of giraffe could be put.

War, for example.

'How'd you think they'd go in a battle with Father?' Mother had to explain what she meant. 'First one of them picks up the thighbone, and hits his neighbour over the head with it. Of course, the neighbour soon gives as good as he gets, and so it goes. It's called war.'

I shall always be grateful for the things my mother taught me. Though she soon decided that war was for the future, she was the first to recognise the possibilities, and the problems. She knew that if we went down the evolutionary path to war, the boys would take to beating up the neighbours, but she could think the whole thing through. She knew that once they got the knack of it, they'd soon take to beating us.

'Murder and mayhem are thoughtless, uncivilised, backward-looking activities, leading us one way only, back to the trees,' said Mother. She stuck to the peace, although she knew the threat of war.

Instead of warfare, Mother substituted cricket.

'See that thighbone of giraffe?' Mother asked my sister Giselle. 'I want you to go and get it for me.'

'What, go down into the valley with all those *Homo habilis* yoicks?'

'Now. This minute.'

'Why does it always have to be me? I always have to do everything.'

'Because you're so good at it,' said Mother, sending her off down the hill with a cheerful shove.

My sister Giselle was always the great whinger of the family, and the effect of whingeing on human evolution has never been studied, as far as I know. Whingeing doesn't show up in the bones, so no-one gives it any thought, but my sister Giselle was the first and the best at doing the least work round the camp and making the most fuss about it. Giselle whinged, and the more she whinged the more jobs Mother gave her to do, to take her away from the trees and out onto the savannah where the boys chased after the gazelles.

Man the Hunter, Ha! Man the accidental-tripper-over of the lion's left-overs, that's what those boys were. According to Mother, all this hunting business was merely a temporary abberation, useful for keeping the boys busy, but useless to anyone who wants to maintain an orderly camp routine centred round hearth and home. Someone has to mind the babies, and Mother regarded hunting as a device invented by Father to get out of his regular child-care duties.

Man the Killer Ape? I suppose when Giselle was sent off to get the thighbone of the giraffe (and Mother was right, Giselle did get it; it was thrown at her when she moaned and groaned about her wretched lot) the idea was perhaps then in Mother's mind, Man the Killer Ape. Hit Father over the head and be done with him forever. But Mother being Mother, as soon as she saw the possibilities shaping the bone into a bat, and a lump of chewed gazelle tendon into a ball, we became instead 'Man the Cricketer'. I have to hand it to Mother. As the ball was sent flying off across the savannah and various scores called 'runs' were marked up on the wet clay tablets, the boys made use of their enormous stock of energy and their oversupply of hormones, and we found a new use for the cuneiform.

As the shadows lengthened, and the seasons changed, and the chill wind blew from the ice, Mother knew that the cricket season had come to an end. Cricket, she wanted to believe, was the game which would best inculcate the team spirit, show the boys how to be good losers, and teach them that eye-hand co-ordination so necessary for leading them gently on to the higher pursuits of reading, writing, weaving and sewing.

Alas, Mother's fond hopes for the civilising influence of cricket on the prosimian male were doomed from the start. Father and the boys soon adapted the game to their own ends, and cries of 'Up yours!' and 'Howzzat?' delivered in an aggressive and unco-operative fashion, the ball hurled down the pitch with the intention of hitting the batter square in the goolies, the ferocity of attack when the bat connected with the ball, the way it sailed high in the treetops and fell to earth on some innocent toddling prosimian, all these innovations were too much for Mother.

Worse, much worse, was to happen once winter started, and cricket gave way to football. The neighbouring hordes wanted to join in, and our pleasant camp site was invaded each Saturday by groups of loutish *Homo habilis*, who introduced the custom of spectator hooliganism and punching up the umpire.

As she began to realise the unintended consequences of her actions, Mother grew quiet and spent more of her time uncharacteristically brooding in front of the fire. It was then that it started to sink in on us that Mother was growing old. Her fur was tinged with grey, her eyesight was not as keen as once it was. Sooner or later, Mother would lie in her grave, and we knew how much we would miss her, when she was gone.

These thoughts marked the beginnings of philosophy.

The way they tell it now, back then we suddenly discovered ourselves the possessors of rather large brains, so we used the surplus grey matter for thinking.

No. That's not the whole truth. The brain was still a bit on the small side when we first fell out of the trees, but down on the ground the hands soon grew strong and skilful in their weaving and sewing. It was the skill of the hands that drove the brain on to bigger and better things.

Try telling that to Father. He simply will not listen. Father believes in brain-led innate male superiority, because he has, by sheer weight of comparative size of everything else, more brains.

'Mere quantity alone,' muttered Mother, 'means nothing. Consider the case of the elephant. Huge brain, no sense.' She explained the steady growth of the human brain as the result of co-operative acts. It takes groups of people working happily together to erect grass humpies, to dig gardens, to create agriculture and a settled pattern of existence. The skilful use of tools in turn affects the neural connections in the brain, as new habits of life are forged, in ways not yet really understood.

Mother only knew that social change must give rise to physical change, and the prosimian brain did not lead this process. It trailed far behind.

We all knew that Father's behaviour was never any kind of argument for intelligence in diminutive prosimians, at least, in the male of the species. The females were different. There seemed some reason, in us, for the existence of sex-linked individual differences. We had the common sense. They had the wanderlust.

There were plenty of other differences.

'Is it, as Father suggests, that there is a good Father in the sky, who will guard us from harm, if we set about approaching him properly?'

'No,' said Mother. 'There is a good Mother in the earth, who asks only that the system of natural cycles of matter and energy go their own way, unhampered, through the systems of air, water, and earth. It's like this, Annie,' my mother would often say to me, for being the youngest in the family I was often about her furry knees, 'Annie, this life must be but a pale shadow of something quite other than it seems. There has to be something more to it than the endless round of gathering food, eating it, and using the sewerage system for its newly designed purpose. What are we training the little ones to collect berries for? For food, I know, but there must be another reason for our existence.'

So Mother reflected on the connections between things. She noticed the pathways in nature, how the berry changed its form and nature as it passed from the bush to become first food for the birds, then ready-mix guano fertiliser, then the new plant germinated from the seed, to berry again. Mother was the first to think this was about nature's bounty, the first to try to keep things moving round, to keep the carbon and nitrogen cycles in some kind of order. She was the first of the great recyclers.

In the rare moments when they were together, Mother and Father agreed on one thing only – the importance of stories for the moral development of the young, to encourage the young into proper patterns of good behaviour. 'Heroic behaviour,' said Father. 'Warm, nurturant, co-operative, sharing behaviour,' Mother would retort sharply, wanting to instil in her brood from the beginning the virtues of co-operation over the sin of competition.

So when Father told the littlies the story of prosimian Lucy and the big bad paleontologist who got the story of our beginnings quite wrong, and the bloodthirsty fate that befell poor Lucy when her bones were later dug up and displayed on TV, Mother told tales of daily life centred on the composition of the good compost heap. And if the eyes of the littlies glazed over somewhat faster with Mother's stories than with Father's tales of goodies and baddies, at least Mother's stories served the function of getting them off to sleep in a reasonably short period of time.

Mother's stories told them what Father's left out, that winning the race to be fully human was not really what it was all about. What matters is the kind of human being we develop at the end of the race, nurturing, caring, someone who will properly respect their mother's grave, when she is gone.

Sitting round the camp fire, combing each other's hair, catching the odd louse, tick, flea or other parasite, gazing into the fire, there we were, a group of happy prosimian women with but one problem in the world, what to do with the men?

'It's them!' said Auntie Elsie, as the dust on the horizon signalled a herd of stampeding gazelle, one sure sign that the men were on their way back to us, making the maximum amount of noise. Back from the away match in the camp down the road, and stoned to the gills on poisonous home brew.

'Why don't we . . .,' said Auntie Elsie. 'When you think of it . . .' She pounced on another louse at the back of Mother's furry neck. 'Why don't we just move on ourselves, leave the home fire burning and the empty cradle rocking gently, and the shelters deserted, leave a mystery behind, and just go off and set up camp somewhere else? Leave the camp to the boys. Just walk out and leave it all, leave the stuff of mysteries behind, leave, just leave.'

'Elsie, you always were a hopeless, mooning romantic,' said Mother. 'What, leave my lovely grave?' and we knew we couldn't ask her to do that.

'The way I see it, men are some small use. In youth, when female passion outstrips common sense, reason, intellect and whatever, and our hormones send us racing in their direction for those few short heady moments of passion which lead we all know where.' To the babies playing around our feet. 'But with age comes wisdom, and the recognition it's not really been worth all that trouble. The way I see it, we still need them, for the moment, to propagate the species and replenish the stock of babies, who, you know, fall all too easily to the marauding leopard or the rapacious fox.'

Ah, those long-lost days of the primal horde, before women invented the incest taboo. It had been all the same to us then, whether it was our brothers or our fathers whom we used to create the new batch of babies. We lived, unawakened, in a state of primitive promiscuity, not realising the future harm inbreeding might cause the human species. It's not true, what they said, that it was Father who unwittingly, through the manner of his death, instituted the custom of exogamy, of marrying out of the family. No, it happened well before Father met his fate at the hands of his sons. (You remember that story, where the boys were so furious when he ordered them away from their sisters, that the boys killed him and ate him?

Afterwards, it was said, they felt sorry for what they had done, and were consumed with a guilt so strong that from that day on they did what Father had ordered back when the fracas started.) Sigmund Freud invented that story, but only to conceal his own dubious motives, to hide the guilt he felt about inventing the crazy story in the first place.

No, the practice of marrying out of the horde into which one was born was the invention of Mother. When she sent Father and the boys off on their long and dangerous pilgrimages, the smartest boys soon got worn out with it all, and dropped off at neighbouring tribes along the way, where the local girls congratulated them on their cleverness, and begged them to stay. Some of the boys settled down happily, far from home, spreading their smart genes through a wider population. Genetic diversity, that's the key to evolutionary success, though we didn't think of it in quite those terms then. How could we use those words, when we barely knew the relationship between copulation and conception? Except that whenever the boys were home, conception happened all the time, and when they went away, we got a bit of a break from the child-bearing side of things.

From time to time Father came home, to replenish the supply of young males, and to take the next batch of boys on his travels. Occasionally, we girls would try to get our brothers to see the light, to encourage them to think that they, too, could be weavers and potters and writers like us, but no, it was in the blood, the urge to follow a male leader, even if he led them up mountains and through bogs and into immense hardship, at all times testing their endurance to the limit.

What us girls wanted to know was, why did they do it? What were they running away from? Us? What were they trying to prove? These questions remain unanswered, to this day.

According to Mother, the men could come and go, grow up and leave, after various fashions, but it was

Matriarchy which provided the solid core to society, the handing of camp fire sites down through the female line to the women. It made eminent sense to her. Through the institution of the matrilinear descent of property, Mother knew she could achieve respect in life, and exercise some control from beyond the grave. Marrying her daughters out to the horde made sense, when she started to think about it in terms of real estate. It multiplied the number of camp sites all over Africa, and round all those camp sites people would sit, and remember the tales of her exploits. Big Mother, the first of her kind.

Everyone knew the camp site belonged to the women, while the men bequeathed necklaces of hyenas' teeth and similar useless objects to their sons.

With respect to the housing crisis of the Holocene who, except Mother, back in the Pleistocene, made moves to protect their descendents in this way? Big Mother, the first and best of them all.

How to explain it, the bond that developed between us sisters as we went about our daily tasks, the feelings that arose in us, for the Earth, our Mother, of which our own dear Mother represented the living embodiment of all the caring, nurturing features we held most dear, the source of warmth and nourishment, rest for the weary, unguent for the harrassed soul. We developed a feeling of unity with the bare earth under our paws. We learned to feel special, because we alone stood upright, our eyes fixed on the stars, our feet planted on solid earth.

If only we could get the boys to see things our way. Mother was starting to work on her plan, except we didn't know what was happening, until it was over.

It was too good to last. The practice of exogamy, together with the invention of team sports, combined according to some relentless inner logic that Mother could hardly have thought through, to present us with problems on a large scale. How to stem the tide of aggressive mindless violence at sporting occasions, and increasingly at weddings, that seemed to be accompanying the widespread adoption of our customs across the savannah? Alcohol contributed, too, and towards the end of her life Mother grew increasingly sad at the use to which her bright ideas were being put.

She made several attempts at civilian control. The police force was brought into being, and the institution of human slavery helped get rid of the worst offenders, but Mother could see that Paradise could never be regained, not in Africa. The years slipped by, and Mother increasingly just sat by her barrow, waiting for the moment when she would enter it for the last time.

'The boys will see it our way, when I am gone.' She believed to the end that with her passing the religion of God the Mother would begin.

When our Mother said her time was come, we knew what those words meant. We knew what we were expected to do. She had grown steadily weaker, and now she could barely move from her bed of rushes to greet the new day with her customary invocation to the sky and the sun, the bringer of warmth, and earth the bringer of nourishment.

We took her announcement to mean that she wished Father to prepare the drink from the cassava root, and ferment the juniper berries for her last meal. We knew what that entailed. Father would get it wrong, for he never properly worked out the difference between the safe and dangerous plants.

Father was pleased to be trusted with a simple action of the hearth. He didn't notice when Auntie Elsie poured the rest of the drink on the ground, once Mother had taken her cup.

Afterwards we laid Mother to rest in her barrow grave, and placed round her offerings she prized, pots of cassava flour, a jar of sloe gin, a few dull heavy stones that she predicted would be called 'gold' in the afterlife, and last of all, her precious tablets of slate and clay, with the mysterious marks of the cuneiform upon them.

According to Mother's instructions, we refused Father's offer to help in eating the remains, and we made sure we sealed up the door with heavy rocks the way she wanted it done.

That is why we are here, today, and why we worship our Mother, the earth, and why we still drink gin.

That was the end of our Mother. Our Father met with a somewhat stickier fate, but that is another story. He may now be the tallest tree in the forest, and you should pay him your respects as you pass, but don't expect an answer from him. He is too busy pursuing the thrills of the chase in that happier hunting ground.

As you pass by the smallest flower in the forest, pause and reflect that it may be our Mother. Speak kindly to her, and avoid trampling her into the dust. She has moved on to a more reflective future.

Who knows, with this simple act of your consideration, the earth may spring a little under your step, your hair may lift with a cool refreshing breeze, and your travels may be a little more joyous along the path, because of her.

1. The story 'Evolution Annie' was written in part as a response to the very funny but very one-sided view of human evolution portrayed by Roy Lewis in *The Evolution Man*. (This was first published in 1960 under the title *What We Did to Father*.)

The Heavenly City, Perhaps

'I was in it for the money,' says the Hottentot Venus. 'But then what with death and all, I learned that what they say is true. What use is money if you're six feet under? It was not what I had intended for myself in life. Death was never part of my great life-plan.'

Paris, 1815. Cuvier, zoologist and anatomist *par excellence*, takes his stand. Dissector of the weird and strange, mixer and matcher of all kinds of animal bones, from the large to the very small, from the hairy Mammoth and the Indian Elephant, to the order of molluscs, not forgetting the structures of the creatures within the shell (as many did). He could sketch the whole animal from the smallest clue, a fossil paw-print, a femur, a piece here or a piece there. Where facts left off, there fancy reigned, and who was there to question him? Nobody, certainly not Sarkey, once she was dead and laid out on a slab.

The great Cuvier hangs his blue velvet coat on a hook, well away from the action. He rolls up his sleeves, catching his rings in the long red hair of his arms. He makes the first cuts. His bright blue eyes peer into the cavities he makes in the flesh. He commits to his prodigious memory all that he sees. He unpacks the body cavity. He orders his assistant to lift this part, toss that aside. Who needs ribs, the heart, or liver? A quick look, then into the bin. The brain matters, and the buttocks, and the mystery of mysteries, just what she kept forever concealed beneath her leather apron.

The assistant helps and listens while the great man talks. Of the Council of State, and the body politic of France. Of the epochs of nature, and the place of the Hottentot Venus, and her time of creation. Of the burdens of public life, and the robe of purple velvet with the ermine borders which he is designing for his official duties.

The assistant murmurs words of praise. The great man accepts them as certain knowledge.

Cuvier talks of the people he despises, the words he is writing on paper, the expeditions he is planning, the expeditions other people have planned without him, the books he has written, other people's books which have got him wrong. 'I never said I believed in the seven days of creation. They put that in, the English translators. What would they know of it? What care I? Let them do what they like, as long as they get the rest straight, the seven epochs of existence of the earth, the seven stages of earth history, the various catastrophes of flood and ice and fire. I never said it was the flood of Noah, the first catastrophe. Let the great unwashed believe that if they need to. I am a dissector in the cause of a higher truth.'

'The books I have been left out of, the ways in which I have been misrepresented, pass the jar, here comes the brain, the stuff I want to keep. Look at the size of it, small, small. To be expected of the lower races. Nothing much in the way of size. Or civilisation.'

'They say, Sir, she could speak three languages . . .'

'A hundred words of each. So?'

'That all?'

'Savage culture, savage mind.'

'Naturally,' says the assistant, as he prepares the pickling fluid.

Later, Sarkey stirs. The memory is there. The brain retains its desire and its dreams, and the knowledge that

2 plus 2 makes 4. Along with the French for 'Piss-off, you bumbling cretin,' though the voice is still.

My soul has left my body, and has gone somewhere else. I know, because I've been feeling very strange lately.

Shouldn't I be dead, though, if my soul has really departed? I hear what you say, and I have to disagree. It would perhaps be the case if my soul has gone for good, but I have evidence to suggest that the absence is only temporary, and that's the difference, between the dead and me.

It's not the living-dead stuff, either. Here I am, business as usual, except that there is one thing that is different from before. I lack a soul. My self has been divided into two parts, and part of me is here, the part that doesn't matter very much, and part of me is somewhere else.

I wish I knew what to do, how to find it, how to get myself together again.

I can't remember when I first realised how strange my life was becoming. It crept up on me slowly, a hint here, a hint there. I didn't see the overall picture developing, until the moment I stepped back – mentally that is, I can't really step back properly, not in my present condition – took a good look (metaphorically speaking) and said, 'This is weird.'

Mistake number one. They must have heard me, the people who have my soul, for immediately the impression of weirdness dimmed, the feeling departed, the light shone again, and everything seemed ordinary, and as it should be. The weirdness went away, but only for a while, and the next time it came back I was waiting for it. Things tried to slide themselves in under the threshold of my attention, but I was awake to them – the way the sky darkened towards midday, the hazy film over the glass. These were small things, but significant.

The people who have my soul don't know what they are in for. I know they've bought themselves some trouble. It's always been trouble, that soul of mine, and to tell you the truth, it's a bit of a holiday not having it round for a while, hovering above my mind and through it, guarding me from harm, perhaps, but not always.

Guarding her from harm, that was my job, and I like to think I did it well, until that moment of parting. Not that it was my fault. Sarkey never would listen to the voice of reason, clear and light as I always tried to be. 'I want to go to London, Paris, Rome and make my fortune,' she said, 'just for one year. Then I'll come back and buy a farm, and settle down, and life will go on as before.'

'You have your health and your beauty,' I used to say. 'Why risk it all for a few gold coins?' But, no.

I'll get back to her soon, and tell her about the deal I'm trying to swing for her. I just have to find my way out of this dump. The Heavenly City? Don't you believe it for a moment. Look at the cracks in the façade, and the places where the glitter is wearing off the streets. It's running down, that's what's happening and, as for the Garden of Eden, there are real problems there and I don't mean the snake this time.

From where I stand, I can look over the city walls and see the Garden of Eden beyond. Remote, of course, and inaccessible, the creation of some mad monk who lived off turnips and hallucinated regularly from malnutrition and too much mortification of the flesh. I know, I met him. He's here. This is what he dreamed up. I said to him, 'Great for you, isn't it? But what about the rest of us? Take me.' I said. 'All my life, my dream of heaven was a little farm of my own somewhere out of Cape Town, my own cattle, my own garden, and what have I got? All this glitter! All this paving over the good earth!'

Wait though, was that my conversation, or Sarkey's? Sometimes I think I am Sarkey, other times I think Sarkey is someone I can talk to as if she were someone else, though someone far away and long ago.

When the self gets divided, the I gets confused with the Me. To keep things clear, she'll be Sarkey, and I'll be Bartmaan. Sarkey Bartmaan, I and Me. When we were together, we were the toast of London, Paris and Amsterdam. Sarkey Bartmaan, the Hottentot Venus with the buttocks *extraordinaire*. Though where are they now? Here in the Heavenly City we're all clothed in long flowing robes which are some kind of seamless web with ourselves, and what is underneath is anybody's guess. A quick feel tells nothing. Since I am a soul discarnate, this body must belong to someone else. Mmmm. That's a problem, thinking that one through.

The Heavenly City is another puzzle. Underpopulated, empty even, for the after-life, considering the vast numbers that have gone through below. Are they all over in the other place?

The other place is never mentioned here. We think about it, or at least I know I do, and I know sometimes with other souls a conversation will start, then cut off abruptly, as if they too are wondering, but don't like to ask. Wondering if it's quite etiquette to mention the missing millions of the earth.

In the Garden of Eden, weird fruits hang overripe from the trees. Flocks of multicoloured vultures flap rhythmically in the sky. Below them, the lion lies down with the lamb and predators have turned fruitarian.

'Cape Town!' I, Bartmaan, told Sarkey. 'You're out of your mind.'

'You don't have to tell me,' comes the answer from the void.

'It's me that's out of your body, your black Hottentot body. Cape Town! Ha!'

'Black body, black soul,' says Sarkey. 'Watch it.'

I am, of course, pristine white, as are all the souls in

Paradise, except this being not quite Paradise the robes with seamless webs are starting to show the dirt. All two-hundred odd years of it.

Sarkey doesn't reply when I point this out to her. She's probably gone into a sulk. Thinking about how to get rid of me for good, I bet. But I know my duty. I shall return, Sarkey, though you spurn me. I shall bring help. I shall guard you from harm, retrospectively. Regard your present state as a slight hiccup in the system. Wait patiently. All I have to do is work out how to get out of here, then, let's see, all I have to do is to reverse the flow of time, just for two-hundred years or so, and then everything will be all right! 'Trust me, Sarkey! Wait for me!'

'Trust her! Wait for her!' Sarkey shakes, and bottles rattle. 'I'd rather be the way I am. I've grown accustomed to this place. It's home, nearly.'

The *Musee de l'Homme* in Paris.

Sometimes in this heavenly place I meet someone who tells me she knows someone who has seen an angel, deep in the dark of night. I've not yet seen an angel, but perhaps they may live beyond the city walls.

How many angels can dance on the head of a pin? I know the answer.

Nothing is impossible in the realm of the spirit, and an infinite number of angels will fit, because that's the usual way of looking at things. If an angel is pure spirit, if it can't occupy space, then it seems perfectly logical that a whole heap of angels, an infinite number even, can dance without fear of falling.

No.

How many angels can dance on the head of a pin?

Answer: as many angels as there are. There aren't an infinite number to begin with. Just some. They have names, most of them, and their population is not increasing. If they exist, that is.

Perhaps I can call on an angel, to deliver me from perfection. Where are the cracks in the city walls? They are never there when you need them. Some things still get repaired, and any path which opens outwards is first priority.

There is one way to go. The ladder of creation stretches from earth to heaven, through layers of water, air and fire and the ranks of plant, animal and human and angelic life. Cherubim and Seraphim. Thrones and Dominions are said to surround the heavenly city, if this is it. There is a path, if I can find it. There is a way, which I may find, if I watch closely the comings and goings. There is a path, and if I can't find it, perhaps I can get a message to Sarkey.

The ladder of creation, up which the angels climb. Though there is something rather odd there – angels have wings.

The glass shades over as the Parisian sky darkens towards midday. The waters close in. I can't look behind, but I know something is happening. I have been chosen especially. To make the transition from this world to the other. Instead of my soul coming to me, I shall be going to it.

There are two worlds, and I shall travel between them. There is a way, they now tell me, just as I've grown accustomed to this place. I must see what is there. To see if the glass, the waters are gone.

Jacob's ladder. Up which the angels climb, or so I was led to believe. A ladder set up on the earth, and behold the angels of God ascending and descending upon it, they said. Climbing the walls of the Heavenly City.

I should have seen it then, the problem with angels. They have wings to fly. They have no need of ladders.

Even then, someone knew that things were not quite right

I know Sarkey is coming to meet me, up the level terraces. I must escape from the Heavenly City, or what will be the use of her coming? She will be on the other side of the wall, and I shall be as far from her as before.

I need to get into the Garden of Eden, and ask the snake for help. Adam and Eve led that way, so long ago, when they found perfection intolerable. Though they tell that story differently as well.

Green vultures hover over red trees, savouring the smell of rotten apples.

Oh, for the wings of a vulture. From this place I shall fly. Far away to meet my Sarkey, far from the Heavenly City, where gold grows in the earth like calcified veins through a sick heart. Useless gold. Pointless glitter.

I lean over the battlements of the city, calling the snake.

A vulture rises from the centre of the garden, and drops a rotting apple in my lap.

Sarkey lived for a while in London, then Paris, until the fever came, caught from posing naked, or nearly so. She posed for the *grands gens* who crowded into her showplace, and watched her as she turned, first one way, then the other, displaying her backside to all who paid to enter. Steatopygous. Large. Enormous. At the extreme end of human variation. They did not think her quite human, then, though she spoke their languages – French, English, and her own. She was different. African. Primitive. Black. 'Though he was wrong,' said Sarkey, 'the great Baron Cuvier, when he said I was a little closer to the apes than the average Parisian.'

Sarkey said she knew what she was doing, then, posing in a cage in front of the populace. 'Better than scrubbing floors and ladling out the pigswill. I was for a short while mistress of my soul, ditto my body. It was my property then, or so I believed. The cage. I was not unhappy. It kept them from me, the people who came to stand and stare. It kept me safe from harm, more than that soul has managed to do. At least I knew where I was, with the cage and its iron bars. I was inside, and the people, the *bons gens,* the *gentilhommes,* those who came to stare, they were on the outside, looking in.'

The great Baron Cuvier. Who now knows the full extent of his errors. Where is he now? I, Bartmaan, never met him in the Heavenly City. He must be one of the missing millions of the earth. He must now reside elsewhere, in the other place which no one mentions.

I am a traveller between two worlds, and it takes some getting used to. It takes time to gather myself together, to chase away the panic.

There are branches of trees up above, where once there was glass. I can see the ground beneath my feet, and it is crawling with creeping plants. There is a path here I must follow, quickly, before the ground opens into a chasm into which I shall fall, a one-way path to the centre of the earth. Which earth? This earth? Or another? This world, or the next?

I turn myself around, to face the truth.

I am on a piece of level ground. Boggy, muddy, my feet in the primeval sludge. Above me rise the terraces, each different from the other. The ladder of creation leads through all the grades of life, each rank in order after the one before.

Just underneath the topsoil, the crumbling bits with micro-fauna wriggling Collembola like vegetarian maggots, guided by blind instinct and a tendency to business. They are so energetic, those tumbling creatures, one stage up the scale of being from the plants. They will flourish on the next terrace up, while plants stay rooted in one spot, steady, solid, centred on this part of earth. If it is earth, this part of the ladder of creation.

Woodlice, too, they will have their day. As the great Cuvier said, from crayfish to squilla, from squilla to Ascidiacea, from Ascidiacea to woodlice, then to Armadillidiidae and on to galley worms. Stages on the ladder of creation, leading downwards. Rungs on the ladder of complexity, leading to simplicity.

The dissection pleased the great man. It showed him what he knew already, that the Venus was aptly named for the lowly sensuality of her nature.

'It is finished,' says the great man. He must keep the parts from harm, defeat the forces of dissolution and decay. Quickly, quickly, place the specimens in the jars, secure the tops, and hurry, hurry from this place, before the decay seeps through into his own bones, infecting him with death.

Slash the pudenda, neatly in one go, and into a bottle of formalin. Poke into the buttocks, noting their wobbling fatty consistency. The head also attracts his attention, for its cranial capacity, the brain, what is its size, how does it relate to race, to a place on the chain of being which starts with the most lowly of mosses and mushrooms, and stretches most surely up to God?

Cuvier knows Sarkey is definitely lower by far than the angels, and just a step above the Orang-utan. He knows he is right. He is a man who knows where true knowledge lies. In his head. He finds the skull a skull like any other, the brain the usual grey and white, though her thoughts do not speak to his knife.

His curiosity is spent. He prepares to leave. What is left on the table is tipped into the boiling vat. The flesh is stripped off. The skeleton will later be prepared for exposition in the *Musee de l'Homme*.

Sarkey will have her farm. It will not be somewhere out of Cape Town, for time does not run backwards, as I discovered. Time marches inexorably one way only, and will not change its innate ways, even if I could persuade the angels to climb off their pin for a few brief moments and perform a miracle or two. Time will never run backwards, not for them, or for me.

We lived happily ever after, Sarkey and I, when I found her again, soul and body reunited. We farmed some land on the upper terrace. There are some animals of the hairy ape type that live in trees, and a small tribe of *Homo erectus* over the hill, but it's 'live and let live' here, each with our own version of Paradise, instead of someone else's notion of the Heavenly City. They never let us into the kingdom of the fully human, Cuvier and his kind, classifiers of animals and plants, rocks and people.

We're better off out here.

If I climb on top of the iron roof of the cow-shed, I can see the walls of the Heavenly City. The cracks come and go, the self-repairing schedule still operates, but at night I can sometimes hear, if the wind is in the right direction, the wailing of the saved as they sink once more into the despair of eternal perfection, eternally not quite right.

Cosmic Dusting

I once saw the end of the world and I was quite impressed. It was in a science museum in London, in diorama. At one end of the room there was our solar system at its beginning, condensing from a swirling cloud of interstellar dust. The stages of planetary history followed in succession, to our time, our blue-green earth. But the scene that really hit me between the eyes was the end of it all, where the sun goes supernova, its outer shell explodes, and the long dead planet earth is caught, consumed in fire, and returned to the cosmic dust from whence it came.

I saw time spread out in space.

I saw myself on the blue-green planet, a coherent mass of cosmic dust temporarily organised into something called 'life'. It was a long haul from the primeval sludge. But the question science does not ask is, why bother? The earth, with its thin veneer of wonderful life, changing, growing, coming in the end, to what? Cosmic dust. All this for nothing.

The diorama haunted me, long after I left London and came back to Australia, where the earth is enduring and the sky is clear, and the end of the world seems remote and untroubling.

I searched the libraries. I tried, oh how I tried, to get people to talk to me about the end of the world, the true meaning of eternity. Cosmic dust.

We all pretend it's not happening. We all go about our

lives, as if the end of the world isn't going to happen. As if the dust wasn't there.

It is as if we live in two worlds. One is the world where it will happen, and the other is the world where it won't happen, the world where everything will always be the same, where this country will be remote, and untroubled, where this universe will swirl forever onwards.

That must be the trick of it, to know when to jump, to know how to leave one world, the world where it will happen, and leap into the world where all is peace and stability.

In the old days, they thought they had the answer to this one. Death, they said, that's the answer. But the more I learn about death, the more I think that it is not the answer to my problem. To believe that death is the gateway to the other world, you have to take on board some weird ideas, and I don't know about them. You have to believe that Giants once roamed the world, and that men lived on earth to the age of Methuselah, you have to believe that men lived 200 years in full possession of ripe masculine urges, before they begat their sons on wives whose age is not recorded, they being the chattels on whom the begetters begat the begotten.

You have to believe that this world is on a pilgrimage, of a different kind from the version given by the cosmic dust to cosmic dust account. You have to believe that this is a world in transition from the Garden of Eden to the Heavenly City. You have to believe that the period of transition which we call earth history, human history, is all rather unimportant. You have to believe that women may be resurrected in the form of men, which presents some problems for the possibility of procreation in the Heavenly City, which we are assured may happen, provided it is pure. You can see my problem. I am being asked to believe in the purity of heavenly lust.

You have to believe that there will be a moment on the path from the Garden of Eden to the Heavenly City when the Millennium will be announced, when the Messiah will come to rule in glory, and the just shall be vindicated on this earth.

There was a man, once, who walked the streets of Sydney. I never saw his message, but others did. Every now and then, down he'd stoop, and take from his pocket a stick of chalk, and there on the pavement he would write a one word message to the world:

ETERNITY

Asking the question, what about the time before the beginning, before the creation of the world, and what about the time after its destruction, which is most properly called eternity?

The man who wrote the word eternity must know by now, what it is, if it is. Or else, in his grave, he lies at peace, not knowing. Not knowing he doesn't know.

Either he knows, or he doesn't.

I read everything I could read about the subject, of eternity, of where was time, before time began, but I didn't find the answer that way. Not by reading.

Life went on, and the intensity of these ideas gradually receded. They weren't with me every minute of every day. They dipped back into the dark recesses, which is where true danger lurks.

I should have known. I should have been on my guard. Dust, cosmic dust. Once you start thinking about it, you see it everywhere. On the tops of bookcases. Along the skirting boards.

I read stories about a red dwarf, and a blue giant, and a galaxy of stars, and the cycles in nature and eternity and the Millennium and cosmic dust.

There are two cities, this city, and the Heavenly City of the philosophers.

There is no cosmic dust in the Heavenly City. The souls of the saved do not spend their time in dusting, or washing down the walls. They contemplate perfection. They spend their days looking at perfection and saying, isn't it perfect?

Dusting is done by angels in Paradise fluttering their wings.

There will be no debates, no arguments, and there will be an end to gossip. Everyone will be perfect, and there will be nothing to talk about, really.

There will be no arguments, because all arguments are based on disagreement. If everyone knows the answer, then there is nothing to say, nothing to talk about. Except how perfect everything is.

To be infinitely bored, for all eternity.

Then it hit me. This story cannot possibly be true. The absence of cosmic dust, the inevitability of heavenly boredom, the imperfection inherent in perfection, these things pointed the way to a different interpretation of the future.

They said at the end of the nineteenth century that it was science which heralded the Millennium, the age of progress. They did not mean, the end of history, progress, they thought, having the knack of progressing indefinitely.

They assumed the Messiah would be male. What if she's female? What if the poor and oppressed who will be vindicated will be the women of this earth? I wanted to add role-reversal to my personal list of Millennial requirements. Think on it, though, how will we know the Messiah, when she comes? I want to know how I'll know her, when I see her, so I won't get excited about the next female prime minister without cause.

Playing the old patriarchal games, though, getting carried away with their stories, their plans. The more I thought it through, the more I realised we need to rise above God the Mother to a truly participatory democracy of the most advanced kind. Why must there be just one Messiah, who will rule 1,000 years? Why can't there be a worker's co-operative governing the Millennium, why can't there be a true participatory democracy of the most advanced kind?

We will know the time is coming when things start to work for us, not against us. We will know the age of the Millennium is upon us when all committee systems function perfectly. We will know the new age is dawning when a committee meets to draft policy guidelines on admission to the Heavenly City, and these guidelines will work precisely, admitting the just and excluding the unjust, without error.

We will know the Millennium is upon us when we choose to elect our Messiah. It will be a rotating position, which will be held by 1,000 people for one year each, a true democracy of the future. Fair will be fair, and another sign of the Millennium will be that of the 1,000 who will share the rule for 1,000 years, 500 will be male, and 500 will be female. The falling out of the numbers will come about not as a result of any conscious policy, but will be decided purely on merit. The Messiah Nominating Committee will not sit and think in terms of last year male, this year female, no, it will happen by natural justice, for the Millennium is when the just shall inherit the earth, or what's left of it.

That brings me to another point. The earth, what's left of it, will, at the end of this period, be returned to its pristine Edenic condition, that is part of the story, and that will come about, at least, that's how I see it, by a core group of Green Guardians, who will non-coercively, but because everyone agrees that Green is good, begin a wholly voluntary 1,000 years recycling project, so that at the end of this time, every plastic shopping bag will be returned to its original petroleum constituents, every broken bottle will be unfused sand, squeaky clean on an unpolluted beach, and aluminium cans will be changed to bauxite under a rolling sward of pristine bush on the top of which the Dodo will gambol with the Moa.

The question of lust in the Heavenly City, and whether it will be pure, is something the relevant committee will have to look at closer to the end of the 1,000 year period. I don't pretend to know everything yet, though of course I will, when at the end of my earthly travels, I reach the Heavenly City of the feminist philosophers.

I think this version of events has greater credibility.

This is my recipe for the Millennium, and it is as likely a story as any other. I shall wait and see. Meanwhile, as I walk the streets of Melbourne, I have a plan.

The key to eternity is here, within my grasp.

It is a piece of chalk, and as I walk, I stoop to the pavement and I kneel before the world.

I write my message with dust, chalk dust, in dust, pavement dust.

I write one word:

ETERNITY

Hovering Rock

Hovering Rock has been part of my life for as long as I can remember. We often took the road from town north through the stone country; and out along the back roads there it was, a curious rock formation standing out from the others, though they were unusual enough, formations of balancing rocks, large rocks poised one on top of the other, dotted here and there around the landscape.

It was, I now know, a special feature of the landscape of my childhood which then I took for granted, that everywhere there were rocks like these; old, weathered rocks settling, with time, through layers of soil, so that years later they stand, one on top of the other, balancing.

None is as beautiful as the two-rock formation I call Hovering Rock.

I was always pointing it out to Dad, whenever he drove past it, because at some angles, at some places along the track, the top rock actually seemed to hover above its base, sitting there on top of what seemed like a clear couple of inches of air.

Dad was never able to look, not properly. He always said, crossly, that he was driving, wasn't he, and someone had to keep their eyes on the road or there'd be a crash. Mum would say, 'I don't see it, Charlie, are you sure?' and then Dad would tell us both not to be so bloody stupid, there is the law of gravity, and rocks can't hover inches above the earth. 'Imagine it, what it would be like, this country, if all the rocks just sat up there and hovered.'

'Easy to clear them off,' said Mother, looking for a spot of peace. 'Just give them a push, and away they'd go.'

I thought so then, as I think now, remembering those places, that it would be nice to see all those small stones, and the large ones, too, just there above the earth, not on it, and we would walk along on the small stones, like kangaroos bouncing over grass, only we'd be the ones in the air this time. We'd help Dad clear the land, easy, easy. The little stones we could just sweep over to the edge of the paddock, and the big ones, they'd be harder, perhaps it would take two of us to get them moving, but once they were set in motion, away they'd go too, and we could build a fence for Dad, too. Or we could pile one rock on top of the other, so that there wouldn't be just two or three balancing stones, but whole vertical spires, and people would come to our farm and marvel at the self-buttressed stone towers and pyramids of Gunya.

It didn't happen that way.

These plans came back to me, years later, when I saw the first men on the moon and the care they had to take with their rock samples so they wouldn't bounce off into the void. It didn't seem as strange to me as it did to other people watching, that rocks could be light, that rocks could be hard to catch, that they might just float away if the astronaut wasn't careful.

Life on planet Earth seemed quite dull by comparison, where rocks adhere to earth, mostly, and where they do not, where the land slips and the rocks slide, it is best to run quickly away.

Hovering Rock. That was a long time ago, and other things have hovered round me since, getting between me and the light.

Too many dark places, too many evasions, too much sorrow. Too much work, too little love. Hovering Rock.

I want to go back to where I began. There is a place, in the past for me. There is no place here.

*

I did go back, one day.

I found myself on the road. I took time to travel slowly. Why not? It was, after all, my time. I planned to go back there and just see what it was that I remembered so clearly.

I thought it would be like other memories of places, that I would go back, and find two small rocks, unexceptional in size, nothing much to remember with such force, such clarity.

I drove through the town and out the other side, into the country. I found the old farmhouse, still there, though crumbling and unpainted since we had all pulled out and left, when first Dad died, then Mum had to leave. It looked as if we needn't have packed up and gone. We could have stayed on because no one else moved in to care, no one cared at all. The wooden verandah sagged, the stairs broken, their treads long rotted through. I went round the back and peered in through spiderwebs on the dirty windows. Bare rooms, curling old lino on the floors, the kitchen still as I remembered it, the wood stove. I could see the remains of the chip heater in the wash-house.

On impulse I decided to set in motion the task of buying it back, because money was something I had, and memories were something I needed to recover from the buried recesses. There may be such a thing as possession of the past, like property, like things. Money frees me from confusion on this issue. If I want it because it will help me think clearly, then I will have it.

I do not ask for peace of mind. All I want is some kind of balance between the good times and the bad. Equal shares of both, I'll settle for that. Not the present continual down swing into the depths, when memory dredges up only the bad things, rarely the joys.

If I possess this house, I shall possess part of my past, and perhaps I shall walk here, and feel that there was something good that happened back then, if only . . . if only.

*

I set out to find the rock. The rock of my memory, the rock that I once saw from the road, hovering, unrocklike.

I parked the car in the shade of a gum tree, and climbed through the wire fence. There it was, across the other side of the paddock, steady on its base, as it should be, according to the laws of gravity. I walked through the long grass keeping it in view, and reached up to touch the top boulder. It felt warm, smooth, sand-worn. At rest. Definitely not hovering.

It was late afternoon and the sun sinking in the sky.

I did not feel disappointed. I knew my childhood vision had to be a trick of the light. It was peaceful, and I sat down and looked across at it, set against the fading light.

What if, instead of two rocks one on top of the other, this place marked the entrance to another world? So many possibilities – a chink in space and time through which travel is possible, the pathway to parallel worlds which exist alongside our own, which spin off at each moment when paths diverge, or the gate through which ghosts and ghouls pass from the other world. It might be the entrance to the Celtic underworld, where all the animals are white, and the sky sits like a leaden lid upon the black landscape, and the people are proud and cruel.

If the rock rests on nothing, nothing but air, then a quick push should reveal any one of these possibilities.

Later, I'll try pushing it later.

On the African veldt there is a custom that if a traveller dies, and he has companions to bury him, on his grave they place a small pile of stones. Passing travellers pick up stones in their turn, and add them to the pile. It is a simple act of reverence before the mystery of death, from one traveller who is continuing on the path to another for whom this place marked the end.

It is not the custom here.

The dead have left this place but their departure has

gone unmarked. They left no monuments. They travelled light, and light as air they passed away into nothing.

Not into nothing. Perhaps that is the secret of this rock. Here there is a gateway. Here there is a pass.

I am ready for the rock. I am ready for my childhood vision to be repeated. I want to tear the veil which stands between me and the light. I have made my decision. I know what I am doing.

I am waiting.

I am in the place of marvels.

Yet how ordinary it is. Some trees are dead, victims of dieback. Their silver trunks stand stark to the sky, but round them the new trees grow green. When the trees died, they all went together, that was the alarming thing. It seemed as if the death of this landscape might be the beginning of the end, might be signalling the death of all landscapes.

There was a fighting fund established, to find the cause of the disease. Some said it was too late, because the real culprit was modern life. The trees were suffering from stress. I gave a donation. Any tree suffering the effects of stress certainly has my symathy.

It wasn't the end of Nature, not that time. It only seemed like it. What appeared, for a while, to be an epidemic sweeping through the country was found on further investigation to be simply part of the long-term cycle of birth, growth, and death. The trees were much the same age. They died at much the same time. One hundred years of growth, then death. New trees germinated in the spaces left by the passing of the old. The death of one landscape signalled the rebirth of another. The bush lives on, though changed.

If I cross this paddock and go over the hill I shall find a creek. It flows round large redstone platforms where snakes and lizards bask in the sun. If I go over the hill at dusk, I shall see platypus surfacing and skimming along the grey-black water, before diving down to feed on the small creatures on the bottom of the river.

Rocks and hills, trees and clear blue sky, the air cool, but not yet cold, brisk, that's the word, pleasant, the autumn sun sinking, with the promise of a sharp night to come.

I remember Marty and the frenzy she felt before her despairing end, the sad desperation of the suicide who must follow certain rules for killing herself. There must be order in the ultimate act of disorder, there must be a logical link of cause to effect in the descent into chaos. There was ritual, too, the tablets, and the bottle of Scotch, and the note, the expression of loss, the statement that the balance of her mind was definitely not disturbed. Indeed, it is a moment of great clarity, she wrote, the act of ending it all. No muddle, no confusion.

Why rest in this world, when there is another? Why keep the spirit bound to just one possibility?

I had not thought like this before. I had always thought 'She is gone' or 'I miss her'.

My mother's life was hard, yet she did not lean towards death with gratitude for its promise. She fought to the end, and won her small battles with her body, forcing death to wait until after the spring, so she could plant seeds saved from the year before, demanding more space still, to sit in the summer sun, always this game, this pushing time back, the creation of just a little more space, for just a little more time.

Death had to catch her when she wasn't looking.

Marty chose her time.

This place has been here, I have known it has been here, since my childhood. I have chosen to come back now. I could have found it then.

It is getting dark. I shall go soon. After the soft sun of this autumn day the night will be cool.

*

I turned to look one last time – and I saw it – a gap at the base, and through it through the gap, a few strands of late sunlight shining. This place is not at all strange. This place is perfectly ordinary. Nothing special. Trees, blue sky, a few clouds, grass, rather dry this time of year. The bush is still. No wind. There are sheep in the far paddock.

It has happened. I can see it. Rising.

No, it isn't.

Levitate, rock.

Rocks do not rise in air.

This one will.

Yes.

My heart leaps.

Bubbling hardening cooling weathering. Lava plains, red soil, point of rest, point of peace, hovering hovering over the rock on which I shall settle, rock to rock, face to face, point of perfect peace.

Water splattering, water flowing, sand, air, smoothing to this round shape.

This is a special place.

Fire, winds, ash, rock. Rock crumbling, grasses in clefts, flowering creepers, ferns, then trees.

First the cold, then the burning. Death first, then rebirth. From the deep places rock extrudes, molten, flowing.

Cycles of change

Balance, harmony, rest, equilibrium, poise here, on this rock, in this place.

Rock talk, rock face, rock art, finger tip to finger tip, hands hands across my belly. Tip to tip, left hand to right, right hand to left, hands painted on me, hands outlined. Rains come, hands go, hands long gone, comfort gone, hands linked in comfort, hands linked in knowing, hands touching hands, good hands, strong hands, wise hands, ancient hands. Hands long gone. Wind and rain, a long time ago. Time flows, earth moves, stars circle, place remains, space is mine to command. I am this space, this rock.

Here, now, here is always here, now is always something different.

Space, my place, hands circling me, hands lifting me up in the air, from this place my place, now placed in air. Hands lifting, hands moving. Healing rock, rock of peace, hovering rock.

Just one rock, several tons of it, lighter than air, floating.

I came home.

The rock floats above its base. I sit here and I can see what lies beyond. Nothing strange. Blue sky shading to grey, pink streaks in the sky as night draws on, trees, some living, some dead. Sheep graze on the distant hills. I can see my car on the far side of the paddock.

Pink streaks in the sky, but where is the sun? Before, when I was looking at the rock, the rays of the setting sun shone in an arch around it. Now I see through the gap, but there is no sun.

I see my shadow. It falls before me onto the rock.

Beyond the rock the sky is blue, the trees are green and white, the sheep move on the hill.

Between me and the rock the grass is green. The sun is behind my head. Between me and the rock . . . my shadow before me, the sun behind me.

Between me and the rock . . . I turn and face the other way. I face the setting sun, where the light falls on me, pushing my shadow onto the grass, onto the rock.

I turn around.

He sees children rolling stones to the edge of green fields. His father is happy with the task so simply done. He sees his mother and his sister. They are bounding along in a field of stones, and their feet are light, and they are dancing with rocks, and his brother hurls a stone along the ground and it skims as if on water.

Are they sheep on the far hill, those white figures? He

strains to see, against the sun. No. They are men in white jumpsuits. They are astronauts without their helmets and glass visors. They are picking up pieces of moonrock. Moonrock? This moon is green and fertile. It is not a cold place of barren rock. The trees are green and thriving. There is no dieback here. This is the moon that might have been, given oxygen and water, given life.

Moonrocks have their secrets. He will soon learn of their attachment to the earth their mother.

If he turns slightly, and looks down the valley, he can see a procession of dark-skinned travellers. They are walking past a rock grave. Carefully, one after the other, each takes a rock from the top of the grave and places it on a small spire in a corner of the paddock.

If he keeps watching he will see what happens when the last rock is gone.

He turns back to the rock, and sees, for the first time, a pattern of painted hands around the circumference. Someone has taken the hands of another, placed them on the rock, and outlined the fingers with white ochre. Finger tip touches finger tip all the way across.

The owners of these hands will soon come forward to welcome him.

The locals point the rock formation out to their children. If you go the back way, then you can see the rock balancing on a fine point, looking for all the world as if the next strong wind will push it over. Sometimes, on very hot days (it must be some kind of mirage) it seems as if it sits slightly above its base and hovers there, just a few inches up in the air.

It's a fairly recent discovery, Hovering Rock, and it's become a bit of a local attraction. People take their children there on hot summer days and endless arguments go on, as to whether it really is a trick of the light, or whether at times the rock rises and hovers at rest in air, the wrong element entirely.

A Pattern to Life

There was once a man who made his mark on the world, and he travelled to Australia. Tom Huxley was a good lad, industrious, with aspirations. He'd been apprenticed to a physician, and at nineteen saw more of London low-life than he could bear. Australia though, that proved different. He joined the navy, and travelled, with time for science and for self-improvement. Sailors fell ill, but there was little he could do for them. Either they got better, or they died. There was surgery, and sea-burials, and time for other pursuits.

So began the wanderings of a human soul. The naturalist examined the strange life of the sea; and the anatomy of the smallest sea-creatures, the gasteropod, the nautilus, the limpet, the barnacle, the sea-urchin, the starfish, the cuttlefish, the sponge. These were the strange members of the sixth class of the animal kingdom, the class Linnaeus called Worms, those left over after he had given everything else a kingdom and a name.

Huxley sought harmony in Nature, and he found passion in himself. He believed that Nature works according to a plan. He wanted to discover the rational order which pervades the universe, nothing less. In 1845 all seemed possible.

The details caused some concern. Did life show variations on a single theme? Was there a unity in diversity? Or an ideal form and endless modifications of it? To each its own spectacular shape and size and symmetry around an axis, and behold the starfish, the sea-urchin, the brittlestar, the jellyfish, the sea anemone, the left-overs in any scheme of classification.

So many different ways to live without a backbone. Nature is prodigal to the spineless. Jellyfish, sea-urchin, each is adapted to life in its own way. Classification, that was the problem, to describe a plan in nature that was both logical and necessary.

There is a mythical classification attributed (by Borges) to a fictitious Chinese sage. There is a pattern in the animal world. There are animals which belong to the Emperor; some are dead, and embalmed; there are trained animals; there are sucking pigs. There must be room for mermaids, and fabulous animals, and stray dogs. There are those animals which are included in this classification and which may be excluded from others. There are creatures which tremble as if they were mad.

The Chinese scheme seems eminently reasonable. Innumerable ones, yes, they exist; those drawn with a fine camel-hair brush, that's a problem. Who is the artist? The author of the plan, or the Chinese sage? 'Others,' the Chinese sage continues, and adds those animals that have just broken a flower vase, a common experience and a link with the stray dogs. Lastly, the Chinese scheme includes those which resemble flies from a distance, and this links the classifier with the classified, the observer with the observed, the human with the insect, the parts with the whole.

Some animals belong to the Emperor, and in Huxley's scheme of things there was the Emperor Linnaeus, Lord of Classification and Creator of Order from Chaos. Linnaeus made room for mermaids, and fabulous beasts, the *Paradoxa*, the Other. The Chinese scheme could be made to fit, just, the new order of life.

Huxley preferred theory to practice, with the architecture

of Nature, and he cared little for the addition of a few new bricks to the structure. He found strange what was thought to be known, and not yet worth knowing, the new organism, the unknown species.

Three months out from Portsmouth he was deep in the study of jellyfish, the *medusae*. He was troubled by his dreams of greatness, not knowing whether they were folly, or prophecy. Jellyfish! Was there glory in *Coelenterata*, or profundity in pelagic life? He gave way to gloom. The waters of Marah, dark and bitter were its springs, and he knew them well. What honour could there be in examining the anatomy of the jellyfish? Aspiration and achievement! How closely he desired the one to follow upon the other. Yet he was insecure and undecided. He asked himself if all was vanity and self-deceiving blindness.

The plan sustained him. He wanted to discover the point of balance round which the whole zoological universe swings, forces which work in the early stages of animal development, forces which direct the embryo to grow this way, or that. Forces the Chinese sage did not know about, nor could he.

The ship arrived in Sydney. After eight months at sea, Huxley longed for life beyond salt-beef and jelly-fish. There was a round of parties, of calling and being called upon. Sydney in 1845, three balls and two dinners in one week!

He met the Fannings, and Mrs Fanning had a sister, a dear little sister, and Tom and Nettie fell in love in quite an absurd way, at first sight, at second sight, and then they must part for a while, she to her sister, he to his ship. They did not meet again for months.

It was the way of the world in 1845. Nettie loved him with her whole soul, she prayed for his advancement in temporal and eternal blessings. She believed the Designer of the plan would guard Tom from harm.

Tom was not so sure, but he still believed Nature had been designed by an Infinite Intellect with Benevolent

Intent. How else could it be, with such a harmonious variety in unity?

'You linked some flowers for my hair,' said Nettie.

'You talked of orange blossoms,' said Tom.

The plan at work again. The plan must have courtship ritual, orange blossoms and a wedding, and hearth and home. The hearth and home of a poor struggling man, moped Tom. What right had he to take her, to disrupt her life, to give her new anxieties, new cares? Still, the plan worked, and he married her, later, much later.

It was Nettie who drew the mermaids and fabulous beasts with a fine camel-hair brush, while Tom's ship was sent to chart the Inner Passage of the Great Barrier Reef.

Hurrah for the hydroid polyps! Hurrah for the corals and corallines! So spoke Tom as he burned with the desire to fit them into his grand design.

He wanted to work, but the rain got him down. There was a foot of water in the cabin, and the stench of timber, drowned rats, decaying starfish, cockroaches, dead and floating.

The plan, he couldn't work on it, when it was hot and stinking. He slept, and read bad novels, and hated himself for neglecting the wonders of pelagic life.

Outside the Reef, inside the waters of Marah.

Two ships sailed north from Sydney, with Tom Huxley still surgeon on the *Rattlesnake*. Edmund Kennedy sailed in the *Tam O'Shanter*. For one, it was a voyage of discovery, for the other, a voyage of doom.

Aspiration and achievement, how quickly they desired the one to follow on the other. Aspiration and inspiration! Kennedy knew the fatal wreck made of the lives of those who mistake one for the other. He dreamed of greatness, but his dreams proved false. He sought the source of the inland rivers, Australia's Nile, and he found Cooper's Creek. He had a plan of a kind. He believed he must follow his calling, sacrificing all things to it. He believed his calling was to lead white men to Cape York.

Black men were there already. No need for them to discover the path. They had the honour without the glory.

Kennedy left for the Cape. Huxley must stay with the ship.

Through jungle, mangroves, swamps, high mountain ridges, Kennedy must press onward to the Cape, or die. Onward to the Cape, and die.

Kennedy dreamed of gentle hills, rolling grasslands, rivers shallow enough to ford, native shepherds for his sheep. The people will be friendly, and curious, creeping out at night to stare at his camp in the green and pleasant land.

His sheep were lost. His carts were abandoned. His horses were eaten. Malaria weakened him, and starvation took his men. At the end he died within sight of his goal, speared through the side, bruised by stones thrown at him in his last agony. Jacky wept for him as he dug his grave.

Kennedy died. Huxley lived. Random life, chance death in the ritual of predator and prey. The wrong place, the wrong time for Kennedy, Cape York, 1848. Chance? No, Tom could not believe in chance. Nature was too intricate, too subtle. Nature was a poem.

Others said Nature was a crazy list compiled by a mad Chinese sage.

Benevolent design, in the pattern of Kennedy's life and death? No design, no pattern, chance alone, chance encounters with hostility. He was lost in a mistaken calling. He was a thief in the Garden of Eden. To the dispossessed of the earth he brought gifts which would destroy them. They killed him. Why? Their land was taken, and they were given in return the mysteries of the Holy Redemption. Fair swap? What did they think? Ask them, and they replied, 'No.'

Huxley linked together the polyps of this world, those that tremble as though they are mad, the coral polyps in their fixed communities, the hydroid polyps, the freely swimming *medusae*, the jellyfish, and the *siphonophora*, those that have a siphon to dredge their food for them.

He became famous. He had a plan for his life. He planned to abstain from petty personal quarrels, and succeeded, for he became embroiled in large and impersonal controversies. He planned to be tolerant, and succeeded, except with humbugs and hypocrites. He claimed indifference to plans for glory, and found he must accommodate himself to fame.

He met Charles Darwin and discovered a new twist to the plan. It was chance alone, said Darwin, that has brought us to our present greatness. Nature seemed fixed and stable, but that was illusion. We were at the summit of creation, but for how long? What we call rest is unperceived activity. Peace conceals a silent but strenuous battle. We live in a scene of strife, in which all combatants fall by turn.

Huxley was convinced.

There's a mythical classification attributed to a fictitious Chinese sage. We're told of the division of the animal kingdom. Some animals belong to the Emperor. The Emperor is Darwin's God of Blind Necessity operating in a universe of chance. Some animals are dead and embalmed. Proof of the slowness of change. Cats from the pyramids of Egypt, cats from the streets of Naples, there is no difference. There are trained animals, where animal intelligence is at work, and learning, and adaptation to the strange environment of the lion cage and the dolphin pool. There are sucking pigs, elements in the festive food chain. There must be room for mermaids, and fabulous animals, for these show the powers of the human imagination, and the inheritance of human culture. There are stray dogs, who teach the survival of the fittest and Nature red in tooth and claw. There are all those animals which are included in this classification, both vertebrate and invertebrate. There are creatures which tremble as if they are mad, and this must mean tube-worms, and sea-whips, and soft coral. Innumerable ones, and these the micro-organisms and the micro-plankton of the sea. Those animals which are drawn with a fine camel-hair brush, that's not a problem, for a classification scheme must have a classifier. 'Others,' states the Chinese sage, with reason, for there will always be others, new species to be discovered. Those animals which have just broken a flower vase are included as an example of a domestication process as yet not 100% complete. Lastly, those animals which resemble flies from a distance are included for their habit of mimicry and their practice of protective colouration.

In the end, Tom found no plan, no planner, no God of Israel, no God of a Beautiful and Benign Nature, but the God of Blind Necessity operating by means of the ruthless struggle for existence in a universe of chance.

Turtle Soup

Coretta woke at five when it was still dark. Some words that Morrie had said the night before were still tumbling through her head. 'This is where it all begins, the cycle of life and death, the measure of nitrogen and phosphorus, on top of the islands, underneath them, in the groundwater, in the shit.'

She woke early, and went out into the darkness of morning. She was on Isabel Reef, the edge of the world, with only a few scattered coral cays between her and the open ocean, then South America half a world away. Everyone else was still asleep from the party the night before.

Sunrise over the reef. Their ship had moored last night in the lagoon. No island, just reef, so no work last night. Most other nights they'd been up late banding the birds on the islands.

At first she'd been nervous with the birds but Alan had reassured her. 'Just do it. Catch one. Make up your mind. Be more decisive than a gannet. It's not hard, you'll see.' She saw. The birds dithered, and as they tried to work out whether to fly or stay, she caught one and tucked its wings under her arm, ready for Alan to clip the band around the right leg. Half-digested fish splattered over her jacket. She counted the ticks on the beak, certain at any moment they would take to the air, leaping like acrobatic snails to land on her face.

'Don't worry, bird ticks won't stick to human flesh,' Alan said, but then Alan never worried about anything.

Booby birds and their nests. Messy, bumpy affairs. A coral corral, a small circle fencing the young chick in, with perhaps an added seed-pod or a few scraps of rubber or part of a metal coat-hanger. Two eggs in some nests, with perhaps two very small chicks hatching, but of these two only one survives. In this place of beauty so much horror, the harsh lessons of existence learned so young.

The sea was calm, too calm for the windsurfers, who liked it windy enough to push them off in the direction of Equador, until one of the coral outcrops sent them tumbling. 'It's OK, Corey,' said Malcolm. 'All you have to do is work it so when you fall off, you fall into the sail.' 'Not for me,' said Coretta. She preferred the sea to the air. She loved the hidden depths.

Above her head the sky was the colour of pale midnight. Clouds circled the horizon catching the glow of the new day. The ocean was flat, clear to the horizon line, where the sheen of the sea left off and the dark shapes of the clouds began. Dead flat sea, the arc where sea met cloud, and behind the cloud the glow of the new day starting.

She knows the earth is round, that there is no edge off which they will fall. Just as she knows which way is up, and the sky is there, the earth is here.

But this morning things were different. In the stillness, pink sea became pink air, and the sea was the sky, and the ship was sailing upside down on air, the waters above instead of below, and the clouds on the horizon were really hills; and the pink glow of the sky, the pink sheen on the water, were interchangeable. The ship sailed upside down, like a plane doing stunts, and she was the only person awake to know what was happening, sole witness to the inversion of the world.

She was suspended in air like the human fly in the circus act, who walks upside down on the ceiling, and smokes a cigarette and reads the paper, though his hat must be glued to his head and his boots slide along magnetised tracks.

Suspended with the sky, the sea, both glowing pink, she

could not tell the difference between them. The waters, once below, were now above the earth, if this was the earth, with no fixed point of reference round which the rest of the world should swing.

Water and air alone, and no way to tell the difference. Up, down, up is down, down is up.

Old distinctions did not count any more.

The moon. If she turned she could see the full moon to the west, in what must be the sky. Reassurance has been sought and found. The moon, rock solid up there in the air, suspended, though heavy, floating, not of this earth.

The sky above changed to pale grey. Blue streaks showed just above the horizon. The row of hills became clouds. The illusion of inversion was broken. Behold the real dawn, the sun breaking through the clouds, the new day setting full-steam ahead for summer.

The spell was broken, or perhaps it was only just beginning. Corey stayed thoughtful, and ate rather less than her usual hearty breakfast.

Her days were relatively free. Bird-banding was night work. Day-work, trying to count the birds, that was a joke as they wheeled aloft in their thousands on human approach. So many birds they must surely stack themselves feather to feather when undisturbed; with others in holding patterns above, waiting clearance to land. The frigate birds were the easiest to count, high in the sky, and never very many.

At Gannet Cay they'd counted five frigate birds, kings of the old weather station, zooming in on the top perches and scaring off any birds of lesser species that might be sitting there. 'So they can be top. So they can shit on everyone else,' said Malcolm. 'That's what I want. That's why I want to be a professor.'

'Malcolm a professor!' Alan asked around. 'Would you take a degree from this man?' Everyone laughed.

Probably not, thought Corey, *though for other reasons.*

Malcolm will die a spectacular if accidental death, and soon. When he isn't scuba diving he's falling off cliffs attached to ropes. Here on the reef he's chasing sea-snakes one minute, going out of his way to stir the small sharks into a feeding frenzy the next.

Corey never went swimming with Malcolm.

They moved on from Isabel Reef later that morning, and anchored at lunchtime near another small cay.

By mid-afternoon she had finished her work for the day, entering up the bird results in the official records.

Time for a swim, in face mask and snorkel and flippers. The underwater world, that was why she was here, why everyone she travelled with loved their work.

The ship was anchored on the leeward side of the island where the reef sloped steeply down into the deep water. Corey took her time, swimming slowly over to the reef edge, revelling in the moment when she would spot the tiny blue damsel fish which marked the place where the perilous drop into the depths shaded over into the safety of the reef flat. The bright colours of the fish first attracted her attention, then the muted colours of the coral. Slowly she made her way over the flat and into the soft blue shallows. Underneath her the coral sand shone white, and two transparent diamond-shaped fish wriggled through the shining water.

According to Morrie this was where the island was tipping over itself, as the wild winds blew the sand across from the other side, and the currents undercut the bank to windward. There, where the ledge sloped steeply, the sand would fall over the edge down into the depths, and would be lost from the cay. Soon the birds wouldn't nest there any more, and the patch of coral sand would be visible only at low tide.

'Why worry?' That had been Alan. 'The winds will change, and the sand will blow back the other way, and who knows, the island might end up getting bigger the next cycle of swings and roundabouts.'

Enjoy the moment. Corey swam up one end of the beach, and back again.

Suddenly, keeping pace beside her, she saw it, her first turtle for that day, larger than life in the tricks played by the underwater light. It was a lovely animal, perfect in its motion, at home in its element.

Swimming easily along together, both she and the turtle reached the end of the island. Then as she turned, not wanting to go round to the wild windward side, the creature turned too, and towards her. The powerful beak-like jaw was close, too close. It was most likely a loggerhead; they were mostly loggerheads at these unvegetated cays. A carnivorous turtle, with a jaw that could crack clam shells in two.

Behold the face of the turtle, and its deep brown eyes. Notice its calm indifference. *All the better to ignore you with,* thought Corey, except during that moment of turning, when she felt a definite frisson of danger. She kept pace as the turtle swam back up the beach. She wanted to keep swimming like this, along with the turtle, for ever. The turtle gave a slight wave of each of its flippers, while she had to work hard against the current.

What if the turtle turned on her, what if it knew that she was a member of a predatory species? What if it remembered past wrongs, what if it bore grudges like she did, what if it started to act like a person with a large list of justified grievances? What if it held race memories of turtle soup and the canneries?

Ridiculous thoughts. Above her the frigate bird, beside her the turtle, bird and beast complementing each other in the chain of life. She felt strange only because she was the intruder here.

Sea and sky, which was which? Easy. The bird belonged to the sky, the turtle to the sea, and hovering between them, flying on the surface of the sea, snorkel in her mouth, flippers on her feet, as birds fly through air, as turtles swim in water, Corey slid in slow motion. The illusion of the early morning returned. The sky below, the sea above. Sea and air, earth and sky, everywhere and nowhere, limbo, belonging to no one element, absent from home, an awkward webbed and goggled intruder in the habitation of other beings.

A brown gannet landed on the water, just behind her head. She found it when she turned and nearly collided with it. *One of mine*, she thought, excitedly. She saw two blue legs under the water, and two webbed feet, and a silver band on the right leg. She looked up through water to air, and saw the brown body at rest on the surface of the sea. Disconcertingly near, curious.

Strong birds, strong necks, the quick swivel, the shake of the head, the deliberate spitting of half-digested fish down her jacket that night, her hand slipping quickly over the beak to clamp it shut, the struggle, until the bird grew passive, resigned to its helplessness.

She could not eat that regurgitated mush. She would be the chick that did not survive, preferring to starve rather than eat slimy putrefying stinking fish. Alan, now he'd be the chick that survived. 'You have to look at it from their point of view. Yum, yum, baitfish, pre-scrambled.'

Turtles. Once they took the females, ripe with eggs, easy to catch as they laboured up the beach to their nests.

Stupid, when you think of it.

Simpler to catch them than the males that never come on to the land.

The death, the mindless destruction in this place.

The turtle swimming beside may be a female, heavy with eggs. Must be, why come so close in to shore otherwise? Waiting her turn to crawl up the beach, to labour and be delivered of her eggs. Sixty at one go.

The death, the destruction . . .

Guilt. Pointless guilt. Sham guilt. She had never killed a turtle, never would.

The booby bird floated on the water. The dallying bird. The sea was warm. The languor of the turtle. Behold the languorous turtle heavy with eggs.

The revenge of the killer turtle. In the midst of so much beauty came the words, the words came from nowhere.

They call loggerheads carnivorous but that doesn't mean, can't mean, people. Fish, mainly, that's all they eat. Crustaceans and crabs. Clams, too. They crunch up the whole clam, then they spit out the shell. In large pieces. Powerful jaws. Beak like a giant parrot.

No, it's a green turtle, a nice algae feeder. Munches ocean grasses. Down there, below, what is there? No ocean grasses here. Not since the mainland.

No ocean grasses. It must be a loggerhead.

Human flesh, though, they haven't got the taste for it.

No, of course not.

Nobody said, 'Beware of the turtles,' the way they said, 'Beware of the sharks. Look out for the single fin.'

The end of the beach again. Another turn. Turn the other way, don't go back. Stop this. Now. Just go on, swim round the edge of the island into the wild side. Don't stop, don't turn with it.

Struggle against it. GO THE OTHER WAY.

The turtle looked her straight in the eye. The connection became more intimate. Gone was the previous indifference. The turtle matched her stride, her stroke. If she stopped, the turtle stopped. Lying in wait.

She will get out of the water. Now.

The turtle was there, though, between her and the beach. The turtle has chosen it that way.

Get out, get out of the water, quickly.

Yes. No. It's only a turtle.

The turtle would not allow it. Corey decided not to go, not for the moment. It was warm in the water, and it was a lovely day, and this was her holiday, and it was only a turtle. She would not get upset. *Only a turtle.*

A killer turtle.

The booby bird, just behind. There. Not leaving, not flying off. Waiting. Lunge for its legs, that will scare it off. Oh. It just moved out of reach. Two blue legs, two webbed feet, one silver band on one leg signifying this bird is banded. It has been caught, labelled and measured, details of its sex and age noted. Alan banded it. Alan is a bird-bander, fully certificated. He is the only person allowed to do the job. It wasn't me. I only caught the birds for Alan. And Alan is gentle with the birds. They have to be gentle with the birds, bird-banders, or they don't get the certificate.

The bird, the turtle.

The frigate bird, what was it doing? Swooping lower now. It was way up before, circling the island far above lesser birds. The flurry when the frigate bird swoops, the way it dives down and takes food from the beaks of the stupid booby. Just on dusk.

Dusk. It is getting late.

They saw it, just on dusk, the booby bird returning to its nest, gorged with fish, and the frigate swooping low, the fight, the booby disgorging, and the frigate flying aloft, victorious. Engorged. Stuffed with fish.

Frigate birds flying high. Why was that one swooping down, so low? Why was it here, what was it doing? Not dusk yet, that's when they feed, and the gannet had no fish in its mouth. No. Yes. The beak came down under the water, and a few dribbles of bubbling fish leaked out. It stirred up the small school fish. They scattered.

She will get out. She was getting cold. She'd had enough swimming. *She will stand on the island, and put her hand up straight in the air. She won't try and swim back to the ship. She will put her hand straight up in the air, and Morrie will see her. He always keeps a look out from the ship, and he'll hop in the tinny and putter over. She won't swim back today. She doesn't feel like it.*

The magic has gone from this reef. Look, over there, where the coral begins. Two Crown of Thorns starfish one on top of the other. Eating each other. Injecting each other with the venom of dissolution. Sucking out each other's insides. Little Crown of Thorns eggs will be discharged, little Crown of Thorns babies will float round her while she swims.

She had never noticed it before. The water felt quite slimy.

No, it doesn't, it just feels wet. Water feels wet. This water definitely feels wet.

A cup of tea.

She will go back to the ship, and make herself a cup of tea, and lie down for a while. Too much sun. Too much sea. Too much sand.

The frigate bird hovered just above her head. She could feel it, even though she had to keep her head down, to keep an eye on the hovering turtle and the blue feet of the booby bird.

Now the frigate bird was so close, surely the booby would fly off.

No. It seemed to be waiting, for something to happen. For the world to turn upside down.

Her arms were heavy, heavy. She tried to move them, to pull herself through the water. Sludge, she was swimming in sludge, and it wouldn't let her move. *Her feet, where were her fins, why won't they fin her over to the sand, why can't she swim to the island?* Her arms were heavy, her legs floated useless, her feet were imprisoned in large pieces of rubber.

Why was she wearing this clumsy gear? To buoy her up. She did not want to be buoyed up. She needed to go down, to sink, to escape. *Where was her weight belt? Didn't put it on. Didn't think she'd be meeting a killer turtle, a fighting frigate bird, and a booby bent on revenge.*

Float, with a hand in the air. Signal for help. Morrie will be watching. He liked to know where everyone was, in case something happens.

Something was happening.

Something has happened. She turned to put her hand up in the air. She lay on her back, floating in the water. Her mistake. The gannet waddled through the water onto her chest. Its beak tapped on the glass of her mask, demanding entry. Chunks of fish dribbled out onto the glass.

A mistake to turn like that. Brown gannet on her chest. Booby bird, booby. Bird. Trying to feed her. Raw fish, slimy with mucus, bubbling with fish digestive juices. Yesterday's fish.

The frigate bird swooped. The frigate bird would take the food and fly off.

No. The frigate hovered instead over her face, black wings flapping. Mouth open. Fish inside. Its feet struck at the snorkel. The birds worked together, co-operating, tugging the snorkel, pulling it from her mouth. Corey's mouth. *She won't open it. Her mask, she can't breathe. She will have to open her mouth. She can't stop, can't stop herself trying to breathe. She can't raise her hands to her face, can't brush off the birds, the one on her chest, the one flapping at her face.*

'Look,' Alan had said, back on the island, back in the safety of the land, the safety of air. 'Let the bird bite you, go on, you've got gloves on.' She let the bird bite her, and she didn't feel it. Not a thing. Just a firm pressure, nothing more.

Today, though, no gloves. *She must breathe. She must move her languorous arms, use her weak hands, find the snorkel, place it in her mouth. She must breathe. One breath, a deep breath, then . . .*

Half-chewed fish dribbled down her snorkel. The birds were stuffing it down, as if she was the baby chick with mouth wide open.

They were small birds. She was bigger than them.

The fish was in her mouth. *She must do something. Move. Spit. Vomit. Add her digestive juices to the mush.*

The birds will eat what she spits out. They they will try to force it down her throat again.

The birds, always just out of reach. More birds were coming. Boobies with bands. Frigate birds, circling above. Uniting together against the enemy. Corey. She was the enemy. *No, no, she wasn't. Bird-banding doesn't hurt. She wasn't stealing eggs, she wasn't going to steal the birds, stuff them for a museum. Mostly all that stopped long ago. She was just someone who wanted to come, to see it all. A passerby. An onlooker at the game of predator and prey. She wanted to see the beaches where the turtles came in to lay. She wanted to see the glories of pelagic life.*

Catch the turtles, turn them over, turn them into soup. All that is over now. It happened so long ago. Most people have forgotten.

The waters, blue, shimmering, translucent, closed over her head. Her mask fell away and down, slowly sinking, carried by the currents down and away, snorkel still attached. Through blurred vision, with smarting eyes, she saw the turtle, waiting. The waters were above, the sand below.

She is innocent.

The turtle waits in the shallows, coming up occasionally to breathe. It's getting late. On the island the birds are settling down for the night. The sun is sinking. There's been a spot of bother from the boat. The small dinghys are out, all three of them, and they're out there looking for something. 'Jesus, this is terrible,' a voice floats over the water. 'You just don't know where to begin to look, when something like this happens.' Round and round the island they go, searching. As darkness falls they go back on the ship.

The turtle remains in the water, circling the island. Round and round. When the full moon rises, she will be able to see, and she will leave the water and haul herself onto the beach. Jerkily, one limb moving after the other, she will pull herself up beyond the tideline. Then over the top to where the coral rubble has been thrown up beyond reach of the tides. There she will lie for a while, exhausted, until some store of energy comes to her aid. She will move her limbs slowly and rhythmically, and with determination she will hollow out a body pit for herself. When it is deep and wide enough, her limbs will rest, and with her rear end she will dig a deep egg chamber. Her lower body will heave as she extrudes sixty round white eggs. Then a short pause to recover, the sand pushed back into place, and off she will lumber, back down the beach again.

Down deep into the ocean, to the hidden places of dark memory.

Blue Venom

A message shot from the fax machine and flew across the room. No sender, no identification, a bare message centred neatly on a bare sheet, and fast, as if jetting through the system at twice the speed of light.

DOWN FROM THE BRANCHES FALL THE LEAVES

Adua noted the time it arrived and placed it on top of the others. There was no signature, no point of origin. That's impossible, Adua was told, when she inquired. There's always a point of origin. It's the way the system works.

'If that's the way the system works then the system isn't working,' Adua said, though no one listened.

The first morning of the conference the delegates swarmed into the office.

Adua did her best. 'Can I help you?'

'Me? I'm the person no one talks to.'

'I'm talking,' said Adua. 'What's your name?'

'Martine Landau.'

Adua searched her list.

'I'll tell you why no one ever talks to me. The last conference I went to was awful. I don't know why I bother. Either no one will talk to me, or they all talk at once and tell me where I'm getting it wrong.'

'You're not on the list.'

'The last time, those guys from Bee Botany, brown shorts

and yellow shirts, wow, those two, they dressed like that to confuse the bees. They thought I was trying to do an exposé on the Bee Botany fraternity. Bee Botany, who cares?'

'Are you sure you've paid?'

'Perhaps I missed something. Perhaps that was the great story of that conference. Bee Botany and its conceptual problems. How the bee gives meaning to the flower. How the flower has an existence only insofar as the bee perceives it. I perceive the flower differently to the bee. Which perception has the more meaning? And perhaps the bee perceives our friends the bee botanists clad in yellow and brown, as one of them, and . . .'

'Who paid?'

'Them. They pay me to go away. I get to all these conferences. By bus. Overnight. When I tell people what I do they say. "It sounds like a right lot of crap to me." Or, "It's people like you who get the money that should come to people like us who are doing the real work."'

A fax flew out of the machine and shot across the floor. Martine picked it up. 'You know what I do?'

'Look, why don't you just go in, and sort this out later?'

'Faxes like this, that's what. Messages that come and go. Ephemera. Minutes of angry meetings. Crumpled up pieces of paper in the photocopier bin . . .'

'That fax, that's mine!'

'Hey, bad news!'

SIR CHARLES WILL DIE

And on a second sheet:

BY MEANS OF 5 MLS OF DEATH ADDER VENOM GENETICALLY ENGINEERED

'Leave this to me,' said Adua firmly, pressing a folder into Martine's hands. 'I'll tell the boss.'

*

Martine circled the scene at the opening party. 'Hi Jenny! How's the job?'

'With old Charley? He's mad as one of his snakes. Still he's got some of the right ideas, and the right connections. I think I may be getting somewhere. At last.'

'Wish I was.'

'And he's onto something, too, something big. Blue daffodils.'

Martine: 'I listen to them. I listen to them talking and work out subtexts and stuff. What they're really saying when they think they're being impartial and objective and just telling about the world as it is.'

'Charley, wouldn't you know it?' Martine turned to find Don behind the bar, helping himself to beer. 'Heard the latest about the boss?'

'Tell.'

'You know how furious he is about the way Charley's been enforcing the cuts in programmes? So the boss decided he'd go hustle his own money. One in the eye for Charley. He found himself a millionaire, wrote to him saying, "Wow, important stuff this, nutrient recycling, basic stuff, dirt, the usual."'

'They need you, Don. Shit-workers in the silt of academe.'

'Got an interview, went off, suit, big deal. Came back. Guess what?'

'More beer?'

'We all said, Tony, how'd it go? And he said, interesting. Very interesting. OK, so what about the money? "No money," he said. "No, I went in to ask him for money, and he told me where all his spare cash was going, orphans in Thailand," and so . . .'

'So, Don?'

'So, Martine, the boss gave him 50 bucks!'

*

Martine: 'I listen to their questions, and work out where they come from. I . . . to be absolutely frank I don't really know what I'm doing. I've got this mountain of data, piles of transcripts, and I read them and I don't really know what to do with them. I just hang around where they are, and just take down what they say.'

'Willey, Charley, aren't you sick of it?'

'Isn't it time they both took themselves off, and subsided into a decently obscure retirement? Why must it be either Willey or Charley, Charley or Willey as President?'

'Because they've always done it that way.'

He was from Gentoch, she was from Radamgene. Companies, not colleges. Explained the air of opulence. The smile at the cameras. The posing. Not truly of this conference. Jetters-in on the way to somewhere else, tolerating the passing moment, slumming it, for now, among the riff-raff.

'Kick out the dead wood.'

'Make room for the new blood. Us.'

'How's it going?'

'Can't complain. How's it with you?'

'Defence.'

'Zurich next month?'

'If the money comes through.'

'Zurich money always does.'

'Who's that girl over there, the one with the notebook? Ducking behind the screen?'

'Media.'

'You'll be wanting our names? Grant Lewin.'

'Sally Yerkovitch.'

'Make sure you spell it right. RADAMGENE.'

'GENTOCH.'

Martine: 'I tell my supervisor, old Prof Dennis, and he says, "Research, Martine, research means getting in there and asking questions. It means getting into a muddle. It means getting yourself out of a muddle. It's all part of the process, and the light will dawn, the light will dawn, and you'll see the path. Or else," he says, and he looks at me over the tops of his glasses, with that look which goes right through me and finds me totally and absolutely wanting, "or else, Martine, you will get in a muddle with your research, and you won't be able to get yourself out of it, and what that will prove is that it's quite the wrong thing for you to be doing, and you should pack your bags and leave and stop cluttering up the place getting in people's way."'

'Charley says he'll dump him in it. The shit. D'you know what Algy's done this time? Came back from the Gobi Desert, so he says. The Gobi Desert, who's he kidding, how do we know it's the Gobi Desert where he got the samples? Anyway, he gave them to Annabel to work on, and she found, so they say, something new, but what they didn't know, was that Charley got another sample, got it tested on the sly, all that filtration, takes hours, boring as hell. They found nothing! There was nothing in it! Gobi Desert? Could have been sand from anywhere. Down the beach.'

'You have to hand it to Charley. If there's a rat around he can smell it.'

'Charley's planning to break the story.'

'It could have just been bad technique. Doesn't have to be the big one. Fraud.'

'Still, it looks bad for Algy, if Charley goes to town.'

'Nothing old Charley likes better.'

'Who's her over there, the one taking all those notes?'

'Media, I bet. Hey, who d'you work for?'

'Whoops, ran like a rabbit.'

'Odd bunch, the media.'

'Seem to be more of them here than us.'

'They stay at the best hotels.'

'My room smells of old jock straps.'

'Beer?'

Martine: 'That's what really grabs me. What really interests them. When they say they do one thing, but what do they talk about? Something entirely different. Who's having it off with whom. Where the grant money really goes. Trips to Zurich and Amsterdam.'

'And I wish he would spell my name right, even if he's put it in Dutch. Rosemarie, I hate it.'

'Weird.'

'Martine, I've got something for you. I found it. On the hard disc. It wasn't meant to be there. A letter in Dutch. He must've made a mistake, and there were a whole lot of files I'd never seen before. I know what to do now, to find it all again. I saw my name, Rosemarie, would you believe, in the middle of a whole lot of Dutch like oop sog de vanvoops.'

'It was a summary of my results. That's what he said, only they weren't my results. Things were changed. I don't know yet, what it was, why he did it. To Willey, it was to him. Charley's up to no good.'

Sir Charles rose to speak. The papers fell from his hands. He collapsed to the floor, dead.

'Those faxes!' Adua was tearful. 'I feel terrible.'

SUMMER TO A STRANGE LAND IS INTO EXILE GONE

The next day. The conference will continue. It was what the old man would have wanted, that's what they said, not having asked him if he was to die that night, if he'd want it.

Martine wants to know it all, but doesn't quite know what she should know in order to know what there is to know, and how, when and if she ever finds it, she might know it's what she's looking for.

'Martine, heard the latest about poor Charley? He's a spy? Was?'

'Never heard that one, Don.'

'They say it. The Sydney mob. Fifty tons of snake venom, that's what it's all about. Said they couldn't do it. So the mob went to Charley.'

'How's he supposed to get fifty tons of the stuff? Milk a snake? Come off it!'

'Bugs in vats. The concrete bunker out the back. Charley, he knew it all. World expert. Was. Bred the little buggers, the *E. coli*, the bacteria, faster than anyone else.'

'So they knocked him off for that?'

'Seems like it.'

'But, Don, where's the sense of it? If they knocked him off, they can't get it.'

'So it was the other side who did it. Knocked him off so the others wouldn't get it.'

'What for? Then they won't get it either.'

'But they couldn't get it anyway.'

'Soil chemistry, Don, you're safe. At least the little buggers in the dirt don't bite you to death.'

THE LAMENTATION OF THE LEAVES

'Charley, who'd have thought it? What a way to go!' Grant Lewin spoke softly into Sally Yerkovitch's shell-pink ear.

'Reckon they did it?'

'Zurich? Didn't know Charley knew them.'

'Zurich! Do you trust them? Sometimes I wonder, what might happen, if we don't come up with the product? Reckon that's what happened with Charley?'

'Sally, you've got to trust someone. Not Zurich, I agree. There may come a time, I can see it, and I think this is what you're getting at, that I may have to present them with a product and run.'

'Me, too?'

'Sally, we run together. We're a team.'

'We are?'

THE EARTH'S WHOLE SAP IS SUNK

'Charley did say he'd dump him in it. Algy. When he heard about Annabel.'

'Algy did it?'

'Pretty impossible, though. Have to rule Algy out.'

'If he's in China.'

'Who can go there and check up? Where they're having the troubles?'

'That's our Algy. In the thick of it.'

'Probably the cause of it.'

'Excuse me, heard the latest about Algy?'

'Gobi Desert?'

'Hell, no. That was months ago. No, Peru.'

'Where are the bugs this time?'

'In the nests of the giant condors. That's what Algy says. Want to argue?'

'Algy has nothing to do with Charley.'

'Shouldn't think so.'

'Peru!'

TREES I SEE BARREN OF LEAVES

'Martine, I bet it was Willey. I saw him last night, the rat. I went up to him last night and said, look, Prof Willey, here I am, I made it after all. He turned white as a sheet. Blue around the eyes with it. He looked frightful. Doesn't want me here. He's up to something. Bet he had something to do with it. With Charley.'

'Why, though, Rosie, Charley was snakes, Willey's the daffodil. Nothing to do with snakes.'

'I don't know what it is, but he's got my results, and if he's playing silly buggers with them, if he messes me around . . . It's all his fault. He could never even spell my name right.'

OH SORROWFUL AND ANCIENT DAYS

The conference called to order. A short explanation from the chair. Sir Charles dead from snakebite, though exactly how unknown. Accident. Conference to continue. He would have wanted it that way. The mystery faxes. Anyone any ideas? Genetic engineering of snake venom? Possible? Desired? Dangerous?

Willey: Let me tell you a story. Once upon a time, all daffodils were yellow. Now they can be any colour we choose, and we have chosen to make the daffodil blue. It hasn't been easy, but now we're reaching the breakthrough. Just a snip of a gene here, from, say, a delphinium. Add a bit of a gene there, say, to a daffodil, and what do we have? Something we've never had before. This daffodil is blue. A questioner: Might there be a problem playing God, meddling with Nature? Might it be, that what has happened to Sir Charles was not an unfortunate accident, but the direct result of growing snake venom, unnaturally, in large vats? Might there be a problem with the blue gene in the daffodil? Might not Nature wreak some kind of future revenge, on people presumptuous to change her time-honoured ways? Might we yet hear tales of the revenge of the killer gene? Willey: No.

A task was set for the questioner. Throw a tin of paint, blue paint, into a rubbish bin. Willey: Quick as a flash, a million mutated genes! Good for nothing, the mutants in the bin. They change alright, they live and die in the space of minutes. Killer genes? Rubbish! A questioner: What if it escaped though, the blue gene? Went from the delphinium to the daffodil, to every blade of grass, every green leaf of every tree, every clump of moss, every pine needle. Things can't go on as before, not if everything turns blue.

Willey paused and frowned and passed his hand across his brow. His hands were blue. His legs trembled beneath him. He fell forward to the floor. His face was blue, bright blue, and he was dead.

'They can't say that, carry on, continue with the conference, Sir Charles, and Professor Willey, it's what they both would have wanted, if they thought they'd both drop dead at the conference, they would have said they wanted the conference to continue. Or,' said Adua to Martine, 'it's what we said they would have said. How do we know it's what they wanted? If they'd been here to say it, there'd be no need to say it. Left unsaid. Now something has to be said, because they're not here to leave it unsaid. So we say it for them, even if it's what they would not have wanted, would never have said. Themselves. Personally.'

'Nothing to do with me, Martine. Soil chemistry, they didn't want to know about it. Except they grow daffs in our soil, and the snakes slither through our grass.'

'Don, though, remember the samples Tony sent Willey? Blue paint in the dustbin dirt? The worms, red wrigglers, two heads each, in two weeks? Or two tails. Hard to tell sometimes.'

'Funny, that. Though this thing, Charley and Willey. Nothing to do with us at all.'

'I didn't do it,' said Rosemarie. 'Even though I said he was a bastard, even if he took my work, and said it was his work, turned it into his figures, my figures with his changes and additions. I thought I was working on the blue daffodil. I didn't know it was war. It turned him blue, he died. I did it, some of it. I never meant it to happen to him, and I never meant it to happen to me.' Rosemarie examined her hands closely for any tell-tale traces of blue.

'I didn't do it,' said Grant to Sally. 'Zurich didn't do it. We just told him what we wanted, a small thing, just a gallon or so of snake venom, for purely medicinal purposes.

The blueness of daffodils, a sideline, lucrative, yes, with potential that one, but never intended to turn the whole world blue. Every blade of grass, every leaf of every tree, blue, all blue. No. Never. It wasn't us.'

THE LEAVES BE BLUE, THE BOUGH BE BLACK

'Nothing to do with the company. Radamgene. They just write the contracts. Money, that's what they provide. Leave the technical details to the experts. Direction, now, the injection of snake venom into the daffodil, the company never said that's what they wanted. The process, that's what was of interest. Not the product. Someone might have given them what they didn't say they wanted, because they might want it when they get it, even if they didn't know it was what they wanted when they started. The gene it was that jumped when someone wasn't looking.'

'In the process of infecting the daffodil with the venom of a snake, we just happened to produce the biting venomous daffodil. It was an accident of fate. These men, Sir Charles and Professor Willey, are martyrs to science.'

THE CONGRESS MURDERS, THEY'VE ONLY JUST BEGUN

Dear Professor Dennis,

This is a note to let you know I shall not be coming back to Sydney to finish my work with you.

Remember you said that if I got myself into a muddle and I couldn't get myself out of a muddle, then it was probably all my fault and I should give up and stop cluttering up the place and getting in people's way?

That's what I decided to do, to clear out.

I don't know where I'll go, what I'll do. Perhaps I'll go to the desert. Central Australia, that's far enough away. The daffodils can't get me there. Death adders will slide through the grass in the traditional manner, and all I'll need to escape them will be my normally adequate reflexes.

It was the fax machine that was the deciding factor, ultimately. The threatening messages kept coming, and they said they didn't know who was sending them. But I knew. Only they wouldn't believe me when I tried to tell them.

Spinifex, the desert sands, that's the way for me to go, away from the city where bugs grow in vats, and who knows what's been added to them, and daffodils bite, and the leaves on the trees are turning blue, and fax machines transmit mysterious etherial messages from a decidedly non-human sender.

The venomous daffodil is another factor in my decision to quit, as I mentioned earlier.

How can I analyse what they're doing, if I don't know what I'm doing, if I walk through territory where the daffodil unites with the death adder, and the delphinium allies itself with bacteria found more normally in the human large intestine?

These are my night thoughts and also my day thoughts, and soon they will be my thoughts in the desert.

For these reasons, I have decided that I can no longer be your pupil. I shall value all you have taught me, and remain,

Yours most sincerely,

Martine

Strange Things Grow at Chernobyl

Three years ago they burned what was left of the forest and buried it. Nearest the site the soil was dead for a while, no tumbling microfauna, but soon they returned, churning the dirt and ash and extracting the radioactive nutrients. Cycles of carbon and nitrogen resumed, but other patterns of life took longer to return. Some things will never be the same again.

Some things will never be the same again. I know this is true, with me. Though I do not live at Chernobyl, and when I am thinking straight, I know the people who live there just outside the zone lead lives which are far weirder than mine.

I rang her, and I said 'I want it back. What you have taken from me. I want my life to go on, as it has always gone on. I want to be part of the great sweeping cycle of things.'

Of course, she knew better than me, she always does, and she told me what was wrong. With me, not her.

At Chernobyl the rats are doing very well. They say they thrive on radiation, but that I don't believe. I will believe some things, but not that one. Cockroaches, yes, I could believe it of cockroaches. Give them a blast of radiation and they grow another pair of sucking regurgitating smacking lip-like protuberences, that I do believe.

They say the rats at Chernobyl show radio-resistance. Those that survive can take higher doses of radiation, before the death threshhold is reached. They are larger and sleek, showing some abnormalities, it is true, but abnormalities that will make the difference, provide them with a boost up the ladder of existence. Watch out for super rat.

She is a rat. She is a cockroach, the person who has something of mine that I value. Something she won't ever give back. The thing is, I don't know how to ask for it. She will think I am silly, not being able to tell her exactly what it is. I should know what it is, so I can ask for it, properly. It would be easy to say, you have my cat, or my book, please will you return what you have that is mine. She has something more. She has my self-respect, and that is why I have all these problems, asking for it to be returned to me.

It was like this, how she captured what I have, which is mine, and which she has taken. She told me nothing, I couldn't work it out that way, what she did. But she told Nicholas one thing, and the others, the people who know more than him, more than me, she told them something quite different, and that is how it happened, how she hurt me, how she has kept what I want from me. Nicholas doesn't know what has happened. The story is about him, but he thinks he knows the story, and that I have it wrong. It is me who is to blame, so he tells me, often. She has been clever. She has taken what belongs to me, but she has taken it in such a way that they say, look, you never had it in the first place. It was never there. It's your imagination. You are the only person who sees it that way.

I am the only person who is right.

Strange things grow in my mind. From the dead forest of my thoughts new shoots are pushing up, but their growth is far from normal. At Chernobyl the young pines grow without symmetry. The needles are large, but the trunks of the trees are stunted and twisted. The oak trees are sprouting giant leaves, white, without chlorophyll.

They are using the plants and animals in the zone as indicators of change. I read that in the paper. Biological indicators of change in the earth, air and water. Earth, air, plants and animals are collected and studied, killed if that's what it takes, and the results are reported somewhere, though not usually until they have been cleared by the appropriate agency, and that can take some time.

There are other ways that people notice things are different. The forest is dead. People have been taken from the zone. There are other ways of knowing.

No one tells Nicholas there is more to the story. No one tells him, and me, I have to ferret the knowledge out for myself, pry at secrets, stir up the dirt, churn out the thoughts, the ideas, work through the problem.

I ferreted out the knowledge about Chernobyl. People ask me how I know all this. I read a bit here, a bit there, I put all this together. I am a sleuth of sorts. Because I care, I really care.

She sits in judgment, she is the censor, the executioner. She is the person who takes from others something they think is theirs, and they will take it by force, because . . .

Nobody meant it to happen. It was an accident. Error just built upon error, sloppy construction added to human inattention, moments of tiredness overlapped with shouted bad-tempered orders, resentment, confusion, a switch turned there, a red light glowing, unnoticed.

'Nobody meant it to happen,' she said to me. 'I thought you wouldn't mind.'

She thought I wouldn't mind, which is why she said nothing to me. Errors built on errors, omissions on assumptions, pain upon misunderstanding. 'I thought you wouldn't mind.' That's what she says now. But then, she knew I would.

She has taken what I value, but she has told him another story, and he believes he is in the right, that she has good reason for what she has done, that she is doing what will in the end be for the best. They say that, when the pain goes one way only.

Wild strawberries are growing, without seeds. Perhaps their sterility is the best, too. Mutant strawberries which cannot reproduce their kind. No one eats strawberries and cream at Chernobyl. Iodised strawberries. Caesium flavoured cream.

Nothing is for the best. I know I shall be thinking like this, forever, thinking that she has taken something from me, and I am searching for it, and I want to ring her to tell her I am searching for it. I want to ask her, where is it, what you have taken from me, give it back to me, give part of me that is my own self, give it back to me, the part that I have lost, so I can become whole again, so I can know I am whole. I want back part of me that is taken, that she has taken because she wanted to go her own way, but she wanted to feel important doing it, she wanted to discard without telling, without benefit of words, for words are hard to say.

I want, I want . . .

Strange things grow at Chernobyl. Storks roost in the chimneys of abandoned villages. Wild animals survived two hard winters, eating the crops left standing in the ground. They say there are moose there, but I have never heard of the Ukranian moose. It must be an error in translation.

She has taken, she has taken . . .

They must mean something different. Not deer, because they talk of both deer and moose. Perhaps it is the wild caribou, something larger than a deer, but smaller than the woolly mammoth. Both deer and caribou (moose, they say, though I do not), show abnormalities in their bone marrow and their blood. Of course they must. They are the indicators of change, and the change is there for anyone to see. They do not need blood tests, to know it.

They are paying the price of . . . progress? More like this. They are paying the price of chaos.

I am paying a price.

In the cooling ponds of the reactors carp have grown to an enormous size. Small fish left in small baskets when the blast occurred have grown to fill their cage, thriving on the radioactive sludge. No one will come to eat them now. They are being observed to see if they will grow to a ripe old age.

Microfauna, strawberries, pines, oaks, fish, rats, deer, the unlikely moose, the lower on the scale of existence, the less the effects of sub-lethal doses of radiation. The rats are the exception.

I have learned to think of her as an exceptional rat.

At Chernobyl people are coming back. They stand with their back to the ruins, having their photograph taken. Old people return to the villages, though it is supposed to be forbidden. They chase the storks from the chimneys and the deer from the streets, and go on with life as they have always lived it. If they feel sluggish and out of sorts, there is a natural explanation. They attribute it to old age.

The children evacuated from the zone are growing in strange ways. They are sluggish and withdrawn, with disorders of the thyroid gland.

My children grow strong and well.

My wife Ruth is a perfectly rational human being. She is one of the most rational people I know. But on one subject – whew! She is quite quite irrational.

I have given up trying to reason with her.

It must be her time of life. They called it involutional melancholia, when the Queen had it, I remember it said so in the *Women's Weekly*.

Yes, I read the *Women's Weekly*. I'm not ashamed to say it. I read it because I happen to pick it up sometimes at the dentist and I like it.

No, it can't be wholly that, involutional melancholia, the menopause blues. Because she doesn't have it about anything else. And she's thirty-eight, that's all, though they say it can happen earlier, the change of life, if something happens, as it has with Ruth. The operation. Still we are blessed, two fine children.

Yes, I was present at the births.

I know it, when it starts, the irrational bit, I know it, but she doesn't know I know it. I see her grow white about the eyes, and then she says 'I heard something about Chernobyl on the news today', and I know that words will flow, and I shall be powerless to stop them.

She has it on tape, the satellite pictures of the disaster. Blurry concrete buildings with flames shooting from their roofs.

Morbid.

Especially in everyday conversation. Not everybody wants to be reminded of these things, not while they're choosing tomatoes at the market. Red tomatoes. I make a good tomato soup. I make it when it's high summer, and the tomatoes are fifty cents a kilo. The secret is, don't add water. Ridiculously simple, isn't it? And basil, you need plenty of basil, and one small onion.

She looked at the tomatoes and she started talking rapidly about fall-out, but I know these tomatoes do not come from the Ukraine. They are tomatoes from Werribee.

She will not listen. Her breathing, it falters a little, she has to catch her breath and start again. Odd, that. It never happens to me. My breathing is flawless.

Being present at my children's birth has made me aware of feelings that were a bit of a surprise to me. There's a marvellous release of a deep instinctual flood of energy. The father's job isn't just a support. It's absolutely critical in the first two months of life, when the other parent, the mother, may be feeling rather dazed by the physical aspects of it all.

The physical aspects of childbirth, I think we've come to see in recent years, are really rather less important than the mental aspects. Yes, the physical in childbirth has always been strongly overrated, that's my view, and the spiritual, the mental, the flow of life energy, the bonding experience, they're where it's really at, and it's high time that it was all got out into the open, so that fathers can assert their importance in the birthing process.

As I did.

That's why I stick to Ruth now, though she is having a hard time. I try not to mention X-rays, or Strontium 90 in passing conversation, not that I usually talk about X-rays, but it's a funny thing, the moment you decide not to mention something, because someone else goes into an entirely irrational tizz then it's amazing how often the word starts to crop up. All these topics of conversation I can't mention, which means it cuts them down, my options. To football riots, that kind of thing. Except Ruth doesn't express much interest one way or the other in football.

She either cares too much, or not at all.

Ruth and Nicholas, what can you say? He's a prick, and she's a clinger. One of the wimps of this world.

I needed him, but I didn't need her. For the club. We have this club. It's not a social club, I have to keep reminding the committee. We're not here to give anyone a good time. We have a job of work to do, and we have to get it done. We don't want hangers on and moaning minnies. They can go off and do something else.

They'd be much happier going off and doing something else, rather than hanging round us, getting in our way.

So this is what I did. I told him to come, but not to bring her.

Then I told her he didn't want her to come any more.

Then I told the committee that their relationship was on the skids, that she was about to leave, he was about to leave. Her hysterectomy. His wanting more kids. Her mopishness. His impatience. Vote her off. Keep him on.

I didn't lie to the committee. I never do that. It was the truth then, if not now. They didn't separate. They should have, in my opinion. Both be better off. Might still do it, go their separate ways. Then I'd be right.

I usually am.

The Palace of the Soul

'Who knows the fate of his bones, or how often he is to be buried?' I was thinking along these lines, though the words are not my own. Sir Thomas Browne, dead some time now, wrote them, prophetically, as it turned out. He was to be buried more than once, himself.

I had the words lodged deeply in my mind, and they kept popping out of darkness into light at the most inappropriate times. 'Who knows the fate of his bones?' I would say in my mind, as I stood to address the students where I work. 'Or how often he is to be buried?' Those words to the plumber as he came to clear the drains. Though I did not say the words aloud.

I first heard the story of the Piltdown skull from Ian Langham at a conference. Later the story appeared in the morning paper. The *Sydney Morning Herald*. Surprising, when you think of it. Someone talks about what happened in the gravel pits of Piltdown, England, back in 1912, and it hits the Australian papers in 1985.

I opened the paper, and there was the photograph of Ian. A lock of straight fair hair hung over his glasses. He was smiling, happy with the story, pleased at making it more widely known. In his hands he held a replica of the skull.

Ian's story was more a progress report on who did what back there and then, and what was in it for whoever did it, and whether revenge is as strong a motive for scientists as it is for other people. He wasn't really so interested in the 'who-dun-it' aspect of the story, but the 'why do it?' side of things. Why plant a fake fossil? What advantage did it bring whoever did it?

There is now no doubt the skull was a fraud. It wasn't the first man, it was something else. It was a modern skull, with the jaw bone of an orang-utan. Though no one knew that, for certain, until the fraud was unmasked in 1959.

I've kept that newspaper cutting, all these years. I came across it just last week, at work. In a file labelled 'file sometime'. I moved it across to the folder labelled 'fraud'. Fraud has a file to itself, in my system, now it is happening all the time.

Perhaps I should have a file labelled 'Ian'. It will have one newspaper cutting, and one article. A special file, a thin one, with nothing more to follow.

Ian gave pleasure to people who heard him talk, because he told the story well, and it was a good yarn. The thing was, though, everytime we met, at conferences, I heard him give a different version. Once it was an Australian anatomist, Grafton Eliot Smith, to whom the finger of Ian's suspicion pointed. The second version of his story, it was someone entirely different.

It pleased Ian, I think, to make one of the perpetrators an Australian. National pride, putting one over the Poms, that's not a bad reason for fraud. Not a particularly good reason, either, and Ian soon dropped that line of investigation.

What happened there, back at the gravel pits of Piltdown, cold and foggy, ideal weather for the doing of dirty deeds, for creating the first man, making him an Englishman? England expected that, back in 1912, when stories of the beginnings of human life took a new turn.

The central actor is the skull, how many times it was buried, how it was changed, how it became the object of so much wonder.

In a painting by John Cooke, 'A discussion on the Piltdown skull', eight men are grouped around a table. They contemplate pieces of the skull. Above them is a portrait within the portrait. Charles Darwin gazes out from the frame within the frame at the men who in turn direct their gaze at the skull.

'Man and the ape share a common ancestor.' Darwin said it first. It's all his fault, the sequence of events that followed. If anyone is guilty, he is. Why look, otherwise, for Dawn Man, something halfway between us and the ape? Why create the skull on the table?

Eoanthropus Dawsonii, named after Charles Dawson, the man who discovered two of its parts, and who stands in place of honour underneath the portrait of Darwin.

The faces in the portrait know more than they can tell. Some say Charles Dawson did it. He found it, didn't he? Others say, yes, but . . . there must be more than one forger. The evidence points that way. There were several separate discoveries, and the techniques used were very different. Some forgeries, particularly the first, were very clever. Later the forgers grew careless, as if they were saying to the world, 'If you believe this, then you will believe anything and you thoroughly deserve to be deceived.'

Some of the people in the portrait must have filed the jawbone, stained the skull, scraped the elephant bone implements, scratched at the tooth enamel.

The faces in the portrait are solemn, as befits the contemplation of mortality. Imagine, though, a photograph instead of a portrait, with the perpetrator unable to suppress a knowing smirk at the vital moment. Then there would be no mystery. We would know.

Ian had some of the answers, or so I'm beginning to believe. He spotted the problem with the portrait. He was on the way to knowing. What if it happened, and he caught them in the act? He caught the act of smirking, in his mind. He knew, as I now know.

Who will believe me, though? Believe us? Ian is dead,

they can't ask him. His proof went with him, and I have only my suspicions.

Turn to the portrait and the men in it. They kept their secret to themselves, back at the beginning of it all. Later, though, as they grew older, they grew confiding, garrulous even. They told the story to their protégés. Each story was different, the cast of characters changing frequently, on the question of who did what to whom, and why.

These men will later find they had forgotten some of the details, what they placed and where they placed it, where the bricks sat in the intellectual edifice they set out to erect. They will forget who did what first. Old men will tell the tale, and get it wrong.

They will remember the skull.

One person is not there, in the portrait, though he was significant. Pierre Teilhard de Chardin, Jesuit and geologist, was absent in France in 1915, on war service. It may be, if anyone is smirking, it will be all the harder to detect, if the smirking is offstage. The cast may know, but the audience will be totally in the dark.

The men in the portrait placed their faith in the skull, not asking the further questions, how much can a skull really tell, and how much they must make of what little it provides? Yet they meet, and argue and know the answers so surely.

'Nature,' said Arthur Keith, distinguished anatomist, and Conservator of the Royal College of Surgeons, back in 1912, 'Nature is capricious, and she does not preserve all her relics. Dawn Man lived and walked in England, of that I am perfectly sure. But he died in the most inconvenient places, on top of hills where his flesh was taken by birds, and his bones exposed to the powers of wind and sun and rain.'

If Dawn Man did not leave his remnants, then it will prove necessary to invent him, to co-operate with the story of evolution, creating what once must have been there, but which was not preserved. Dawn Man must be a million years old, a relic of the Pliocene.

Arthur Keith bends and scrapes and stains and files, in the most expert fashion, for is he not after all the up-and-coming young man, whose fate it is to be surrounded by incompetent bumbling old men who hold their positions of power and influence because they were in the right place at the right time, and to whom he must kowtow in daily life, but aha, in his secret life, he files, polishes, and stains, and plots where to place the skull, how best to have it found – not by him but by an amateur digger, someone who will find things because he is always out there tramping the gravel pits.

Arthur Keith prefers the warmth of the hearth, crumpets and cups of China tea. Let Charles Dawson find it, someone who truly believes that the first man must be an Englishman. Someone who will find the evidence, because he has faith that it exists.

Smith Woodward, that's the man Keith wants to show for the fool he is. Expert in fossil fish, what would he know about Dawn Man? Yet he pronounced, so surely, that human history was short, a mere 300,000 years. He knew the answers though he knew nothing about the subject. This skull will tell him a thing or two. This skull will change his tune. This skull will make the difference, says Arthur Keith. Only, as it turned out, one skull was not enough.

'Take this skull,' says Smith Woodward, holding it aloft to the assembled meeting. 'This skull, which I, with Mr Dawson here – stand up Charles, take a bow – which we have found, and I have pieced together, this skull is the skull of modern man – large brained, but apelike in its jaw. The brain has led the way. The divine light shone at Piltdown, and breathed into our ape-like ancestors a soul and mind elevated above the rest, and in that place, that holy of holies, the first man stood erect, generous in his mental endowments, striking for the strength and nobility of his brow, and that man was, I am pleased to tell you, an Englishman through and through.' Lily-white in skin colour, that goes without saying.

Arthur Keith leaps to his feet, a critic in for the kill. 'What about this?' he asks. 'The strength and nobility of the brow. Why reconstruct it this way, why not that?' Arthur Keith must know. He was, after all, the creator.

Smith Woodward looks down his nose, and is so certain in his replies, so sure, so sweeping in the picture he paints of Dawn Man walking the gravel beds of ancient rivers, so certain of the date, the Pleistocene . . .

'Pliocene, surely,' murmurs Arthur Keith, bravely. 'The river gravels, surely, the Pliocene.'

'Quibbles, mere quibbles,' says the great man, who has not risen to greatness through listening to the nonsense of minions.

'The tooth,' says Keith, 'the canine tooth is missing. What would it look like, do you think?'

The great man describes a canine tooth more human in form than the other teeth in the ape-like jaw, less like the great fighting teeth of a creature that lived by its brawn.

Arthur Keith sits down and seethes. Smith Woodward rises serene above the fray, his dignity and his theory intact. Keith is the apoplectic young man, exceedingly ungracious in defeat. Smith Woodward towers above the mêlée. Evidence means nothing, one way or the other, once the mind has settled in its ways.

The portrait tells one story, the meetings another. There were other meetings, other stories. Ian told his versions, often, with evidence pulled in from here, from there. Sometimes the cold gaze of others turned on him, savagely. They muttered, those who sit in judgement, censors, judges, executioners. Critics in for the kill, with the question intended to show how clever the question, and how dim-witted the response. Ian had his share of that. He could not tower above the mêlée. He possessed humility before the evidence, the one sure path to truth, though also to self-doubt. There may be nothing, nothing but air.

When Ian went north to work so far away in Sydney, someone said, 'We must look after him, because he is there, alone, the only person caring for the subject that we teach. It will be tough for him, the isolation.' Too much may have been expected. Wisdom. Fortitude. Endurance. Then there was the end.

Ian is dead, I can't ask him.

In the portrait, the first knowing smirk must come from Arthur Keith, though it will, in the end, be a smirk of fierce regret.

How to explain, though, the rest? There had to be more than one actor in the fraud. There was not one fraud, but several. Two skulls, one canine tooth, and twenty stone-age implements of various kinds, found over a period of some five or six years, and created by different hands. Some of the fakes are skilful, others clumsy. Some are stained with potassium bichromate, others with colours taken from an artist's paintbox. Vandyke Brown and Burnt Sienna.

The portrait provides clues, but now the going gets tougher. Pierre Teilhard de Chardin was not there when the portrait was painted. He is the Jesuit in this story. 'Let your words be few,' words of some wisdom, though they are still words, and 'let your actions speak,' and this action spoke. It spoke to Arthur Keith, who certainly sat up and took notice. The tooth was just exactly as Smith Woodward had described it.

When it was discovered, Smith Woodward sat back, immensely satisfied. Arthur Keith seethed even more.

The canine tooth. The second forgery. Who did it? Why do it?

*

Gobi Desert, 1930. The American Central Asian Expedition.

Pierre Teilhard de Chardin, Jesuit and geologist for God, looks out over the desert and meditates on discovering, undergoing, growing old, and waiting.

The Citroën has broken down again.

'I am distressed,' he wrote to his sister. 'I see nothing in this voyage but traces of a vanished world.' But where has it vanished? He looked out over the Gobi, wide shallow basins which caught, not water for life, but the flowing detritus of the desert, the pebbles, the gravel and sand, relics of the earth's eroding crust.

The French engineers crawled over and under the truck, cursing the desert.

Teilhard started another letter. 'In the desert,' he wrote to his spiritual confessor, 'I find that the mystic impulse is inseparable from the scientific impulse, and needs equally to be given a chance.'

'I seek your guidance,' Teilhard paused in his writing, to speak with God. 'That small affair at Piltdown. It seems your enemies have won, and the Piltdown skull is everywhere taken as genuine. Now you and I know how much that is affecting our work in the Gobi, creating havoc with the new discoveries here in China. Peking Man, twelve specimens already, they are no fakes, yet they must live in the pale, false shadow of Piltdown, unnecessarily, as you and I know is the case.'

The Citroën sprang into brief spluttering life. The Chinese bearers stirred. Teilhard did not rise. The sound of the engine ceased. The bearers settled back in the holes they had hollowed in the shady side of the sand basin.

Teilhard traced a circle in the desert sand with the tip of his tightly laced boot. He scooped some sand in his hand and let it slip through his fingers to cover the dull-grey pebbles he had earlier placed carefully together in admiration of their smooth water-fashioned shapes. He continued his talk with God. 'This place is dead, where once life flourished. Ancient waters flowed here, once; behold these pebbles, relics of a vanished land.'

On the horizon two dust-spouts appeared in the stillness of the day, stately *kwei* of the desert. They moved as a pair, one male, the other female, the forces of wind contained within them, their cloaks of sand about them.

Teilhard watched without moving. His Chinese companions scooped their hollows deeper for protection. The engineers shouted to each other, and rushed to reassemble the truck. Teilhard continued in prayer, his hands clasped, his lips moving. 'Round me the sands of the desert stir with the life of brute matter, the dust on the surface of the world which each new dawn is granted anew some small part of your divine presence, invested with some small vestige of life. Now is the time, swirl with the wind, return to another vanished world, Piltdown, 1913. Let the gravels of Piltdown move in mysterious ways, let this canine tooth reappear at that time, that place. There they will see a tooth too good to be true, too close in agreement with Smith Woodward's predictions. They will suspect it, then check the skull and find it for the clever fake it is. All the subsequent nonsense will be avoided.'

Teilhard watched the two dust-spouts draw closer. 'Dust of the divine breath,' he whispered, 'fold me in your loving arms.' Dust, then darkness, faith, then one canine tooth, one prayer answered, though not in the manner directly requested.

When later they dug the man of God from the sand, they marvelled at the fact that he lived.

At Piltdown in 1913, Teilhard de Chardin bent down and shouted to his friends. He had found the missing canine tooth.

It didn't work out, though, the way it was meant to work. No one grew suspicious. The tooth was slotted into the story as glorious confirmation of an inspired guess. Smith Woodward sailed serenely on, unknowing.

It meant more to Arthur Keith. He grew thoughtful, and less pushy. He thought it meant that someone knew, someone who figured in the portrait. It was as if a message had been sent to him, 'Stop what you are doing. Stop your fraud, or I shall tell him, the great man, Smith Woodward.' That is what Arthur Keith took it to mean. Though it didn't mean that, not at all.

And so the story goes. More implements of various kinds were made, and planted. Fraud within fraud, fraud upon fraud, but all failed their primary intention. Arthur Smith Woodward did not notice. The great man rose above the mêlée, his theory intact. He kept the faith in Piltdown, to the grave.

As for Sir Thomas Browne, whose words forever haunt me, he knew the fate of his own bones. They lay in peace for some two hundred years, before his skull became a prized object for the new science of the mind. His grave was robbed, and his skull was taken by phrenologists. Better to be the object of scientific curiosity than a drinking bowl for his enemies, he might once have said, had he thought of it. His skull was weighed and measured, and held up for the crowds to see.

'Here is the skull of the man who meditated on death, who accurately predicted the fate of his own bones. Look at the shape and size of its parts, sure signs of the mind that once dwelt therein. Bump of veneration – for religious feeling, very high. Bump of comparison, inductive reasoning on the fate of his bones, large, too. Bump of acquisitiveness, on the low side, and as for the size of brain, large, as befits a physician of a speculative and melancholy disposition.'

On his open tomb a skeleton is carved, a skeleton holding a skull. Around it twines an inscription, 'This is man'. In knowing the skull the living know themselves, that is the message, know what they really are, though not quite. The living are warm and breathing, and alive, and know it, know that the skeleton is still beneath the skin, still comfortably clothed.

The skull is centre stage. The stories spin out of fossil skulls, but not from femurs, ribs, or ulna. The skull is the palace of the soul. The skull is what is truly there, once the veneer of culture, then life, then flesh has been stripped back, to the bare bone.

This is part of the story Ian Langham told. This is the story I am hearing, so many years later.

I stand in front of a class of students. Some are, as usual, bored. Some are, as usual, interested. I place the portrait of the Piltdown men on the glass plate of the overhead projector. The portrait has been copied and recopied onto a transparent piece of film, so that the colour has changed to black and white, and light shines through the men and out onto the wall of the room.

I always see something, whenever I place the transparency on the projector. I see it as a holograph, hovering just above the glass plate.

I adjust the focus from the remote edge of fuzziness. Charles Darwin does it first. He winks at Arthur Keith, who looks up and out to me. Then Keith turns his head and winks at someone beyond my line of vision. However quickly I turn, I've never yet caught who it might be.

It's enough to make anyone nervous, and sometimes I take the picture too far out, blowing it up too much. Then I must backtrack, and as I bring it back into focus, slowly this time so as not to overshoot, I see the jawline on the skull straighten, and lift, and at that moment the winking ceases, and the skull smirks out at me, unblinking.

Holiness

The young priest sat on a donkey, gazing across the desert to the distant cliffs. 'In the time of the First People,' so many local stories began, 'In the time when Giants roamed the earth . . .'

Michel had come to the desert to find the First People, or what was left of them. Peking Man, they called him, back in Paris, *Sinanthropus pekinensis*. But here, in the vast plains at the edge of nowhere, the time they talked of was the time before this time, the people who lived then were truly the First People, and the Latin names of the Academicians of Paris were dusty irrelevancies in the harsh realities of this wild place, this strange time.

Michel dismounted and picked up some of the ancient flints from the gravelly sand. When he lifted his eyes to the horizon, he caught the glint of fierce sun bouncing from the steep walls of the Flaming Cliffs. He walked on, leading his donkey.

In front of him the truck moved slowly across the desert. In its train it cast a plume of dust into the air. Dust of the earth, thought Michel, dust, the holiness even in dust, dust with its ration of the life force which flows through all things, the significance of the apparently insignificant, each mote of dust part of a plan that he felt he was at last beginning to understand.

Tonight they would strike camp, not far from here, where the cliffs met the sand. Tomorrow, they would start digging.

He came to a place where two roads crossed. A severed head swung from a pole. Michel bent down to examine it, his trained eye noting the sap still oozing from the raw wood. Not long cut. In the desert, with not a tree in sight. Someone had woken this morning, cut the pole, met the man he murdered, hacked his head off, tied it to the pole, and gone on his way.

This head here, the severed head, united with the means of its suspension in the air, at the crossroads, beside the cliff, at this time, and no other. The life force had passed from this man, and now it inhabits this dust. Michel paused, his head bowed.

He was roused by the sound of someone approaching and a soft voice saying, 'There is but one hour of death.' It was of Babao, his assistant, who had climbed down from the truck, and gone in search of his master. Michel nodded his agreement.

'Do you require this head for your collection?'

'Not old enough. It's the skulls of the First People that I'm after.'

Babao grasped the head by the hair and gazed on its blood-encrusted features. All of a sudden the head gave a quarter turn in his hands. Babao jumped back. He looked at Michel. 'You saw that?'

Michel was white about the eyes.

'It moved! The head moved!'

'The land whirled round, too. Did you see that?'

'A jump forward, the head, the place, together. What's happening?'

'It was the earth beneath our feet. A tremor. A quake.'

Babao shook his head. 'The head jumped in my hands.'

'Of course it did. The earth shook, the head jumped.' Michel turned his attention to the severed head. 'Poor wretch, killed by his tribe, his head hung here in warning.'

Babao looked sharply at Michel. 'Is that what you think?' he asked in his careful French.

Michel looked equally sharply at Babao. When he spoke,

it was in Babao's dialect. 'These people are savages. I have come to this place to show them a better way.'

In the distance the Citroën spluttered to a stop, the dust plume still hovering in its train. Michel mounted his donkey and hurried to join the rest of the expedition, Babao running along behind him.

That night the dust in the air above the truck glowed bright red and the sunset, far from being remote on the horizon, seemed suspended directly above their heads. When the dust looked like settling to earth, gentle breezes wafted from the caves in the cliffs and kept it suspended in the air, as if the earth had exhaled a deep breath especially for the purpose.

'The earth is sighing,' said Babao. 'First, the head spins, the earth shakes, and now the earth is sighing. There is a message in these signs.'

Michel agreed. 'Dust of the desert. Held there for this glorious moment, to remind us that the material part of its being far outweighs the element of spirit and makes it a fitting image for the lowliness of man.'

'Dust of the desert,' said Babao. 'Glorious dust which holds the promise of the future, when the troubled spirits will depart, and all life will be as dust, serene in its unknowing.'

Matter and spirit, thought Michel, with spirit the stuff that really matters.

Matter and spirit, thought Babao, with matter the stuff that will triumph, in the end.

So it was that Michel looked upon the severed head of a man, and assumed it was punishment. Babao looked upon the same head, and saw it as liberation of the tortured spirit, a reward for high virtue. Michel sighed, and thought, 'Life is sweet,' as he gathered the long folds of his soutane around him, its heaviness a barrier against both the sleet of Paris and the sweeping winds of the high plateau. 'Come, sweet Death,' thought Babao, buckling his belt more firmly on his round belly, round his long cloak, with its warm lining of soft fox fur.

Babao had his orders from his masters. 'Watch closely. If he finds out too much, it may be necessary to take him into the desert. To pay him the ultimate honour of liberating his body from the evil of the spirit. The First People are our people. Their secrets are our secrets.'

'He wants to find their bones and take them to Paris.'

'The relics belong with us.'

'It shall not happen.'

'You must do what you must do. There are no choices. Only blind necessity. Come. Eat.' Babao recalled the last exquisite meal his master had given him, and his words of comfort, 'Eat. The flesh is weak. It needs all the strength it can get in its daily struggle with the spirit.'

Time gave another forward jerk. The tongues of the camp fire were etched like small bolts of lightning in the black air.

Strange, thought Michel, as he spooned his dinner from his cup, the things which are happening here. Where previously there had been continuity, now there was discontinuity, yet daily life goes on, just as before, though everything is, in fact, quite different. Michel put down his cup, opened his notebook and jotted down his thoughts.

Babao took a handful of melon seeds from his pocket and munched on them hungrily. Once more he had been forced to stand in line at the six-gallon drum for his hunk of bread and his cup of gruel, and listen, incredulous, as Michel blessed their food. Babao watched Michel as he ate without thinking for a moment of what passed between his lips.

How easily Michel gazes into the abyss, thought Babao, without knowing. It is the dark abyss of time which he is opening here, by the very act of his presence. He seeks the First People. They know it, and are talking to us, through the earth, through its movement in space and time. If between one moment of time, and the next, there is a gap, if instead of jerking forwards, the seconds separate, and between the two instants there is the void, the moment when the mind pauses, perplexed, and strives for the next pulse from the distant centre of the world. What if it does not come? The ear strives to listen, but it cannot hear. The body strains to feel, in the air, in the rocks, but there is nothing there. The gap has opened, between one second and the next. There is the void, there is the place where matter has departed, the cosmic emptiness. Void of matter, full of evil. What if the gap opens, and does not close? The next minute never comes. The slide commences, deep into the abyss.

Time cheats.
Time is the agent of decay.
Time is a tyrant. It imposes its will.
Time is playing tricks.
There was a time when Giants roamed the earth . . .
The end of time is the condition to which the universe aspires.
Time is the villain.
Time obliterates.
Time destroys.

Michel sometimes thought of time as something as vast as the plain on which he stood, stretching two ways, one towards the past, which was the subject of his study, and the other towards the future, which was the object of his desire.

Dust is the detritus of matter, cycling and recycling through the earth and its atmosphere. Where, though, do those lost seconds go, the detritus of time? Seconds slip by, minutes fall, hours pass, but, to where? Not even to dust. Yet time has carved these monuments, these cliffs, time has created these fossil bones. In the strata of the cliffs, in the petrification of the bones, there time has left its traces, in the substance of our earth, its crust.

Dust as it falls adds to the substance of the earth, mountains wear down, valleys erode, the river bed silts up, sea becomes land. Land becomes weary, land wears down, the land passes away, into dust. Seconds slough off time, like a snake sloughs off its skin. But there is no physical presence, no empty shell; the present takes leave of the past, without physical residue.

What if, though, the relics of past time are left, but not in this place, not in this universe? Here, there is only room for one kind of detritus, dust. The dust of time goes somewhere else. There is a dark abyss into which the seconds fall, the minutes, the hours. It is the abyss between this world and the next.

During the night, the soft breezes which blew from deep in the caverns died down, and dust descended upon the sleeping camp. Where it first rose in the air as the brown dust of the desert, it now fell as red as the glow of the setting sun, as if in its sojourn in the air sand had become fused with the substance of light. Where the red dust fell thickest, the straggling dry grasses died, and men itched where their skin was exposed.

Early the next morning an old man came walking from the south along the line of the cliffs. He entered the camp and spoke with the men, ascertaining why they had come, welcoming them when he found that the object of their visit was the pursuit of knowledge. His name was Laka, and for forty years he had lived in the cliffs, guarding them from those who sought to plunder them, welcoming those who came to learn.

Michel presented his letter of introduction from the Central Government and waited respectfully.

'Safe passage! You are safe enough from me,' the old man said. 'I am no threat to you. But before you go any further, you must come with me and I will show you something.' He asked for a lantern. 'The First People. Are you sure they're what you want to find?' He led the way into one of the caves.

When their eyes adjusted to the dark, they saw faded pictures glowing on the walls, patterns of flowers and dancing flames, and in the centre, a large representation of the Buddha.

'The artists have come here, and left their mark, for us to cherish and respect,' said Laka. 'This is surely what you seek.'

'We esteem and value your work here, in this place where so many have come in worship. But I seek the people who lived in a time before this time,' Michel replied.

Laka motioned them further into the caves, and pointed to another part of the wall. Here a fringe of leaves round a lotus-flower the colour of the dawn, there delicate tracery, but overlaid with the scrawl of an alien alphabet, a frenzy of white characters in a carelessly scrawled Cyrillic script.

'Russians,' Laka scowled. 'They left their names. And that's not all they left.' He motioned to the two men to bend down low with him as he slid back a wooden panel, and shone the light of his lantern through a hole in the wall into the depths of a cavern below. Michel and Babao saw, in the far corner, a pile of bones.

'The First People?'

'The Russians.'

Things jerked forward, once again. Then twice, three times in quick succession.

'Earth tremors?' asked Michel, though the rocks on the cliff did not slide.

Laka laughed. 'Is that what you think?'

Babao looked sharply at him. 'Then what is it?'

'Time-slips.' As they emerged from the cave into the desert the old man pointed to a cave further up the cliffs. 'There, by that Tilb tree,' he said. 'Enter there.' He gave the lantern to Babao.

'What is a time-slip?' asked Michel.

The old man looked round him, muttering, 'I must go.' He left, walking quickly in the direction from which he had come.

'Time-slips? The earth slips, yes, but slips in time? Have you heard of that?'

Babao shrugged, and gestured in the direction of the cave. He busied himself with sorting out Michel's tools.

Michel looked around him, at the wildness of the place, and knew that, try as he might, he would never fully understand this place, this time, these people. He picked up his knapsack, and walked with Babao in the shadow of the cliffs.

As they came to the tree, Michel noticed that a branch had been freshly cut from it. Sap was oozing from the wound, and a line of dark red ants made their way through the bark shavings on the ground. 'We must take care. It looks as if the murderers have left their mark.'

Babao nodded. 'Laka?'

'Those Russians . . . But it's not as if we came, like them, for gold. We have come for knowledge. Laka knows. He seemed to welcome us.'

Babao shrugged.

'I know, who can tell what the old man thinks?'

Michel accepted a cigarette, his fingers trembling. 'Time-slips, the old man said. Earthquakes, why not have jolts in time? This is a place to which few men have travelled. It is, by all accounts, a special place. You know, Babao, my theories. You know why, in Paris, they are pleased to see me gone.'

Babao nodded. He, too, had been sent on a long and difficult journey.

'Time is playing tricks, because of who we are, and where we are. When we are, too, that goes without saying. There are three great truths, Babao, Buddhism, the Catholic Church, and Evolution, and because I say that, that is why they have sent me away from Paris. They don't like the way I bring all three together. But I know I am right, and that there will be a point in time when these three truths will start their convergence towards the Omega Point. It could be here, now, that it is starting to happen!'

'I, too, have seen the dark abyss of time. But you seem to welcome it. I fear it.'

'I cannot fear a future which has been planned by God. You fear the future, because you do not believe.'

Babao made note of the fact that though Michel professed no fear, his hands still shook, and his glance about him was anxious. 'I believe,' thought Babao, 'I believe you are wrong.'

Michel paused, looking at the far horizon where the sand met the sky. He continued, 'This may be the point of maximum divergence from our common origin, some time before the First People. Ahead in the future, the time lines will converge again. The present is the base of two triangles, one emerging from the past, the other stretching to the future. This is the place of holiness. Here is where time will pause for a moment before beginning the rush to convergence. Perhaps.'

'If that is so,' thought Babao, 'it must be stopped.'

'Holiness, yes, but perhaps, first, there will be the plunge into the abyss, the dark night of the soul, the testing through torment, then comes, at last, the light.' Michel's heart raced, his brow grew damp with sweat. Babao passed another cigarette, touching his fingers lightly to Michel's clammy hand.

They entered the cave, climbing over a pile of loose sand blown high in the entrance. Light filtered from behind and the lantern lit up the gloom of the high, vaulted space. Bats started from their sleep and flew high in the roof. Their droppings covered the floor in splattered profusion. Small insects scrunched under their feet as they walked.

Michel turned his back on the shadows of the cave and

looked out towards the desert. 'Once this was a green and fertile land.'

Babao turned to look, and dreamed of pomegranates, bright red against the orange leaves of autumn.

'Look,' said Michel, 'you can see the water channels. Conduits where the waters from the cliffs spilled onto the plain, and rich crops grew between the spring thaw and the summer drought. Melons and palm trees, groves of lemons, valleys rich with grass.'

Babao touched the melon seeds in his pocket and longed to plant them, to see them grow.

'And that line of boulders there, look, it marks out a road.' The path led off into the desert and stopped after a short distance. 'Once the desert bloomed, in the time of the First People. But something happened to turn their lands to desert and to drive them away. A change in the climate, perhaps.'

'I knew it,' thought Babao. 'The power of the spirits grew, until it overcame them, and destroyed them.' The evidence lay before his eyes. Paradise, in ruins.

The two men turned their back to the light, and walked to a large mound of dirt at the rear of the cave. 'This feels right,' said Michel, as he began scraping back the earth. 'I know this is the place.'

Their efforts were soon rewarded. Michel yelled in triumph as he uncovered some large bones, vertebrae, and a femur the size of a man.

'They ate that?' With noodles, and strips of fat, thought Babao.

Michel shook his head. 'These bones are very old. Older than the First People. They might be the bones of dinosaurs, giant animals that died long before the people came. The floods must have come to this place, swirled the litter round, and turned things upside down.'

'They say, that before the time of people, Giants roamed the earth.'

'Both our stories agree in certain most interesting ways.'

They worked steadily through the rest of the day. Just as night drew near, and they made ready to leave, Michel let out a shout, and called for Baboa. 'Look,' he said. 'A clutch of eggs!' Six eggs, each the size of a human head. One was crushed, the others intact.

Babao saw thin strips of egg floating in a bowl of steaming soup.

'Eggs! They've been here so long they have turned to stone.'

Babao sighed.

Michel took his hammer and pried one loose. He picked it up. 'Not nearly as heavy as it looks!' He put it in his knapsack.

Babao looked anxiously at Michel. 'You mean to take it with you?'

'Of course! It's quite a find!'

'It belongs here, to the First People.'

'No, it doesn't. It was before the First People. That's what I keep trying to tell you.'

'It belongs to the time of Giants?'

'I think so.'

'Laka won't like it, if you take it.'

'I'll ask him. Tomorrow.'

Babao let his objections lie.

Together the two men walked back to the camp, their lantern bobbing in the twilight gloom.

'We have a story,' Babao told Michel, as they sat around the campfire that night. 'It is a story about an egg. It is a story which goes like this. In the beginning was the Egg. Long before there was anything else, there was a large Egg, and inside it were kept all the stars, and the essence of pure matter. Then, everything was in a state of perfection. There was no pain, no death, no war, no famine, indeed, no life, but then, one day, the evil spirits broke open the Egg, and the stars fell out, and all the matter of this world fell with them, and everything became infected with the spirit of evil, and the evil spirits laughed at their triumph, and that is how and why we are here today.'

'I have a story, too,' said Michel. 'I believe this egg might be the egg of a dinosaur. Once giant animals roamed the earth, but then, for some reason, they died and left only their bones behind.'

'For the reason I give,' thought Babao. 'I know why they died. I try to tell him. Once again, our two stories are consistent.'

'What if,' said Michel, 'what if this is the moment when the past finishes and the future is about to begin? Not just as is always true, that this moment is the beginning of the next, but this moment is the turning point, the end of our beginnings, the beginning of our end. What would you choose to do?'

'There is never a choice,' said Babao.

'Imagine, though, for the moment, that there is. What will you choose, to take the path forward, or the path back?'

'I would choose to go back,' said Babao. 'So I can stop the Egg breaking, right at the beginning of time.'

'I would choose to go forward,' said Michel. 'To the point of convergence, the Omega Point of pure spirit.'

That night, the red dust descended once again. It fell on the tents, it drifted over the two guards fast asleep underneath the truck, it fell on Michel's knapsack in which he had hidden the egg. In the red moonlight, Laka walked silently round the sleeping camp. He must check on the safety of his charges, the caves, and their contents. He noted the excavation tools, the collecting sacks, the apparatus of the scientific expedition. 'They will take their wagon,' he thought. 'They will fill it with my treasures, they will take that which I guard, that which belongs here. Others will come after them, and soon all will be destroyed.' Silently he walked, feeling his way to the place where Michel slept, feeling his way to the sack Michel had brought back from the cave, noting its rotundity, feeling, in his mind, the nature of its contents.

'They have come to steal from me,' thought Laka. 'Like the Russians. Like the Russians, they will go. The cliffs have their secrets. The cliffs have their powers. The First People will come to protect their dwelling place. They will come today, as they have come in the past.' Laka shuffled from the camp, feeling his way back into the familiar shadows of the cliffs. Swiftly then, he moved, his age lifting from him, as he entered his holy place where the walls gleamed with the radiant images of the pilgrim artisans, and the holy fire kept the powers of darkness at bay. His acolytes bowed before him, and the flame on the shrine quivered with the soft breath of the caverns. 'Prepare the abyss,' said Laka. 'We have two more travellers. The time has come. These people must be sent upon their way. Behold the signs. The red dust falls. The caverns of the earth sigh deeply. The time-signs are appearing. We must be ready.'

'Summon time, the destroyer.'

The calls went round the caves. 'Summon the dark tyrant, time.'

'Summon time, the trickster.'

The word has power when it is spoken. When the time is ripe they say, don't they, the time is ripe, but that means the time is appropriate, when time stops in its progress, because the time is ripe for the appropriate moment to be, in its full intensity, in its full ripeness of time, they say, and at that moment, to savour the intensity, to appreciate the justice of the moment, time stops, the pulse ceases, to allow time for the knowledge to sink in, and so we have the appropriate moment, the rightness of time. You might think, if a chasm opens up, you will see it, like a crack in the earth, so that there might be some possibility that it could be avoided. But that is a crevice in the earth. A crevice in time is different. It is invisible, it cannot be anticipated or avoided. You may feel yourself near it, in those moments of dread awakening, the sudden start just before sleep falls, or just as the nightmare lifts, the jolt awake, the sudden re-entry into consciousness. It is the feeling of waiting, for the next beat of the pulse, the next throb of the heart, the next drawing of the breath, the next link in the chain of thought. The gap is there, the chasm opens by stages, and the thought first comes, no, this can't be true, then the next thought, just before all thought stops, yes, this is true, this is the moment of death.

The next day, when Michel and Babao returned to the cave, all seemed as they had left it the day before. The eggs lay uncovered, the femur and vertebrae carefully placed to one side.

'I would choose to go back,' Babao had said.

'I would choose to go forward.' That had been Michel's choice.

Babao stared at the eggs until the six eggs became one egg, and the one egg grew, and glowed.

Michel stared at the dark between him and the light.

The egg became the Egg. Babao stared in disbelief. Then he started, shouting, as a large fissure rent it from the top to the bottom. 'It must not open!' he shouted. He darted across the cavern floor, and tried to embrace the Egg, pleading, 'No! No! No! The Egg must stay whole this time, enclosing the purity of matter, the divinity of light. The world must be saved!'

The Egg shrank beneath his hands until it rested, small and whole, on the floor of the cave. Ferns grew, lush around the cavern mouth. The crack widened. Within the shell of the egg, the life force surged, triumphant yet again. The sharp sawing sound continued, until the baby dinosaur opened the roof of its shell and looked out.

Babao sprang back, looking round for help. But Michel was not there, and from the world outside the cave mouth he could hear the roar of strange animals, and the swish of large animals in the swamp. It was a new day, a new dawn for new life. The dinosaur opened its eyes. There, cowering against the wall of the cave, against the brilliant background of lush green ferns in the dripping wetness, stood Babao.

Life is good, thought the young dinosaur, dimly, as it ambled across for its first dinner.

Michel sees the future rushing towards him as multiple tracks of convergent lines. He had a grand sense of time rushing joyously past his ears, his eyes, his skin, so sensuous, this onward rush of time, he had not imagined it would be this way. Paradisical. Edenic. Pure.

Faster and faster though, he travelled, now with a sense of time in turmoil. He must be getting closer to the Omega Point, the end of creation, the end to time. He was confident, still, in the sense of his own privileged access to truth, his being at one with the Creation. He has worked hard. He has kept the faith. He has observed the fasts. He is unafraid. He has found the path to the Flaming Cliffs, and he has found the path beyond.

Round him wheeled the stars. Though, what was happening to them? The dark was growing round him, the stars were going out. The darkness was growing, and the void. Where was it, the place in which he believed, the place to which all human ideas had departed, rising as grains of thought to a place beyond this earth, thoughts sublime assuming the form of etherial matter, thoughts never lost, thoughts always influential, flowing from earth their place of origin, to the heavens, their place of rest.

This must be the place that is filled with spirit, invisible, ineffable, all-wise. This must be the place where matter has ceased to be.

Spirit, it must surely manifest itself to him. Here, now. But there was only the sense of time passing in his mind. Round him was the void. Emptiness, the world is emptying. Fear started to take hold of him.

The voices of Babel started to sound in his ears, louder

and louder. He could not understand a word. He could not speak.

If this is perfection, if this is the end . . . it cannot be. This is the time of testing. This is the time when he must keep his faith.

At last, the end of turmoil, the end of noise, the end of disagreement.

The void.

There was nothing there.

Except holiness.

The end of holiness is nothing.

He found the cloud of unknowing. Knowing nothing, he knew everything. There was nothing to know. The void. There was nothing.

Michel fell, screaming, into the emptiness. He had attained his heart's desire. He hated it.

During the night dark figures moved into the cave of the First People. There were two new piles of human bones to be buried. Laka kept his acolytes busy until the morning. The next day the remaining members of the expedition packed up the Citroën and left, and the report to Paris was of an unfortunate accident, a deep chasm in the cliffs, the bodies never recovered.

The Daughters of Darius

Chapter 1

Whenever Vonnie and Freda and Roxane asked their mother, Eva, about their father, Darius, a dreamy look would come into Eva's eyes, and she would sink into a trance, and not answer them for a while.

Freda and Roxane and Vonnie remembered nothing about their father, or so they said, though Eva would say, 'Surely you remember, Freda, when he sat down on that carpet with you, and pretended the carpet could fly through the air round all the countries of the world, and do you know, he was so convincing, that for a moment I thought so too, that the carpet hovered in the air, just a few inches above the floor.'

'Mu-um,' said Roxane, 'you're not still on about that? You've got to stop it and wake up. You can't keep living in a fantasy world.'

'I suppose you know what the real world is like then?' Eva would reply, a retort which irritated her daughters, who knew that whatever the real world was, it could never match their mother's wild stories.

'That rug?' Vonnie asked, staring at the warm red carpet on the floor, with its patterns of intertwined plants. It was a rug from Persia, their mother said, though Vonnie would ask, puzzled, in distraction from her geography homework, 'Where is Persia on the map?' Freda explained to her that Persia was an ancient place that no longer existed, another example of their mother's wild imaginings.

The rug had patterns of peacocks' feathers on it, and behind the glowing blues and greens there was a tree which twined its way, emerging here as a branch of leaves, there a pattern of flowers. 'A tree of life,' said Eva, tracing its pattern for her three daughters. 'That's what he used to say.'

'He left you, Mum, even if he left you with a rug.' Freda bounced her baby Mickie on her knee, and tried her best to sort her mother out. Mickie waved her right hand in the air in a regally circular motion.

'He left me with much more than that.'

'What, where is it? I don't see anything.'

'Look at dear little Mickie! She's doing the royal wave again.'

'Come on, don't try to change the subject. What did Dad leave you with?'

'He left me with my memories.'

'Mum, what would you say if I'd come home with a man like him? Instead of Sergio?'

'Half your luck, I'd say.' Eva sighed into her coffee and pushed a strand of light brown hair from her face. 'He said it was just the way he was. That there were times when he just had to go.'

'And you fell for it?'

'Take me or leave me,' he said. 'It's just the way I am.'

'Sergio would never behave like that,' said Freda with grand conviction.

'He was a huge man, full of warmth.'

Freda grew silent.

'It all seemed so reasonable, while it was happening. He came here, now and then, and gave me three beautiful daughters. He was delighted, Vonnie, when you were born, he wanted three daughters, and there you were.'

Vonnie looked pleased. Freda scowled.

'He was a king in his own country, that I know.'

'Come off it, Mum! You said he was in import-export.'

'The two things are not incompatible.'

'You said it was rugs and silver trays.'

'The lovely things he left me here.' Eva sighed, and gestured at the walls and floors where the rugs glowed in the sunlight.

'We're certainly the best set up house for rugs and silver trays I've ever seen,' Freda agreed.

'And dear, when you left home, when you went off with Sergio, there were plenty of silver trays to spare for you.'

'I never said I wanted silver trays! I wanted a father when I was small.'

'Some people have a father, dear, others have, well, rugs and silver trays.'

A house hung with oriental splendour, that was what they grew up with and took for granted. When Vonnie was small, she loved it when her friends came home and played in caves they made in the carpets. Now, at fifteen years old, Vonnie was more critical of her mother for the way they lived, as she came to see that her friends had houses which were more like houses ought to be. Not so many rugs and trays, for a start.

Then there was the question in the census, the year it happened and Eva sat at the kitchen table, filling out the forms.

'Religion,' muttered Eva, to herself.

'What are you going to put?' Roxane was still at home, and Freda too, the year the census happened.

'C of E,' said Eva vaguely.

'What religion was he?'

'Who?' Though Eva knew they meant him, the absent father. 'I was never quite sure,' she added.

'Go on, tell us,' said Roxane.

'He was more of . . . I don't know . . . there was always

a bit of an altar in the fireplace, nothing obvious, he kept it fairly out of the way, discreet with it.'

'A discreet altar?' Roxane yelped.

'A flame in the fireplace, what's wrong with that?' Eva was nonchalant but it didn't fool her daughters.

Freda looked at her mother with horror. 'I suppose there were blood sacrifices there, on that altar? In our fireplace?'

'Of course there weren't any blood sacrifices in our fireplace!' said Eva, exasperated. 'His offerings were all quite dead when he left them there.'

'Mum, how could you?'

'They were only flowers. Flowers in the fireplace, what could be more natural? More a kind of offering of love. We all have our little ways, Roxane, and let me tell you some of yours are worse than his ever were.'

'Blood has flowed on our hearth.'

'Go and peel the potatoes.' Off Freda and Vonnie and Roxane would go, grumbling.

'You think Dad was a king of another country? and I'm a princess?' Vonnie asked whenever they had this kind of conversation with their mother.

'Yes, and I'm a banana,' said Freda.

'And it's no used writing "Zoroastrian" or something down in the census,' said Roxane to Eva. 'It won't show in the records. All they'll do at the other end is lump us in under "other". With the Moonies.'

'Vonnie, you laughed the day of your birth, and that mattered to him.'

As usual, Eva left her daughters feeling thoughtful, as if even though they could tell their mother the answers, there was still an elusive something that they could not quite pin down.

'I shall never, never be like Mum when I grow up,' said Vonnie to Freda.

'Of course you won't,' Freda comforted. 'We can learn from her mistakes. Look at me.' And Vonnie looked at

Sergio, Freda's lover, and thought about his regal airs, and his airy dismissal of conventional niceties where and when the fancy took him, and wondered at the pattern repeating itself from mother to child. 'It will never happen to me,' Vonnie repeated to herself, 'because I use my brain to think. He didn't do the right thing by her, and the sad thing is, she doesn't even know it. Or if she knows it, she doesn't even mind.'

This was how Eva explained to her three daughters, from time to time, what their father Darius was like, and how, though it must seem to them that he loved her and left her, still she remembered him with great affection.

'You shouldn't have let yourself be used like that.'

'You wouldn't be here, if it hadn't happened that way.' Eva's logic was irrefutable.

'He might have thought of us, that we might need a father.' Freda was reproachful.

'I don't know, fathers can be a bore sometimes,' said Eva.

'Mother!' said Vonnie.

'Sometimes it just happens that way,' said Eva. 'And you have to say to yourself, at least I had something great while it lasted, even if it wasn't going to be forever. How often is it, that it isn't forever, and people kid themselves that it will be forever, and give themselves a bad time, and it still isn't forever. The way I look at it, I enjoyed myself when he was here, and though he was, well, the way some men are, rather intense in his demands while he was present, and yes, it appears he left me to do the hard work of bringing you all up, you could also say, that when he went away it was a bit of a break, and I could get on with the rest of my life, and make of it what I would. He was different. He was good to have around while he was here, and it was a rest to have him go away, and so, you could say, I have had the best of all worlds.'

Roxane scoffed, incredulous. 'You are suffering from delusions of romantic love.'

Eva sighed. 'He swept me in his arms and took me into the desert of my dreams.'

Freda had a talk with Vonnie, and asked her to keep an eye on their mother. 'Let us know if she starts saying too many silly things. It comes from living a life of hopeless fantasy. She's starting to believe her own stories. How many years has it been since she last saw him?'

'You should know, I'm fifteen,' said Vonnie crossly.

'Fourteen years and three months. I ask you, is that the act of a loving father?'

'Not in a conventional sense,' Eva replied, when they challenged her. 'But you must remember it's how royalty has always behaved, and women have always loved them for it.'

After Roxane and Freda and Mickie went home, and Vonnie sloped off to watch TV, Eva took down the photo album and sought out the images of her lost love Darius.

She remembered the day they'd met, so long ago. It had been on the beach at Sandringham. She'd gone down there with a gang of girls from school, one hot day in summer, and they lay on the sand waiting for the boys.

When the boys came, everyone else ran off into the water leaving Eva wrapped in her red towel on the sand. It was early in the summer and the sea was cold, and though Eva knew her friends would sooner or later come running up the beach and force her into the water, still she lingered in the sun. She sifted sand through her fingers. 'To see the world in a grain of sand,' she said, the warm sand sliding through until only a grain was left, stuck in a crease in the palm. 'Look into the grain of sand,' she said to herself. 'See if you can see another world.'

Another world which has spun off from this world, which exists within it, as the world of spinning electrons exists within the world of the atom, as the world of DNA exists in every living cell, imagine, that in the grain of sand, there is a desert, and in the desert live the desert-dwellers, and these are people going about the ordinary business of the desert; trade, and barter, warfare and weddings, tending their camels, erecting their tents. Except I, thought Eva, who am all powerful, have picked up this grain of sand, with a small world within the large world, and look, I place my lips to the sand, and blow, and see, it flies off and falls through the air, and the people in the desert kingdom are troubled by fierce sandstorms followed by a great upheaval of the earth beneath them, and I have caused their problems, I have been the god of the desert; savage, unpredictable, wrathful, capricious.

As Eva watched, light shone around the grain of sand in flight, and spread rapidly, flowing over her like a wave, expanding the grain of sand into a sphere, which pushed over her, and beyond, so that the sand-world became her world. Or did it? She looked around. All was comfortingly familiar, as before. Her friends swam in the ocean. Small children played at the base of the cliff. Two dogs chased each other, barking.

Then along came Darius as if from nowhere, striding along the beach clad in a full suit of armour. He looked as if he'd stepped down from a film set, *Quo Vadis* or *I, Claudius*. Darius seemed puzzled, and kept looking round as if wondering where the rest of the army had gone. When he saw Eva and looked at what she was wearing, he seemed alarmed, so Eva recalled from the blurred details of memory where present desire colours the interpretation of past events. He stopped, stepped back a few paces, looked out to sea and saw Eva's squealing companions, then back to her. Eva was looking good that day (so Eva remembered it) in her black one-piece bathers and bright red towel.

Eva smiled in reassurance. 'What's the matter? Lost your army?'

The stranger looked relieved. He nodded and hesitantly returned her smile, and Eva knew then that she was lost forever. She stood up and dusted the sand off herself, and wrapped the red towel round her waist. 'I'll help you look for it.'

The soldier fell in beside her and urged her on. Together they walked briskly up the beach, the object of considerable interest to the people they passed. Dogs barked at Darius, excited by his clanking armour. Small children squealed, and small boys followed them as they rounded the sand spit at the end of the point. The soldier looked desperately down the beach on the other side. He turned to her.

'Nothing there,' said Eva.

Her companion had to agree.

'Nothing!' he repeated, speaking for the first time, helplessly, sadly. 'Nothing. Nothing.' He sat down on the beach and put his head to his knees as much as his breastplate would allow.

'You look lost.'

'Lost. Lost. Yes, I am lost.'

'So am I,' said Eva. 'I am lost, too.' I am lost to you, she said to herself.

'Though I have been here before.' The soldier raised his eyes from his knees, and looked down the beach. 'It's a good place.'

'Yes,' said Eva. 'We like it here. We come down most Saturdays, me and my friends.'

Wearily, the soldier unbuckled his breastplates and let them fall to the sand. He was wearing a loose cloth shirt underneath, of some rough brown fabric.

'You must be hot,' said Eva.

He smiled and nodded. 'I have been here before, and there are no armies here.' He lay back on the sands, and it seemed to Eva that the weariness of war suddenly passed from him.

'I have been here before.' Eva thought about it. His English was good, but accented in a strange way she'd not heard before. 'Where do you come from?' she asked.

Her visitor laughed. His face lit up. He gestured to the sky.

'You're having me on.'

He shrugged, and lay back in the sand with a graceful languour that Eva found instantly appealing. 'I'd better get back, or they'll wonder where I've gone,' she said after a while. 'Come back and meet people.'

That was how it happened, so swiftly, so simply. He moved into her life. Eva had just turned eighteen. She'd finished her last year of school, and had the summer before her, waiting for her exam results. She didn't know what she was going to do next, work or study, and Darius decided it for her. She would do neither, but the next six years would pass in a whirl of activity which at the time engaged her full attention, though she could never give her daughters a coherent account of what, exactly, it was all about.

Effortless ease, that was Darius. It was his manner of relaxation into the pleasure of the moment that Eva loved about him, right from the start when he so easily got into the swing of her friends at the beach, falling into the moment as if this hour, this sun, this sand, was all there was. It was not long before Eva and Darius were living together, and Darius quickly picked up the domestic arts expected of him, the etiquette of flat-sharing, taking his turn at washing-up and cooking, and only once did he ask, and never again, where were the slaves to do all this?

This was the life that Eva fell into for some six years. She scandalised her family and friends, back then, when people were easily scandalised by such things, but such was her pleasure when she was with him, that she never regretted it.

Darius scorned money, though when the going really got tough, he would produce gold coins of a rare antiquity which he sold at a good price. He moved easily into the barter system, living on the fringes of the coin trade, the oriental carpet trade, and the silver tray trade in ways that Eva only later found strange, so natural did it seem at the time, the ease with which a soldier turned to peace. As a result, Eva learned a lot, and some of it would, surprisingly, stand her in good stead as a single mother. Nothing practical, but she developed an eye for quality in a rug, and her life after Darius was not as tough financially as it otherwise might have been. Her children grew up in a comfortable and cheerful household.

Darius had talked about the Land of Giants, and the Great Sea at the Edge of the World. He often mentioned the stars, and took a keen interest in amateur astronomy, until he learned that others did not believe, as he did, that there were people like ourselves living out their lives out in the remote reaches of the galaxy. Nor did he want their scientific tools of analysis, their astro-chemistry and astrophysics. Eva wondered what was happening, those long nights when Darius could not sleep, when he sat out under the skies, and looked at the stars, lost in dreams.

After Darius left, Eva continued her interrupted studies. She studied sociology and ancient history, a surprising combination of subjects, she was frequently told, when she faced the clashes on the timetable. She studied sociology for the job security, and she studied ancient history to search out some understanding of what had happened to her, for she knew, whatever the secret was, that it lay in the past. It seemed through the study of ancient wars she grew closer to Darius, and learned more about what life must have been like for him. She heard the ancient language in her dreams of Darius, and bit by bit, she grew to understand it.

She got good marks in history, though she was commended on her historical imagination, rather than, more correctly, on the accuracy of her observation and interpretation of what happened in her dreams.

That night Eva flew through the skies in her dreams, the carpet firmly beneath her, keeping her safe as she flew over two of the seven seas, curling around her as she skimmed the tops of the Himalayas, zooming in close to whales, veering off fast from vultures. 'A city lost in time,' the words kept ringing through her mind, the lost city of Bazaklik, where East met West, and made best use of each other, a city set in a cliff, a city of mystery.

She flew as if with wings to her lover, yet Darius was not her lover any more, he was an idea in her mind, the lover of her dreams, the lover of her memory, who, if he still lived in this world, might be someone rather different.

Eva knew the impossibility of loving a man from ancient Persia, yet the reproductive urge, the nesting instinct, transcended time and place. Love she could explain to herself, in terms of the tenderness, the ease with which he settled into new situations, taking command, as if to the manner born.

How to explain it, this love? A surge of hormones? Memory traces in her neurones, of facial expressions, gestures, or a graceful languour in repose, calm in adversity, joy in the moment, and what did she give him in return, that he should come to her? Three daughters, in whom he took great delight, though swaddling was more his style than nappies, and at first he seemed to expect that the child would be placed somewhere else and kept amused until it reached an age when it could fire arrows, if a boy, or run after them and pick them up, if a girl.

One thing was certain. After he left, Eva never found another man who matched up to him in any way.

He was her knight in shining armour, her paramour from the East (or was it the West?), her bronzed lover, her friend and companion, her romantic hero, and the silly thing was, she knew enough about knights in shining armour, and romantic heroes, to know it was all in her mind, as were her dreams. Yet she loved him, and try as she might, she could not stop herself from loving him, nor from missing him, in every moment of every day.

At the end of one day, he had walked out of her life, and never came back. Eva knew he never intended it that way. He just stepped out for a moment into the garden, and that was the end of him. The police looked, but found nothing. They explained it as something they saw from time to time, the man of the family for whom it was all too much, who goes off and sets himself up again somewhere in another city, where he can shake off the daily grind of family care.

Eva knew that the common explanation was not good enough. But she knew she could not tell the police that Darius had gone back to the stars as easily and effortlessly as he had come. Her children would never understand that a man who fell from the skies wearing a full set of armour was no ordinary man. They should be lucky, that he chose them, to be his daughters.

Chapter 2

Behind every great god there is a goddess. So it was with Alexander the Great, King of Macedon, when he proclaimed himself a god. The goddess behind Alexander was his mother, Olympias.

They said of Alexander that one world could never be enough for him. He wanted to travel to the Great Sea at the Edge of the World and lord it over all the earth, and he wanted more. He wanted to travel beyond that place to find new worlds to conquer.

When he became a god, he proved he could do it, that he could pass into an infinity of other worlds, and move on in continual eternal conquest. He found the Edge of the World and fell into other worlds entirely.

Olympias, his mother, knew that something was wrong when Alexander returned from the Edge of the World. Everyone rejoiced when he came back with wild tales to tell but, 'A mother always knows,' said Olympias. She knew that the Alexander who returned was not the Alexander who left. The Alexander who returned was mortal, and soon died. The Alexander who stayed beyond the Great Sea lived on, immortal, and conquers new worlds still.

Alexander, King of Macedon, and Olympias, princess of Epirus; one world could never be enough for them. They made that most unusual of transitions. Both were born mortals but became gods.

They said of Olympias that she embraced a serpent when she conceived her son. Philip, her husband, spied on his wife and saw the serpent resplendent, voluptuous, sinuously entwined around her sleeping body. Later, when he grew blind in the eye that saw the deed he grew afraid. He would not lie with Olympias fearing she would bewitch him further.

What if the snake was not really a snake, but the great god Jupiter in disguise? That could be the secret of Alexander's immortality. It does not quite explain how Olympias became immortal, though it may well be the case that a man may become immortal through inheritance or merit, while a woman gains it by sleeping with a god.

Philip said he refused to lie with Olympias out of respect for the god. Then he divorced her for adultery, relinquishing her, he said, to please the gods.

Olympias did not accept his story, as, indeed, he had not accepted hers.

Perhaps the story of the serpent was the stuff of dreams, with a basis in ancient custom. In Macedon the women tamed snakes and carried them round their arms and necks to keep themselves cool, and in Pella the women went so far as to give suck to serpents. The story of the snake upon his mother was a story Alexander allowed to circulate, though he neither confirmed it nor denied it, and so excited even more curiosity.

'A woman has to have her snakes about her, and if in travelling she has to leave them behind, then it's a good idea to catch a few more along the way. Snakes will stand you in good stead where men forsake you,' Olympias remarked.

Before Alexander went on his last expedition, Olympias said to him, 'Prove yourself worthy of so high a birth.' That's what he said she said, he said to his confidant, who wrote it down verbatim for his memoirs, together with this record of a mother's advice to her son: 'Alexander, as you are a god, pray do not tell Juno that Jupiter was your father. It's never a good idea to tell the whole truth, and in this case, there is a certain room for doubt if the serpent was really there. I was sound asleep at the time. I'm not the best judge of the truth in this affair. So pray do not openly hail Jupiter as your father. He might appreciate the discretion.'

Two things reminded Alexander he might be a man; sleep and the enjoyment of women.

There is a story about Alexander, how he voyaged into the Land of Darkness, with his donkey, his cook, and his tutor Aristotle. Of his mother Olympias they tell another story, of how she travelled safely through the Land of Giants, finding her own food, doing her own cooking, looking after her own donkey, and without benefit of a tutor skilled in the ways of argument. She had to create her own arguments for herself.

In her travels through the Land of Giants she met the giant Eudymedon. Had Alexander met Eudymedon, then Alexander would have known he was in trouble, but not as much trouble as was Olympias. Alexander would go in fear of his life, but not in fear of his virtue.

Olympias was a princess, or so they said, later, but that was not strictly true, not at the beginning. She was just a girl who lived in a village, who tended the goats, ground seeds for flour, knew what hard work was like, and because she was smart, she knew it was not for her. She plotted to escape, once she realised that across the mountains there were other places, other ways of doing things, ways in which others would do the work, and she would be in command, lying back in the cushions with many men to leap to her bidding.

This is how they kept the girls in the villages, back then. 'If you leave home,' they said, 'you will have to travel through the Land of Giants, and no-one who left that way has ever come back.'

'Because there's a better life out there,' replied Olympias, 'that's why.' She took her donkey and left early one dark morning. She took to the hills, and no-one was brave enough to come after her.

'They said he was a giant, Eudymedon,' she said later, 'but by that they didn't mean he was twenty feet tall. They meant he was a giant in a particular manner of speaking. Parts of him were more gigantic than others, proportionally, and no, I never bore his son, that's not the case. The son I produced while I was in the Land of Giants I got by striking the ground with my staff. My virginity remained intact until my marriage, as Philip, dear Philip, will testify.'

Philip refused to testify. From the first time he heard the story, he had his doubts.

'In my travels,' Olympias continued, 'I came to the river Chenab, where there were pythons twenty feet long, and cobras of great speed and ferocity. I showed people how to tame them and extract their poison, and use it on their spears. They were very grateful for it, and yes, they saw it, my staff striking the ground, and the ground parted, and there lay this small child Tryphon, who was not strictly speaking my son, but a son of the earth. But someone had to look after him, and so I took him with me, and that's how he came to be, and how I came to take him in charge.'

Eudymedon was a giant, lewd and stout, and Olympias had little choice in what happened when he caught her. She granted him her favours, for he would have taken them otherwise, and quite likely her life with it. Keeping his mind from his worries, that's what she did, until she escaped, relaxing his erect member so that it lay limp, a simple task, one not calling for great powers of concentration or habits of mind.

Alexander came later, a child of the lawful union of Olympias and Philip, born in the usual way, though his manner of conception may have been unusual.

'Not all that unusual,' Olympias said reproachfully, when Philip first raised the question of divorce. 'Look what happened to Juno.'

'Juno was a real goddess,' said Philip.

'It was the wild lettuce, that's what Juno said. If it happened once, it can happen again. Juno ate wild lettuce, and she conceived a child.'

Philip looked doubtful.

'Three times it happened to Juno, unusual conceptions. The first time, she conceived by the touch of a flower.'

Philip laughed.

'Jupiter believed her. A god accepted the story that Flora gave Juno a flower, and such was its wondrous virtue that Juno grew with child.'

'That's what Juno says.'

'The child was the god Mars, conceived by a flower.'

Philip signalled to his secretary that he should write down the evidence of his wife's wandering mind.

'Then there was her second son, Vulcan. She conceived him by the wind. The wild lettuce was Hebe. I tell you, all this is true, and if it is true of Juno, then it is true of me. I prayed to the gods, that I might become a mother without benefit of a man, and after I prayed, I struck the ground with my staff, and lo, there came forth the baby.'

'Tryphon,' Philip whispered to his secretary. More evidence for the divorce.

'He was a mistake, something of a monster. Fate, woman's lot, you have a moment of madness, and you pay for it, you pay for it. I won't go round striking the ground again. As for Juno, I think she had her regrets. Mars and

Vulcan, what can you say? Look at all the trouble they've caused. And though Hebe was a nice girl, and good with it, until that fateful feast when the gods demanded to see what was under her petticoats and she showed them and they chose never to bless her again. Then that's the gods for you, they get what they want and then they punish you for it.'

'It was the snake, I saw it upon your belly.'

'He was a snake,' thought Olympias, wronged wife. 'But who will ever believe my story?'

'Dear, little Alexander,' said Olympias to Philip. 'Don't you remember him, as a child in his basket, so small, so determined even then to bend us to his will?'

Philip did not remember Alexander in his basket, nor, indeed, did Olympias. Alexander was given to others to rear, as was the custom. Olympias thought it only natural, especially for the sons of gods. Surely Jupiter would not expect her to change his swaddling clothes. If Jupiter knew the problems of infant hygiene, which quite likely he did not, that being the province of mortals and women at that, he would not wish that task upon her.

'Alexander cannot be my son,' said Philip. 'I never lay with you from the day I saw you with the serpent, and that was enough to turn me blind in the eye that saw the deed.'

Olympias replied. 'Perhaps I conceived the child Alexander by myself. I don't remember what I was eating at the time. It might have been wild lettuce that did it, for me, as well as for Juno. As for Tryphon, I travelled through the Land of Giants and preserved my virginity intact. I am a woman of no mean accomplishments.'

She was very definite on that matter, and Philip, though sceptical, knew better than to argue with a woman who has conceived a son from the eating of wild lettuce, and whose virginity was, Tryphon notwithstanding, intact, until he knew her. Or so he thought he knew her.

*

How can it be known, so far from her day, that she was a goddess? If she was the mother of a god, that gives her some claim to the title, but there were other signs. Once, she washed herself in a spring, and from that moment, the waters of the spring had a most agreeable smell. Another story has it that in the imprint of her feet there sprang forth sweet-smelling herbs, called by some heartsbalm, and that from the village that she left as a young girl, her path can be traced by the presence of these sweet plants along the valleys.

With Olympias began the custom of giving court to women, and honouring them above the other sex. In the family of the Macrians, they had a custom which was that the women carried around with them engraved upon their rings the likeness of Olympias, and if pressed, they said, 'We do it for good fortune, for the likeness assists us in our tasks.' On their headdresses was embroidered the crown of Alexander, but it sat above the effigy of Olympias. This was a most curious custom, and no-one of the Macrian tribe could say why they did it this way. Even on their lace petticoats the women embroidered these themes.

Someone will ask, 'Who has heard of these Macrians? Alexander went out and conquered the whole world.'

'But it was Olympias who stayed at home,' will come the reply, 'she who ruled Alexander's kingdom for twelve years while he went off on his travels.'

The Macrians did well at home, honouring Olympias, while Alexander did well abroad. Alexander may have travelled into the lands of the gods, but Olympias it was who first came from those places, travelling from the Land of Giants. When Alexander's troops first passed by the great mountain Mir Samir, and camped in the valley below, they knew they were following in the footsteps of the gods, and Alexander saw the sweet herb heartsbalm, and grew mindful of the stories his mother told him.

*

Two things reminded Olympias she might be a goddess, her magically preserved virginity, and the fact that once she slept with a god, and who knows, perhaps in that act some measure of divinity rubbed off upon her. It was after she passed through the Land of Giants with her donkey, and added to her baggage the baby Tryphon that she met the god Dionysius. Though she did not confide this story to Alexander until just before he went on his last great travels.

'I came to a wondrous place, with laurels and myrtles and ivy. Ivy, imagine it, so far in the strange lands to the East, but ivy it was, of a lush and generous nature. It was there I met the god Dionysius.'

Alexander poured himself more wine. Tomorrow it would be far fields and distant pastures. Tonight it was his mother and her stories.

'He struck the ground with his rod, and from the rock sweet water came to wash me. When I grew hungry, he dug his wand into the earth, and milk came forth. And, as for wine, fountains flowed with it, and honey dripped from the trees. All these things I have seen.' Olympias shook the wineskin in front of her. 'Fountains of wine, from the sweet earth.'

She told Dionysius that it was her destiny to offer herself in marriage to him. 'It was long before I met your father.'

Alexander waved away the boys his admirers kept sending him. They made him angry by their presence. (One day people would say of him that Alexander was fired with the love of boys even to madness.)

Olympias sighed. Dionysius, of course, had been no fool. Marriage with a mortal was not for him, and he knew he could easily enjoy the favours of Olympias without benefit of contract. And he did. When he woke, he said to her, 'It's a problem for you, that you are mortal, and slept with a god. You know what they say, that mortals who lie with gods are not long for this world.'

'On the contrary,' said Olympias who, you must remember, went travelling without benefit of a tutor Aristotle, and had to make up her own arguments for herself, 'surely the opposite must be the case. A mortal, in sleeping with an immortal, takes on intimations of immortality, tending to a longer, not a shorter life. So that is why,' said Olympias to Alexander, some time later, 'I sometimes think I must be a goddess in disguise, and the mother of a god.'

'Why leave that place, if wine flowed from the earth, and honey dripped from the trees? Shall I see it, in my travels?'

'I'm sure you'll pass it by. I left because of the trouble people like you and me have when we meet with the gods. The trouble with gods,' said Olympias, 'you give them what they want, total devotion and all, and it's never enough for them. They move on, from one thing to the next, as soon as the first taste palls.'

Alexander grunted.

'With Dionysius, life was just one long party, and it soon grew rather boring. And if I ever should disagree with him! He didn't like me having my own opinions, not one bit. Thunderbolts would form, and lightning fly, and it all got to be too much. All that dancing and singing and leaping about the hillsides, I thought to myself, I might as well be back at home in the mountains, before I crossed the Land of Giants, milking the goats instead of milking the ground. I wanted to think a bit more about things, about the world, and how it came to be, and whether there are more worlds than this one, and how a woman might travel to them. So I ran away, one day, when the others were off rampaging through the hills.'

Alexander left the next day, unsure whether he was descended from a god on his father's or his mother's side. Or perhaps he might be doubly blessed.

Olympias did not see him for twelve years. They wrote letters to each other, but no-one knows whether the letters were delivered, or whether they were intended only for the historians of Alexander's reign.

When Philip divorced Olympias, she resigned herself

to ruling Alexander's kingdom in his absence, some said most cruelly.

They said she died a brave death.

Alexander travelled to the village that Olympias left so many years ago.

'I am the son of Philip II, King of Macedon,' said Alexander, when he reached the city of Bazaklik, on the edge of the Great Sea at the Edge of the World.

'And who was your mother?' asked Prizansis, chieftain of Bazaklik.

'My mother is Olympias, princess of Epirus.'

'This Olympias, does she wear snakes round her neck, and is she a half-wild woman, visionary and terrible?'

Alexander was surprised. 'How did you know?'

'She was a local girl,' Prizansis said, 'and she ran away. We thought she perished in the Land of the Giants. But obviously not. How did you come this way?'

'Through the Land of Giants. They were sleeping at the time,' said Alexander.

'You won't get any further. That's the Great Sea at the Edge of the World out there, and no one who set out on it has ever returned.'

'Didn't you say the same thing to my mother, when she went into the Land of Giants? Look at me!'

'You may be proof she lived to bear a son, but one thing is true, Olympias never returned to us.'

Alexander died when he was thirty-three. In the year of his death he became increasingly superstitious. He believed divine protection forsook him, and perhaps it did, for the Alexander who returned to Greece was not the Alexander who left, and it was the Alexander who still lives beyond the stars who took divine protection with him. His house was full of priests and soothsayers, and he spent his time in sacrifices, expiations and auguries. Terror often seized him, and madness, at the end, clouded his judgement.

After so many expeditions, so many battles, so many mountains, so many rivers descending from unknown countries, and so many seas, in all which he had come off with safety, Alexander was at last killed by drinking too much.

That was the official story. The poet Dryden hinted at another answer:

One world suffic'd not Alexander's mind
Coop'd up he seemed, in earth and seas confined,
And, struggling, stretched his restless limbs about,
The narrow globe, to find a passage out.

In support of this view, it was said of Alexander that he wept when he heard the philosopher Aristander say there were infinite worlds. His tears flowed because he knew he could never conquer them all.

Aristander said that it seems obvious at first glance that there is this one world, and it looks like that is all there is. Take, however, this flower growing here and look inside its cup, and see there a small green beetle, which lives its whole life in that flower. The flower unfolds from the bud, within it the germ of the beetle, and the germ of the beetle unfolds, and the life of the flower and the beetle pass as one life, for one short period of time, one week. A short life, too short, but to that flower, and that beetle, and the still smaller fleas upon the beetle, and the juice-drinking ants still further inside the flower, that week will be as long for them as our lives are for us. Just as there are worlds within worlds, so there are worlds parallel to our world which spin off further worlds in which all other things are possible.

This is what the philosopher Aristander told Alexander, before he left for the East, and what he told Olympias, after she suspected that the Alexander who returned to her after his travels was not the same Alexander who left.

'There exists a world in which Alexander went beyond the Great Sea at the Edge of the World. There exists a new Alexandria beyond that sea, my lady queen, in which your son, your true son Alexander, lives. Alexander is dead, yet still he lives.' Aristander said all this, when news was brought to Olympias that the Alexander who returned had lost little time in drinking himself to death.

There may even be a city Alexandria among the stars, said Aristander, in what Olympias took to be his cups. He was a prodigious drinker, and his stories at the end of the evening were often wilder than seemed likely. 'It may be that Alexander discovered the pathway that leads to the stars. What are the stars for, otherwise, if not created to inspire in us the challenge to find a way to reach them?'

'I thought the stars were the milk of Juno, that spilled from her breast when the infant Hercules sucked too vigorously.'

'That is a story the women tell about the Milky Way. It is a story which belongs before the time of philosophy in the time of magical romancing.'

'You mean it isn't true?' Olympias frowned.

'True, yes, it must be true,' replied Aristander, awaking too late to the danger he was in. 'Magical romances are true because powerful people believe them to be true, and that has the effect of there being no question of it.'

'Say, though,' said Olympias, a woman who had to construct her own arguments for herself, 'say the stars were once the milk of Venus, that was how they were created, but now they have changed to something different. They have become suns like our sun, and there are worlds like ours that those far-off suns circle, just as our sun circles round us.'

'There, madam, I think you have it.'

'Alexander found the way.' Olympias sat in quiet admiration. 'Surely, then, he must be the son of a god, to return to the places where the gods rule, to Mount Olympus in the stars. Olympus, Olympias, it was written in my name.'

'Surely he must be the son of a goddess,' murmured the philosopher.

'I think so, too,' said Olympias, quietly. 'Did I ever mention my virginity to you? Its quite miraculous intactness, still, at my age and despite my many lovers, and my children.'

'That is a sign of a goddess,' said the philosopher, sinking to one knee, and making his devotions. It did him no good.

'How might I find my son again?'

'You, too, must travel to that strange land.' But Olympias suspected the motives of Aristander, who clearly wanted her gone for reasons of his own. She told him she would think about it and sent him on a mission from which he never returned, to the river Chenab in the land of snakes.

'Besides,' said Olympias, after Aristander was gone, 'I've done all the travelling I want to do for my life. Time to settle down and rule Macedon. If Alexander still lives, in some place beyond the Great Sea, then it may be the case that he will come back and visit his old mother. I don't see why, at my age, I should be the one who has to set off in pursuit.'

The story comforted her, that Alexander had discovered the door to infinite undiscovered worlds, and that somewhere, out there, he was busy taking charge of them.

Chapter 3

Eva woke suddenly. She stared at the comforting familiarity of her bedroom, the soft curtains at the window, the pink sky glowing through the glass. Yet something was different.

She stood. Her feet encountered sand, as if she was on the beach. She bent down, puzzled, and touched sand, warm, as if from the sun. She picked up a handful, and ran it through her fingers.

Eva sat on the bed, stunned and excited. This was how he had come before. Darius. She remembered the warmth of the sand on the beach that day. Then, she let the sand run through her fingers until there was only one grain left in her hand, and he had come. Now, as the sand lay in the palm of her hand, she raised it and once more let the grains fall, until only one remained, then down it, too, fell, and as it fell light shone from it and expanded into a radiant bubble, and the bubble grew and pushed past her and away into the dark recesses of her bedroom. The walls around the window dissolved until it hung suspended in air above the desert sand.

Darius had been with her, in her dream, and now she was awake he had slipped away again. She hovered at the edge of waking, reassured by the warmth of the rugs on her bed, puzzled by the window floating in the air, the pale pink sky, the soft whisper of the desert wind.

It's true, she thought, he's come back. I always knew he would. The call was clear, and her answer came from deep within, her voice a little shaky. 'Darius,' she called. 'Darius, where are you?'

The silence of the night greeted her. Eva got up, and turned on the light.

'Mum, are you alright?' Vonnie came to her door, half-asleep. 'I woke up. I heard you calling.'

'Oh, Vonnie, I thought he was here.'

'You're having those bad dreams again. You've got to give up, stop living in a dream world. Roxane says so.'

'Vonnie, don't you see? The sand, the desert? Look out the window.'

Vonnie saw the sand, the desert, in the bedroom, at two o'clock in the morning.

Darius called again, this time from close by. 'Eva, Eva, where are you?'

'You heard him!' Eva shouted with joy as Vonnie jumped and looked behind her. 'Darius!' Eva called, 'It's me! Here

I am!' She rose from her bed and looked in the direction of the voice.

Darius came running. Eva reached out her hands to him. They touched. She felt his grasp. This was the real world at last. Her long separation was over. Eva smiled, then laughed. He had called her. She had woken from her dream.

Darius said, 'Come!'

Vonnie said, 'Who are you?'

Eva laughed and said, 'I can't come like this.' She picked up her jeans from the sandy desert floor, and pulled them on, tucking her T-shirt into her belt.

Vonnie glared at Darius. 'Mum, what's he doing here?'

'It's just your father, Vonnie darling. He's come back!'

'What, him?'

Darius smiled at his daughter.

'Are you sure?' Vonnie was suspicious.

'Don't be silly, darling, of course I'm sure he's your father. Hurry up, get dressed. We're going! Darius, darling, this is Vonnie, your daughter. I don't believe you've ever met.'

'You must hurry, hurry!'

'You just can't come back here and order us around,' said Vonnie. 'Where've you been all my life?'

Darius looked at her dismissively. 'You don't have to come. You can stay.'

'So? What if I want to come?'

'Hurry, then hurry!'

'Vonnie, get dressed.'

Vonnie looked down at her jeans and jumper. 'I am dressed. What are you going on about?'

'Shoes. Take mine. Those runners.' Eva pulled on a jumper.

'Yes, yes,' said Darius. 'Come now.'

Eva made one quick phone call, to Freda, to leave a message on her answering machine. 'Dear Freda, don't worry about us, Vonnie, and me. We've just gone off with

Darius. I can't explain now, I haven't got time, but I'll send you a postcard when we get to where we're going.'

Darius strode to the window, pushed it wide open, and climbed through. He leaned back to help first Eva, then Vonnie. Behind them, the bedroom faded fast into the haze. The desert stretched out around them, and Darius walked proud and free, a king in his own country.

They strode through the desert. Eva soon slipped several paces behind, as if to the manner born, while Darius strode ahead, keeping a swift watch from side to side as he did so, guiding them surely through the shifting sand. Eva had to work hard to keep up, her feet slipping on the sand, her breath coming with difficulty. She was beginning to wonder whether she had climbed a mountain in her sleep. Worst of all, here she was, reunited with the lover of her dreams, and there he was, without her, striding ahead, deep in conversation with Vonnie, who had never really believed in his existence.

They had arrived at a strange place. It was desert, that seemed obvious, with sand hills like waves of the sea, rimming shallow basins of rock-slab and gravel. Here and there grass struggled through cracks in the stony depressions. A few trees, stunted willows, and shrubby wormwood struggled to survive among scattered clumps of sagebrush.

Vonnie glanced sharply at her father, noting his bronze breastplates, his sword swinging at his waist. 'You're not really the emperor Darius III?'

'I am.'

'Aren't you going to ask about me? How I'm going? What I'm doing?'

Darius looked at her and shrugged. 'You've got a lot to learn.'

'If you were the emperor Darius III, then you crucified 3,000 people in your kingdom.'

'They say that, do they?' Darius spoke bitterly.

'It's horrible.'

'They said it was me,' said Darius. 'But I don't remember. If it was me, then it was at another time, another place. If I don't remember, then it wasn't me they said it about. This is me. Here. Now.'

'Is that an excuse or something?'

'I've changed. I don't do it any more. Crucify people. If that's any help. I've lived a long time, because of him. Alexander the Great.' He glared at the portrait of Alexander on the coin he held out to show Vonnie. 'I would have just died, like everyone else, if he hadn't wanted to go on, and on, and on, in eternal conquest. It was me, wasn't it, the person he had continually to vanquish? I tell you, life has been tough, and eternal life, or the near enough to it that I've experienced, has not been worth it. Conquering, being conquered, marching, tramping on throughout the galaxy, ever onwards, why can't he find something else to do, and leave me alone? There must be another way. That's why I came to find you. There has to be a path of peace, of harmony, of living together in tranquillity, that we can show him, so he'll stop all this. Then I can come home, to you, dear Vonnie, and sweet Roxane, and, what was her name? The other one?'

'Freda,' said Vonnie, with dark suspicion. Darius home to live for good! Eva had neglected to mention that possibility to her. Vonnie looked behind, in the direction of home. There was nothing but desert. Ahead lay a low line of rocky hills, and it was to these that Darius was hurrying.

'What about all this war stuff?' asked Vonnie.

Darius started and looked swiftly behind him.

'War is wrong,' said Vonnie, sternly.

'War is very, very wrong,' Darius agreed, gloomily. 'Especially this war.'

'What war?'

'The one that's happening now. Look after your mother,' said Darius peremptorily, as he strode ahead and disappeared over the top of a sandhill, leaving Vonnie behind.

Vonnie waited for Eva to catch up. 'So? I've met him. The great father. What's the big deal? He's a creep. I want to go home.'

Eva sighed. 'There were some things about him that I had forgotten.'

Vonnie said, 'And we seem to be in the middle of a war of some kind.'

'There always is a war. Somewhere.'

'Mu-um, I came with you, you needed me, and we've left home, to come to this?' Vonnie gestured round her. 'This dump! And in the middle of a war!'

'I'm sure there's some explanation,' said Eva vaguely. She was, much to her own surprise, unworried, and expectant. She had lived in her dreams for so long, that now the dream world had become real she was prepared to wait and see what happened next.

Vonnie tramped on across the desert, cross and tired. 'What about me? You don't care,' she wailed. She grew hot, and took off her jumper and tied it round her waist.

'He says he'll soon be back.' They were greeted by a man of large proportions, dressed in black-and-red canonical gear. He introduced himself, in Germanically accented English, as 'Wolff.'

'Eva,' said Eva. 'And this is Vonnie.'

'How did you get here?' Vonnie asked.

'One travels,' said Wolff, waving a beringed hand in the direction from which they had come. 'I was on a mission. I set out to seek the lost. I found them. Then, it would appear, I joined them. I was accompanied by an incompetent guide who lost the way.'

In response to his waved invitation, Vonnie and Eva sat down beside him on a large carpet spread in the shade of the cliff.

'Water?' asked Wolff, gesturing towards a jug and brass cups on a silver tray. 'Jerome!' he called, waving his right hand in the air, his gold rings catching the light.

'Water, wait, is it safe to drink? The water?'

'Safe? Safe water? It's water. Drink.'

A young boy slouched out from the recesses of a cave in the cliff. 'Mrs Robinson?' he whispered, excited, when he caught sight of Eva.

'Not yet, Jerome,' said Wolff. 'Faith requires patience, and faith in Robinson requires the greatest patience of all. Jerome is my acolyte,' he explained to Vonnie and Eva.

'What is an acolyte?' asked Vonnie, smiling at Jerome as he poured water for her, with great sorrowful sideways glances, as if these were not the visitors he had expected from the other world. She drank the water thirstily. 'It tastes fine,' she assured Eva.

'If only I'd known I'd have brought the tablets. But we didn't know we were coming,' said Eva to Wolff. 'Where are we?'

'An acolyte,' said Wolff to Vonnie, as he too drank deeply, 'is someone who is receiving training in the word.'

Jerome stood silently by.

'Where are we?' asked Eva. 'Who is Robinson? How do we get home?'

'Here,' said Wolff, 'one soon learns to look upon that other world, the world you have just left, as something that has passed. Here I am, you must say, as I say, and here I must stay and make the best of it. Have no expectation from this world, and no desires from it, and you shall be happy. What you must now do is sit yourselves down in the desert, where we pass the time, as best we can, waiting on the great ones. There is no point in travelling on, since we do not know where we are. Since we are here, God has given us this time. What we do with it, is up to us.'

Vonnie turned to Jerome. 'Why did you think my mother was someone else? Are other people coming?'

Wolff turned to Eva. '*Robinson Crusoe*, are you by any chance acquainted with the book? I brought a camel-load of the book with me to the desert, translated, by a Mr Zarock, of Malta. Very popular the book is, in this place. Four camel-loads of the Bible, and one of *Robinson Crusoe,* I brought with me. Should have been the other way around, as it turns out. The people here have taken to *Robinson Crusoe* as their sacred book. Still, at such times one learns to pray, and I look upon *Robinson Crusoe* as a book from which it is possible to learn the virtues of hard work, the economics of trade, and the Protestant ethic.'

'Robinson,' Jerome said softly to Vonnie. 'It is the word of Robinson I have come to learn.'

'*Robinson Crusoe,*' said Vonnie. 'It's only a story.'

'The greatest story of them all,' Jerome was happy to agree.

'Go,' said Wolff to Jerome. He spoke to Jerome's departing back. 'At least I try to spread the word. I say the right words, and he hears the wrong ones.'

'Where are we? Are we really stuck here? Where is Darius?'

'These caves,' Wolff waved behind him. 'People have lived here for thousands of years. There is something about them that draws people to them and by and large keeps them here.'

'I didn't mean to leave home for more than a few hours. What do you mean, that we can't get back?'

'Look upon it, that world you have left, as a place you once lived in, but are come out of.'

'I want to go home,' said Vonnie. 'I said I'd come, but I didn't mean forever.'

'Between you and there, there is a great gulf fixed, a gap in space, and in time. Look on it this way. You are removed from your former troubles.'

'Only to find some new ones!'

'He didn't promise you a garden with pomegranates, and honey flowing in soft streams?' Wolff turned to Eva.

'No.'

'Just as well.'

Eva sifted warm sand through her fingers and grew thoughtful.

Vonnie leaned towards her. 'Don't worry, Mum, it's only a dream.'

Eva smiled in gratitude. 'Of course. That's what it is.'

'As you please.' Wolff turned to Vonnie. 'Save the whale?' he read out the words spelled out on Vonnie's T-shirt.

'Oh, that,' said Vonnie, stretching out her T-shirt and looking down at it. 'It's just an old shirt, but I really like it.'

'Save the whale?' queried Wolff. 'Save it, for what? It is, I suppose beloved of Christ, as are we all. Is it for that reason, then, that it is to be saved?'

'Save the whale means, save the whale. I suppose, if you've been here for a while,' she gestured at Wolff, his clothes, the desert, 'you might not have heard of them. Greenpeace. No more killing whales. You know?'

Wolff took an elegant hanky from his pocket, and twirled it round his fingers. 'You mean, save the whale from the good whaling ships?'

'The bad whaling ships.'

'Tell me, my dear, if the whale is to be saved, whatever will happen to Jonah?'

'Jonah who?'

'How can he ever escape? Think of him, poor Jonah, imprisoned forever in the belly of a whale. No whalers to kill the whale and release him from his prison.'

'Robinson Crusoe will rescue him.' These words came from Jerome, who had returned to his servant duties. He could not stop himself. 'Robinson Crusoe will rescue us all, and Jonah, and he will look after the Emperor Darius, yes, and you too, my father, though you deny it!'

'I do deny it, Jerome. To your duties. Go!'

Jerome shook his head in sorrow, and resumed his mournful place back in the dark recesses of the cave.

'A little knowledge,' sighed Wolff. 'How dangerous it is! Where was I? Ah, yes the whales.'

'Perhaps you don't know much about whales. They're very intelligent. They have more brains than we have.'

'For what purpose is the brain of a whale? Their blubber, I grant you, that is some use. They make good oil for candles. The good Lord watches over us in mysterious ways.'

'Where I come from,' said Vonnie, 'we have electric light. We don't need candles. So we don't have to kill the whales any more.' Vonnie settled some more cushions behind her, and glared at Wolff, her mother, and the desert, in turn.

'Let me tell you a little of my story. My father was a Rabbi, and I was born a Jew. As a boy, I was called by different voices. I had a burning ambition, which I knew, as a Jew I could never accomplish.' Wolff paused, waiting for Eva to ask him.

'Yes?' prompted Eva. 'What was that?'

'One day, when I was some seven years old, someone asked me what I wanted to do, when I grew older. I remember it most clearly. I was asked, and I responded, while my dear father stood by, and my mother waited fondly. I answered that I wanted above all else, to be the Pope. Popes were then, back in those days, not infallible, so I knew I had some chance. Of course, my father, the Rabbi, did not like it. He grew sorrowful, and as soon as I could I left home, eleven years old I must have been, and I began my life of wandering. I rather like wandering. It's why I'm here. I had a guide, but he lost my way.'

Vonnie stood up and stretched. She was listening hard, but pretended not to be.

Wolff continued, 'The thing to do, in war, is emphasise the difference. I travel in full canonicals, like this, red and black, and I carry the Bible, open, and I tell the soldiers I meet that I dress in red to show I am ready to give my blood for my faith. If you kill me, I say, I shall die the death of a martyr, and live in Paradise. They don't want to do me a favour, so they don't kill me. It works every time.'

'I don't think that will work, for me,' said Eva, doubtfully.

'You are a scholar?' Wolff turned to Vonnie. 'I was a scholar once, at your age. I travelled to England, and there learned English, at Cambridge, though I had as the main object of my studies, Persian, Chaldean, Syrian, and Arabic.'

'Of course,' said Vonnie, faintly. 'I study, too, biology, and French, stuff like that.'

Vonnie stood up. 'I'd like to look around a bit,' she said to Eva. 'You can wait here if you like. Probably for another fifteen years. I want to go home.'

'My acolyte will show you round.' Wolff summoned Jerome.

'Is it safe?' asked Eva.

'As safe as water,' Wolff replied.

'How safe? Isn't there a war going on here?'

'There's always a war going on somewhere. It's Alexander's fault.'

'I don't need anyone to go with me,' said Vonnie.

'Ever seen a Time Gate?' asked Wolff.

'Only on TV,' said Vonnie, in surprise.

'We have one here. Show her,' he said to Jerome, who nodded his head.

'A Time Gate? It's only a story.'

'It's true,' Jerome assured Vonnie. 'As true as Robinson.'

'Is it safe?' asked Eva.

'Go on,' said Vonnie. 'You're having me on.'

'Come with me,' said Jerome. 'I'll show you.'

'Come back soon,' said Eva. She waved an anxious good-bye as Vonnie walked off with Jerome, along the path beside the Flaming Cliffs.

Chapter 4

Robinson

How the book of Robinson Crusoe came to be the holy book of the people of the Flaming Cliffs, and how it led them to the good life.

This is the story of Robinson and his desert followers. It is a story of an ordinary man, born to a middle station in life, who was impelled, against his will, on a great quest. He became great, as all may rise to greatness, through troubles and through resignation to them, through trials by water and wild beasts, through despair at imprisonment, to attain in the end the knowledge that escape was possible, at least from the prison of his troubled thoughts. Robinson passed from despair at his calamity to the joyous recognition of divine wisdom and goodness working through it. At the end he was rewarded with great riches.

Robinson travelled from the great Town at the Edge of the World, called London, to the Great Sea at the other Edge of the World, and somewhere on the way between these two great places, his ship was wrecked and he was cast adrift. He lived for many years on an island, which at first he called the Island of Despair, but which later became, under his careful management, something more akin to a new Garden of Eden. His fall was fortunate. What looked like calamity turned out to be a blessing.

His ship was like a camel, which carried him in his belly across the desert seas, and cast him up, like Jonah, on a green and fertile island.

To the people of this desert, he arrived at the happy land. To live on an island is to live in a state of blessedness.

The cult of Robinson is an eminently practical cult, and

Robinsonians have become quite rich, with the goodness of Providence consistently translated into material as well as spiritual benefits, as fits the ambitions of a desert-trader. Money is the general dominating article in the world.

Some are inclined to say that Robinson Crusoe *is only a story. In one way, that is true. There are stories in the book, but they are fables to enlighten the ignorant. There are stories told, of the life of Robinson, events which are known to be fictions. For example, Robinson cuts down a large tree, and then endeavours, through the daily labour of some two years, to turn it into a canoe. He then says he found it too big for him to lift, and too far from the water for him to push it there, so his labour was wasted. But Robinson knew in advance his labour would be wasted. He was no fool. He told the story to show others, that they should not embark on activities beyond their competence.*

Robinson was a great worker of magic. He rescued a male kid, but look, later, the kid turned female, and brought forth young. Here, at this place, Robinson took off his clothes to swim from the wreck, but lo, at this part of the story, but half a page on, he wore breeches, into the pockets of which he crammed ship's biscuits.

If we become like him, our male camels will turn female and produce young, when that is what we want, but will turn male again, when we need them for long desert treks, or for waging war.

Here it said that Robinson had no salt, but there he taught his servant Friday to eat salted meat. The magical creation of salt, that was no problem for him, and for others, likewise, when they find the secret. The believers say, of the inconsistencies in the book, that all things are possible for the mighty Crusoe, for he is the best of gods.

The book provides eminently practical information, on how to conduct war, how to sail on the sea, how to become rich, how to channel the powers of Providence to material ends.

It is a story of how he came home to his partner who did not forget him, in his absence.

He came home to his partner, but it was not his wife, for he met her after his return. It was his partner in business who greeted him most warmly. He did not have a wife to come home to, and indeed she played little part in his later story. She bore him three children, and died in the same half-sentence as she was first mentioned, on the second last page of the book. This proves the unimportance of women, and the real significance of sand. Sand is the receptacle of footprints, the sign of the signs of life.

The sand has seventy names. The sand which flows, the sand which sticks, the sand which blows uphill, the sand which blows down hill, the sand in which footprints may easily be left, the sand which marks the passage of time, the sand which dessicates, the sand which deprives of life, the sand which preserves the body from corruption.

Chapter 5

'Remember, how he sat on that carpet with you, and pretended the carpet could fly though the air round all the countries in the world, and he was so convincing, that we all believed it, and you know, the carpet hovered in the air for a few moments, just a few inches above the floor.'

Roxane sat on the carpet, remembering what Eva had told her about her father. She leaned forward and with her fingers traced the arabesque of stylised intertwined branches, with here a leaf in bud, there a flower, here the tendril, there the leaf in full display.

Darius said the carpet could fly through the air. He said so many things which had become part of their family history. Where once Roxane scoffed, now she doubted. Eva had always told her stories with conviction. What if they were true?

Roxane, as she kept insisting to herself and others, was

a sceptic, a modern woman, who believed in modern ways of doing things. Hence, part of what was happening to her she could explain in terms of biological urges, the desire to search for her genetic ancestry. She found herself listening, with rapt attention, to stories of adopted children who sought and found the mothers who had relinquished them, of the children of the new birth technologies who needed to keep tabs on their biological past. Stories of conception *in vitro*, semen donorship *in absentia* and squabbles over frozen embryo orphans and the riches they stood to inherit, all these stories swirled in her mind, asserting the dominance of the gene, the power of biology. Though the sceptic in her head said, 'Rubbish!' the romantic in her heart said, 'Well, I really would like to know a bit more about my father.'

Half her genes were his genes, 25,000 of the little wrigglers, the genes of the absent father, if her mother was right, which Roxane, in her rationalistic moments, did not believe. Eva had to be somewhat deluded about some things; he couldn't have fallen from the sky wearing a full suit of armour. Yet, if her mother was only half-right there might be a touch of royal blood in there somewhere.

Her father, thought Roxane, might never have heard of the concept of the gene, or have any idea of the nature of biological inheritance, but primogeniture, the right of the firstborn, or, the right of the firstborn son, but there was no son in their family, and though Roxane was the second-born daughter, she might just have a few rights in her father's kingdom.

Remember, Darius had said, the carpet could fly through the air. There was in what she heard the kernel of truth, the grain of the real, some dark memory of an experience in her early childhood. Roxane sat and traced the pattern, trying to dredge up from the mists of memory the elusive idea that was there, slipping in and out of the dark recesses.

Her mother's stories were impossible. Yet now Roxane wanted to believe. She pulled the phone across the floor to where she was curled up in comfort on the carpet, and rang Eva.

No answer.

She tried Freda and got her.

'I'm going. I've decided. I just had to talk to someone about it.'

Freda juggled her baby on her knee. 'Mickie sends you a wave,' she said, as Mickie bestowed a gracious wave on the phone.

'Aren't you going to ask me where I'm going?'

'Yes, sorry. Where?' Mickie picked up trails of the telephone wire, and wrapped them round the top of her head. 'Oh, Roxane, Mickie has made herself another crown.'

'Bazaklik. You've got a thing about Mickie, did anyone ever tell you?'

'You don't understand. She's always doing it. Acting like the Queen. Bazaklik, though. Wow, Roxane, wild.'

'You know what I mean?'

'I think I do. What about your job?'

'Resigned. Chucked it in. Cleaned up my desk at work, tossed everything out. My parting present to Michael, in the big office. I went in. Place was in a mess. I sorted it out. Then I said I was going. Why not go? Find out if there's anything to find out. Going on the trail of the long-lost father. To the romantic East.'

'Romantic? Do you know what you're in for?'

'I feel I'm being called.'

'Called? Roxane, are you feeling quite all right?'

'This guy in the travel agency says Bazaklik is the place to go this year. Ancient Greece and ancient Asia, best of two worlds. East met West. Once. Back then.' Roxane looked through the intertwined branches on the rug, and caught glimpses of an ancient city, its dwellings set in the face of a cliff. The clay walls of the houses lay crumbled in ruins, the city was deserted, the desert wind was blowing, the sand was almost between her fingers.

'East meets West. You mean, like here? Like this street? Mrs Giannakopoulos down the road, the Ng's next door? Why leave home?'

'Ha, ha, very funny.' Roxane looked more closely into the pattern, and saw people dressed in white togas sitting in the desert sand, languidly drawing triangles in the dust, debating geometry. Saffron-clothed monks walked and talked in pairs. Roxane saw herself riding on a camel, guided into the city by a strong brown youth who, from time to time, paused in his work to look up at her, his eyes shining in adoration. 'I need to find out if these memories are really my own. Or if they've been implanted by some alien invader.'

'I can see you on the back of a camel, the guide asking you for more money before he'll let you off.'

'You know, I thought of the camel. I'll have someone lead me, but some dignified inhabitant of the region, a descendant of Alexander the Great, dark of skin, Grecian in his profile.'

'Roxane, I see you in this strange dusty place where you don't speak the language, having an awful time. What language do they speak?'

'I shall communicate by means of mime. Take me to the city of my fathers. I shall act it out.'

'You'll manage somehow. You always have.'

'If I go, then you can follow,' said Roxane. She put down the phone and stretched out on the carpet. Funny, how lately the carpet had figured both in her waking moments and her dreams. Her nights were full of stories, and she felt she was beginning to understand that Darius might well have been caught in the grip of forces greater than himself, that he never meant to leave them, and indeed, in the dreams she was having, he had not. Roxane would wake in the night to the sound of the noise of clanking armour. Then she would wake in the day and everything was back to normal.

The carpet felt sandy. She must vacuum. She looked at the grains of sand where they clung to her fingers. Size, she thought dreamily, all is relative, these grains of sand, to see the world in them, to see each grain of sand as a world, to see the bridges which connect each world to the next, between one grain of sand and another. She has picked them up in her fingers and separated them. She has broken the bridges between those tiny worlds. She looked at her fingers, and saw through the gaps between them, Eva and Vonnie, trudging through the desert.

If she closed her fingers, and opened them again, she saw her sister Freda, looking in on the sleeping Mickie, checking to see she was warm and covered. Parallel worlds, worlds within worlds, worlds in grains of sand, bridges which exist, bridges which she has broken, bridges which she must mend. The world in the grain of sand may be a world like this world, a world which might grow around her, enveloping her as she lay.

The carpet rode above the ground, on a cushion of air.

Through her fingers she could see the block of flats where she lived, and Mike and Jenny in the yard sweeping sand out of their flat, sweeping sand which has blown in from somewhere. She sees the brooms working, she sees the sweepers talking about it, wondering how it got there, so far from the beach. There was Kevin, with a dust-pan and brush, standing uselessly looking on.

Roxane tried to get up to join them in their activities. So much sand to shift. She felt too languid to move. Mike tied a handkerchief around his nose, yes, she could see it, there was a sandstorm, and the sand was blowing in his face.

There is no desert in Melbourne. The sand-world must be somewhere else. Yet that was her house, that was her yard, they were her housemates.

As Roxane drifted more deeply into sleep, the carpet

rose higher in the air, until it slipped over the window ledge, and vanished into the night.

Chapter 6

'Mr Wolff,' said Eva sharply. 'Can you please explain what has happened? How you are here? Where we are? And what has happened to Darius, who brought us here, and left us?'

'My dear, we are all left. Bereft. Forlorn.' Wolff gestured at the retreating figures of Jerome and Vonnie. 'You have come to join the lost. This is a place of secrets. Here you will learn the ways in which faith and reason interact in the world. Faith does not have to be faith in fairies, or faith in God, or faith in oneself. No, faith is the way in which the mind operates, from one minute to the next, the way it keeps going, not sliding down into the abyss of unreason.'

'If I wanted to know all that,' said Eva, 'I would have taken a course in philosophy.'

'On the other hand, if you want the Emperor Darius III,' Wolff said, rising magisterially to his feet, 'There he is.' He pointed to the figure of Darius, who was walking swiftly towards them. Wolff made a low bow in the direction of Darius, and swiftly disappeared into the cave in the cliff.

Eva leapt up. 'Darius!' she called, and he saw her and smiled in her direction, so warmly, that once more she was lost.

'Eva!' he called, and she went towards him. He took her hands, and gestured at the cliffs. 'Let us go!'

'Darius, you haven't explained. Where I am. Why we're here.'

'You are at the City of Sands in the Desert of Lob. These are the famous Flaming Cliffs.'

Eva looked to one side at the cliffs, to the other at

the ranks of sandhills, with their sharp contrast of light and shade. Ahead of them the sandhills yielded to a low outcrop of conglomerate formation, like a tesselated pavement marking the path from the desert to the Flaming Cliffs.

'This is a place that is very old. This path, look how smooth it is. It has been worn deep by the passing of many feet over many thousands of years. It is a place where people of one age make contact with people of another age.'

Darius walked as one on whom the affairs of state hung heavily, perpetually getting in the way of his intentions to rekindle the flames of his long-lost love. Together they followed the path beside the cliffs. They crossed a shallow stream which barely wet the sand. Along its edges small plants sprouted leaves of a tender green. When Eva looked up, she saw long rows of openings in the cliff walls.

Darius looked where she pointed. 'These caves, too, are very old. The people who came here made them. They carved them out of the cliffs. Here you will find there's some stuff about Robinson. Elsewhere you will find other caves, still tended, which tell the story of the Buddha, a thousand times over. Further on, there are caves more ancient still, places which tell the stories of Gilgamesh and Mani, Barlaam and Joasaph.'

Eva pointed to some words scrawled in white on the cliff walls. 'That doesn't look ancient. That looks like Russian, to me.'

Darius nodded. 'They left their names. As if they mattered.'

'Robinson? Russians?'

'The Russians weren't interested in the Robinson stuff. They wanted gold, but there never has been any gold here. The only gold that is here is the golden thread of reason, which binds all people together, the cord which stretches from earth to heaven. This is the take-off point.'

Eva was impressed.

'Come!' said Darius. 'See what is in here!' They stood in front of a statue of a large cherub with folded wings, its sightless eyes staring at the desert, its mind turned inwards on its cherubic thoughts, a guardian of the caves, without weapons, but with a brooding air of power waiting to be unleashed on any unwanted intruder. Behind lay the entrance to a cave.

'I don't know,' said Eva, doubtfully.

'Trust me,' said Darius. Eva glanced at him sharply.

Darius led the way into the dark recesses of the cave. It was far deeper than Eva had imagined.

'We need to wait a moment, to let our eyes adjust.'

'Where are we?'

'Inside the Flaming Cliffs. That is their name, because the sun lights them in flame as it rises and sets. You must see the sight sometime, from the desert.'

As her eyes grew used to the gloom, Eva saw that the walls glowed with scenes painted on them, and she moved closer to look. Some light came from above, from windows cut like a clerestory, high up in the cliffs. Patterns of leaves and flowers had been painted on the walls, the colours vibrant and glowing, delicate blue-greens, soft pinks.

'They are the colours of the bloom which lies on the surface of the young lotus,' Darius explained.

A narrow passage at the end of the cave gave way to a room, then other passages, other rooms, each lit a little from each other. 'I'll never be able to find my way back,' said Eva.

'Don't worry. You'll have me,' replied Darius.

'Yes,' said Eva, doubtfully. She was distracted by a distant vision, further into the caves. Beads of light hung in the air. From a brass saucer-lamp, Eva saw, as she moved closer, with someone tending it. The reverberating sounds of a gong made her jump and turn, trying to catch sight of what was going on, this time from another direction. The beat of the drum was soon joined by a harp and a flute. The smell of incense wafted from the lamp towards her.

'This is the cave of lists,' said Darius. 'It's supposed to be special.'

Eva saw a map of an island set in a golden sea, and on the island was painted a thick grove of luxuriant green trees.

The tender of the flames hurried forward to greet them, bowing to Darius. Darius grimaced, and hurried Eva along, with the caretaker in breathless attendance. 'Here Robinson is filling his pocket with biscuit, there he found rum to drink, here shows where he assembled large spars of wood to make his raft. Here we see three chests of bread and one jar of rice. Look, three Dutch cheeses, as it says in the book.'

'Dutch cheeses are red,' said Eva.

'Dutch cheeses are wrapped in goatskin,' said the attendant, firmly.

'No, they're not,' said Eva, to no avail. Darius moved as if to brush the caretaker away, but Eva stopped him. 'No, let him continue. I'm interested. This is the kind of history I never knew existed.'

'Three cheeses wrapped in goatskin. There are the five pieces of dried goat's flesh, that is the bag of European corn, here are the rats that ate the barley and the rice, here is the flask of cordial waters, there his clothes he rescued. Tools from the carpenter's chest, ammunition, and arms, pistols and powder horns, a bag of shot, two barrels of gunpowder.'

'We must hurry,' said Darius.

'I am hurrying,' said Eva.

The caretaker trotted beside them. 'This is the place of lists. Look, over here, these are the animals on the island, these are the trees and shrubs, here is a list of the food crops he grew, here the stages according to which he built his shelter, his castle, the enclosures for the animals.'

'This is a map of the island. They are the places of pilgrimage. Here he meets the cannibals, there he is on the beach of bones.'

'What's it all for?'

'A man is tested not in the desert, which is, after all, the nature of daily life here, but in the sea.'

'What about me? I'm not a man.'

'There are no women in *Robinson Crusoe*.'

'What's that supposed to mean?'

'It is one of the mysteries. How he managed,' said Darius. He led the way more deeply into the caves.

'This is the cave of life. The life of Robinson. Here is his disobedience, there we have his punishment in shipwreck, there we have his feeling of isolation, his alienation from his life, there his repentance, here his conversion to seeing that whatever happens, is good. There we have his redemption, here his deliverance from the island, and his triumphal return home, to great wealth and great fame.' The caretaker bowed, and left them.

'It's only a story,' hissed Eva. 'Why don't you tell them?'

'What does it matter? I'm tired of it all, tired of everything.'

'Where are we going? Why am I here?'

'We'd better talk.'

'It's about time,' Eva agreed.

'It's Alexander. I keep trying to get the message across to him. There has to be a better way than all this conquest and conquer stuff. I try to keep him off this planet as much as I can, with my limited access to power. I'm not a god like he thinks he is, I'm just someone who's been around a long time and learned a few tricks. I'm just someone who got caught up in the plans of someone else, and is doing the best he can.'

'It's hard for me to work out. You've lived on, too, like him?'

'It's hard for me to explain. Dust, I think that has to be the secret. Some of the dust of immortality has twinkled from Alexander onto me. In intimate skirmishes, the rough and tumble of thrust and parry, that's how it happened. That's how I became somewhat immortal, though I do not think I am completely so. It remains to be seen, whether, one day, I shall die. I'll say this for Alexander, it's nothing personal he has against me. It's the idea of conquest he's in love with, and he's been doing it for so long, he just can't seem to stop himself. He can't slow down and return to more peaceful ways, growing ivy, tending snakes, like his mother. Ah, how I long to be able to grow geraniums. To potter around doing just as I please.'

'Darius, are you feeling quite well? You never used to talk like that.'

'I've grown old, I think, and a little tired, within, though without, I look the same.'

'True,' said Eva. 'While I have aged outside, but remain the same inside. Alexander, where is he now?'

'Over in the stars somewhere, but from time to time he finds the passage back, and then, what can I do? He keeps coming after me, and I just have to act to defend myself. I don't wage war. I just act in self-defence.'

'I think this must be a dream. These caves, this place. Am I really here?'

'The desert is a place which is very full of dreams, and some of these dreams have escaped from their prisons in the mind. Here at the Flaming Cliffs some elements of the dream world have worked their way loose and fly where they will, and sometimes it is very hard to tell which is which, whether one walks in the dream world or the real world.'

'Perhaps,' said Eva, 'there is no real world. That is the way I feel just now. Perhaps there is just a succession of dreams, and our lives never touch the real world, not once.'

'Here, some would say, that world, the real world, is the world of the chosen few after death. Others of us die and then return, and we enter another dream, and are minor characters in the dreams of others. Only I am a major character in the dream of Alexander, his dream of world conquest and domination.'

'It's not what I've been used to.'

'Here dream worlds intersect. It is a place of junction, a place where you will see many strange things. You can't escape it. Shut your eyes sometimes, you must, and when you drift off to sleep, who knows what scenes will pass before your eyes, and when you wake, who knows which world it is, to which you will waken?'

As Darius said this, the light grew brilliant again, and they were outside, having made their passage through the cliff. They had left behind the dust and sand of the desert. Here, inside the cliff walls, the desert bloomed.

'An oasis,' said Eva. 'It is what I've always thought, that you reached a place of refuge. It's beautiful.' Eva saw a golden city set in a green and grassy valley. Goats wandered through the streets, and chickens, and washing flapped in the breeze. 'Where are we?'

'Bazaklik.'

'This is Bazaklik? The place Roxane's been talking about? She showed me something different though, a picture of a ruined city set in a cliff.'

'This is a city set in a cliff.'

'Not yet in ruins,' said Eva, thinking of Roxane and her travel plans.

'You begin to understand.'

'I have travelled, not only to this place, but to this time, the time before the time that Roxane will visit here?'

'Travel,' said Darius bitterly. 'It used to be much easier, before Alexander came along to order us all about.'

'Let me get this straight. I have travelled, in space and time? How? Why?'

'You always did ask a lot of questions,' said Darius. 'Why did the Lake of the Crescent Moon not silt up with sand? It was because the ceaseless winds of the desert were always at work, blowing off the Lake, and upward. Then, one day, the gods deserted this place and the winds turned treacherous, and the sands bore down relentlessly. The water was covered in sand, and the desert bloomed no more.'

As they walked through the city women kept joining them, women who seemed to have some kind of claim on Darius. He greeted each with an absent-minded affection, though making it clear to each, in various languages Eva could not understand, though she caught the gist of the message clearly enough, that they must not bother him just now. Each woman in her turn gave Eva a sharp and knowing look before moving on. Though, after a while, Eva, looking back, realised that the women had not walked on their way, but had fallen in behind, and were trailing them through the city.

'This retinue,' said Eva, nodding over her shoulder. 'Those women. Who are they?'

'Them?' Darius looked back, gesturing vaguely at the trail.

'Them,' said Eva firmly. 'Who are those women? All those women?'

'Some of them are my wives,' said Darius, with reluctance.

'How many?'

'It's not quite what you think it is,' said Darius.

'Oh? And how do you know what I'm thinking?'

'Oh, Eva, darling, I know your thoughts, I know you have been a good and faithful wife to me, as I have been a good and faithful husband, in my fashion.'

'Really? Am I expected to join the procession?'

'It's always hard to explain. Women find it hard to understand, but I say to them, it's all perfectly comprehensible, once you look at it from my point of view. You will always be number 1 wife to me, though of course, I suppose after two-and-a-half-thousand years, it must be, let me see, number 2001 or thereabouts.'

Eva yelped. 'So there's a list?'

'Not a list,' said Darius. 'I never thought of it as a list. Look, these people here, they have a way of looking at life that helps explain these things. They don't look at time like your people, as if it was beads strung out on a string, as if we were part of the way along a time-line that stretches from here to there, with us in the middle, in a state of transit, from here to there, at this bead on the string, with those to come, and those which have past.'

Eva knew her heart was listening to his words, though her mind remained rebellious and questioning. 'Strung out like wives on a string,' came from her head, though her heart went pitter patter.

'I have been caught in forces totally beyond anything that has ever happened to other people. You know me, dear Eva, how could I go without the comfort of women in my long life?'

'It's rather too much for me to take in just now,' said Eva. 'But I suppose, making allowance for the peculiar circumstances of your life, to expect total devotion, absolute fidelity, would have been rather impractical.' She could hear the sceptical voices of her daughters in her mind, 'Mum, you're always making excuses! This is it! This is just too much!'

'Of course, I have been faithful to you, within the limitations imposed on me, by each time and place. You have my word, as a king and warrior.'

'It takes a bit of getting used to,' said Eva. 'For me. Being a bead on the string.'

'Don't think of it that way, that's what I'm trying to say. Time, and love, and the relation between the two, it's much more than that, much more. One thing I have found,' and he slipped his arm around her, and drew her to him, 'I have discovered that time does not diminish love. Rather, memory tricks the eye, and when I behold the beloved, she is to me always as I first saw her, in the glory of that first day of freshness and youth.'

Eva looked into the eyes of her lost love, and saw there were small creases in the surrounding skin.

'Time, for me, was living in the moment, because I never knew when that moment would be replaced by something so totally different, so wholly beyond my previous imaginings. These people with their love of Robinson, they have taught me so much. Like the man who is shipwrecked, I live with devotion to the present task of survival. Yet the reason that I survive is that I can remember another life, and when I ask myself, why it is that I bother, it is because I can imagine a better life in the future. I never know, when I go to sleep, where and when I shall wake, or with whom, with which past or future love.'

'I knew you would come again.'

'I knew I would never truly leave you in my thoughts, though I might leave you in the more usual way of looking at it. We are the playthings of Alexander, and only he can stop this game with time.'

'If it stops, though, where will you be?'

'Back where I started, I suppose, and I tell you, that is not the best time, the best place I have been.'

'Which is?'

'I take the view that the present time and place is always the best.'

'Here, now?' Eva looked around, and saw the city set in the oasis, and the women trailing along behind them. 'I thought there was a war going on somewhere.'

'There always is, with Alexander. Never worry, you are here now and it is to you, dear Eva, that I look for a solution to my present problems.' They had arrived at the centre of the village. A broad sweep of steps led down to a large well. The inhabitants of the city were going about their business collecting water, gossiping, glancing with curiosity at the new arrival.

Eva looked at the murky water of the well and saw a dead rat floating in it. She pointed it out to Darius, who ignored it, and continued musing. 'It is you who shall empower me.'

'Darius,' said Eva, 'I have to tell you something. I'd like to help you, but I don't see how I can. Do you see that dead rat? Is this the water that everyone's drinking?'

He smiled. 'The water of this spring is famous for its sweet taste.' He gestured at the women who were following, and pointed to the rat. The women in turn tried to persuade the next person with a pail to remove the rat, a task which, Eva saw, was destined to be passed from person to person until, in the end, someone else would be found to perform the task. 'Just like home,' she said. 'Only at home, it was taking the garbage out.'

'Eva. It's because of what you are, of what you've done. You are the answer to this mess. My soothsayer says so. He found three worms in the entrails of a slaughtered goat.'

'Oh. Darius, I have to say this. I think you have changed. You are not the man I married. You never used to slaughter goats for their entrails.'

'What significance has the number three in your life, the soothsayer asked, and I replied, why, it is the number of my daughters by my wife. Then he said, it is your wife that holds the secret, and, look, this first worm, he has a knowing look. It will be the first daughter of that wife who holds the key to your escape from your present predicament. The problem then is, I have had a number of wives, to whom the number three has been significant. Excuse me one moment. The rat.'

Eva sat down on the steps leading down to the well, and thought about her problems.

Chapter 7

'Is this the Great Sea at the Edge of the World?' asked Alexander the Great when he reached the Caspian Sea.

'It could be,' said a local shepherd who knew better than to argue with an emperor in armour.

'Looks like it,' said Costys, a soldier who had walked for long enough.

'Of course it isn't,' said the philosopher Aristander.

'Alexander, set sail on this sea and find where it will take you.'

The shepherd waved farewell. Alexander set sail on the sea and got to the other side more quickly than was likely for the Great Sea at the Edge of the World. Costys ran from the gaze of his emperor.

'Is this the Great Sea at the Edge of the World?' asked Alexander when he reached the China Sea.

'This is a great sea, and this is the Edge of the World,' the Chinese agreed with him. A fisherman tried to sell him a boat, and a magician offered him wings to speed him through the air. 'The active ingredient, with wings, is faith that they will lift you,' the magician explained. Alexander declined.

'Of course, this isn't the Edge of the World,' said Aristander, who daily grew in Alexander's respect. 'This is the Great Sea at the Edge of this World, that I won't dispute, but look at the stars, and see what other worlds are there for you to conquer! An infinity of worlds, and all for you!'

Alexander wept. How could he conquer all those other worlds which twinkled so brightly in the heavens?

'There is a problem with this world,' murmured a Chinese sage. 'This world is round, there is no edge to it, as you imagine. If you set sail on this sea you will come back again to where you started.'

Alexander grunted at the wild notions of the natives. Who would set sail only to arrive at the place he had left? Step up to the stars, though, to go on in eternal conquest, that was more what he wanted. 'I am,' he replied, 'a god, so eternity is no problem to me.'

'Step up to the stars,' and Alexander led the charge. 'Who will come to the stars with me?' he cried, and those soldiers round the camp fire roared back a drunken 'Yes!'

'This way,' called Alexander. 'Let us go!' He led his men into the darkness and out of this world.

When Alexander saw strange seacraft sailing in a strange

sky, he knew he was a god, and that this was a new world for him to conquer.

All dreams signify something.
None of them is in vain.
It is only because our knowledge is imperfect that we do not understand our dreams.

These words Alexander told his historian Aristobolus to add to the official account of their travels. They sat together near the fire, emperor and scribe, on the shores of an alien sea. Aristobolus was tired and troubled by their rapid transition from one world to another. What Alexander accepted as the natural order of things, that he should push on in eternal conquest, Aristobolus wanted to question, though he knew better.

'I remember my native Telmessus, as if it was a dream,' said Aristobolus, staring at the stars which twinkled in the alien sky. 'It was by the sea in another place, another time. Lycia, how far away it seems.'

'Telmessus, Lycia. Tell me, they say, that people from that place have the gift of prophecy. Surely, you must have known, that these great things would happen.'

'The gift of prophecy is a great mystery. It is shared by many who share my place of birth. Nature smiled on Telmessus, and made it a place of marvels. The sea is warm, and from the mountain behind come sweet rains, and the land brings forth prodigies by reason of its fertility. Things which to others seem strange, happen quite naturally in Telmessus, and we think them commonplace. Whales swim in to our shores and onto the land, mistaking their element. Comets light the sky by night and sometimes by day. Cascades and cataracts of fire fall through the air, presaging times of strife in human affairs.' Aristobolus sat sighing, remembering the lost land of his birth. 'My king Alexander, when do you imagine we shall return, you to the mountains of Macedon, and me to my beloved Telmessus?'

'Why? Are you finding my campaign tedious?' asked Alexander with a sharp sideways glance.

'Strange, but never tedious.'

'Continue then. The gift of prophecy? How is it to be explained?'

'People come to us, and say, 'This happened to me. What does it mean?' And we tell them what they should do, what path in life they should follow. We are often right. If there is a reason for our gifts, some say it was because Telmessus, the founder of our city, was the son of Apollo.'

'We sons of gods are blessed, true, though I do not have the particular gift of prophecy.'

'Dreams are the world in our heads, and sometimes, to us, it seems that world is the real world, and this,' Aristobolus gestured at their alien surroundings, 'this world is the dream. We think we have travelled to the stars, but perhaps our bodies lie safe and warm at home.' Aristobolus' voice was full of longing, that this might, against all odds, prove to be the case. 'Imagine, Alexander, that this city in the stars is an illusion, something that exists in your mind only.' Aristobolus warmed to his theme. 'If only . . .'

'I thought you were happy here.'

'In my dream, you mean, I appear to you to be happy, in your dream? What is happiness, but often an illusion? Like this place, this new place in the stars at which we have just arrived. If this is the stars . . . What will we do here?'

'Find some people, conquer them, and found a new city I shall call Alexandria in the Stars. What else is there to do?'

'I agree, that is a fine thing to do, but surely there must be something more than this, if this is truly the stars, where marvels may be found. Where shall we find the abode of the blessed, where is Mount Olympus, which, I grant, you, but not I, could enter. Where are these places of marvels, fabulous places, weird beasts, machines which fly through the air, ships which sail under the water?'

'You are right, Aristobolus, when you say that no dream is in vain. Everything means something. Whether we are awake, or whether this is only a dream, either way, it is our duty to press on, and find what it all means.'

Alexander marched his men far from the sea until they came to a walled city. 'At last,' said Alexander. 'Prepare the siege.'

'This is a strange land,' his general cautioned him. 'The city is a strange city. Are you really quite sure that is what you want to do?'

'I am not unreasonable. Perhaps before we make war we ought to make further inquiries.'

Soldiers went into the country and returned with some people they found labouring in the fields. 'They look rather like us,' said Alexander, disappointed. 'One might expect the inhabitants of the stars to be more extraordinary.'

'The atoms have fallen through the void, and they have created people in the stars as they have created them on earth,' Aristander hazarded a guess. 'Perhaps the atoms which fall here, fall there and clump together, two arms, two legs, a head on top, a heart beneath, here, as there.'

'We march under a different sky, yet much is the same.' Alexander shrugged. 'I expect difference when I travel, but perhaps the problem is my expectation.'

The barbarians were old in years. Old men, old women, leading old donkeys. No-one young, no children, and no young women.

'Did the young men and women run from you in fright?' Alexander asked his men.

'No. We saw no-one young, and, as for fear, those we caught do not seem scared of us.' That was true. Curious, yes, about the armour, the shields and the spears, but unafraid.

'It is because they recognise my presence for what it is.' Alexander glowed with the authority of a god.

'Who does he think he is?' The old woman Marissia asked Aristander, but no-one understood her.

'This old woman acknowledges your eminence,' Aristander reported to Alexander. Marissia looked sharply at Aristander, took hold of his shield and spat upon it. Then she rubbed it with her apron. 'A mark of great respect in their culture,' Aristander explained to his stunned leader.

Aristander sat each day with Marissia, and learned her language.

One day Marissia asked, 'You have come because of the city?'

'Alexander plans to conquer the city as he has conquered you.'

Marissia laughed. 'You cannot conquer us, because we are not free, and you too, are conquered men, though you do not appear to know it.'

Alexander vigorously denied he was a captive.

'We are all captives to the city.' Marissia accepted it as her fate, and was more interested in the tea they brought with them all the way from China. 'It's good to have young people around, men with a hearty appetite, men who want our food. There's not many that want our food these days.'

As for Aristander, he ate more sparingly than the soldiers. There was something odd about the food. Strawberries, big as plums, with seedless skins and leaves divided into seventeen parts, not the five-part leaves of the wild strawberry of his native Macedon. The local fish in the ponds near the city, giant carp with green eggs the size of grapes, were not what he was used to, nor were the red deer with purple blood that lived in the strange forest where pine trees grew crooked, their cones sitting oddly on branches without a trace of the usual green needles.

Alexander ate as heartily as ever.

'Ask where all the young men have gone. And the

women. How can I replenish my army, if there are no young women for the breeding? Have they all fled into the city?'

Marissia laughed. 'If you want to renew your army, you must send your men much further into the forest. As for the city, don't take all your men with you. They will all die, and you with them.'

'I am immortal, so death is no problem.'

'They will all die, so leave some men behind for your return.'

'You are telling me how to conduct my campaign, old woman?'

'Sir, I cannot tell you anything.'

'True.'

'It is myself I am telling, that the city is not for everyone. The city of Sher is the city of the dead. You will need new men to replenish those you will lose.'

Alexander took her advice, though he never admitted it to his official historian. He sent half of his men off to found a new Alexandria along the river bank, and gave instructions that they were to bring their manly qualities into the wild hearts of the local barbarians. 'So the glories of my rule, the stories that are told about me, will go down through the ages, though of course, I shall have moved on, elsewhere, in eternal conquest.'

Marissia looked sharply at Alexander and went her own way, muttering.

'The barbarians believe that after death their spirits fly to the city,' Aristander explained. 'That is why she says our men will join their dead, if they breach the city walls.'

'Rubbish. An error in translation. Never in all my travels have I heard of barbarians who build a city for the dead.'

'Remember the towers of silence.'

'I stand corrected. Ask the old woman if it is a city where bones are exposed to the birds.'

Marissia recoiled in surprise. 'Bones, the bones. You know about them?'

'We come from the skies,' said Alexander, pointing upwards. 'We know everything.'

The rats were sleek, good for roasting, and the snakes that lived off the rats were glossy in their skins and fat and long. Alexander thought of his mother and her love of snakes, and as he lay thinking, not sleeping, not dreaming, but lazily wondering how he could send some snakes for her playthings, Alexander felt himself in communion with her, though she lived so far away.

'Alexander,' said Olympias, 'They tell me you have reached the stars. How very clever of you.'

'Mother! I was just thinking of you, and here you are, so close to me in my thoughts! How are things back home? Laying siege and defending everything, as usual?'

'How kind of you to think of me,' said Olympias, smoothing the pillows upon which she lay resting from her latest conquest. 'What is happening here is more a kind of consolidation. We call it peace.'

'What? I see I must soon come home, to stir things up again.'

'We need you there, among the stars, where you are doing such good work.'

'Yes, of course, I can see that, but . . .'

'I know why you were thinking of me. It is, of course, soon to be my birthday celebration . . .'

'And I have just the present for you, Mother! The good snakes of Sher, black and glossy, and very good at catching rats.'

'I need something to show those women of Pella. Send the snakes to me.'

'I'll do my best. It may take some time. But Mother, now you are with me, may I consult you about my latest siege?' Alexander often asked Olympias her opinion on how he should proceed, though he did not confide this fact to his official historian. 'There is a city here, a walled city which no-one enters or leaves.'

'Alexander, you must have it! A city that is self-sufficient, the ultimate fortified city, the city which cannot be starved into surrender. Conquer it and learn its secrets.'

'They call it the city of the dead.'

'Then why is the city sealed? The dead will not escape. They say that only because they do not want you to have it.'

'True.'

'Is there no way in that you can see?'

'Not a crack.'

'Send in the rats. If it is truly a city of the dead, they will find a way. Send rats, and then the snakes to chase behind them. Then follow where they go. Dig if you must. You must not let this city defeat you, or the people will hear of it, and mock your plans.'

'I'll think about it,' said Alexander, preparing to dismiss his mother from his thoughts. But, 'A mother always knows,' said Olympias, and she refused to leave until she was ready. She gave him more advice, telling him not to drink too much. 'Avoid the local goddesses, they will only bring you trouble. Choose ordinary mortals. That is a mother's best advice. A mother knows what is best for her son, even if he is a god, and an emperor,' said Olympias, closing off her end of the conversation and allowing her son to rest at last.

The next day Alexander climbed a hill and looked over the city. The walls were higher than any he knew from his previous conquests, and were made of some grey substance, smooth and cool to the touch. Though he was high on the hill, he could not see into the city. Where the walls stopped, there the smooth grey roof began, and though he sent one of his men to climb to the top of the tallest tree the view remained the same. Grey walls, a single grey roof. No courtyards separating dwelling from dwelling, no ramparts round the city walls, no defenders, no sign of any kind of life.

Alexander took twenty of his best men and travelled for

a day and a night round the city walls until they found a weak place that might serve them. It was a place where large pipes pushed out through the walls into the ponds. The pipes went deep down under the mud. There was no entrance. But high up on the wall one of the pipes had been pushed from its mountings, and a large crack ran down the weakened wall.

First the rats were sent through the hole, with the snakes in swift pursuit. They did not return. The men worked on the hole, enlarging it for entry.

There was no sign of life from the city. No-one came from inside to inquire what they were doing.

After a week, the wall was breached, and the hole was large enough for entry. Alexander led the way.

They found the first dead rat in the mouth of the first dead snake. 'This is the city of the dead.' The alarm ran round the men.

'Dead rats, dead snakes?' Alexander was scornful. 'Carry on!'

They forced their way through the rubble into the ruins of an ancient room. 'This place has secrets worthy of us,' said Alexander, as he saw pipes which wound over and under each other, coming out of the gloom and disappearing into it. 'This is a palace of marvels.'

Still no-one came to greet them or to throw them out. They moved on into the spacious room, following the flow of the largest pipes in the glow of their burning torches. Their feet stirred up phosphorescent dust, and wherever they walked they left a glowing trail of shining footsteps behind them. As they moved into a passage on the far side their flares died down and some went out in the sour-smelling air.

'Quickly,' called Lysimachus, the commander of the lifeguard. 'Onwards, and up to the light at the end of this tunnel, where it seems the roof must be open to the skies.'

They walked through the empty corridor towards the

light, their sandals glowing in the dust, and found a place where light came, not from a hole in the roof, but from a far wall, shining and soft to the touch.

'The city seems deserted.' Alexander consulted with Lysistratus. 'This place, this wall, the dust on the floor that glows like the Caspian Sea at dusk, all is strange to me. The city cannot be what we thought, a place of retreat to a new life free from old battles.'

Here and there in the dark places a phosphoresecent snake chased a phosphorescent rat.

'What kind of ruin is it, free from rats and snakes of its own?' asked Aristander. 'And where are the defenders? Every citadel must have its defenders.'

Alexander looked round impatiently, his hand to his sword.

'Look! Here they come! They float through the air to meet us.' Lysistratus drew his sword.

Out of the gloom came a row of slowly moving shadows, large round bladders hovering just above the ground, bumping through the benches. Like large bubbles of froth they swam as if on the surface of the sea. When a rat ran into them, the bubbles silently engulfed it and rolled on, leaving the animal dead.

'Do not fight the bubbles,' called Alexander, as he sniffed the poisonous air. 'Let them pass unpricked. It does not matter, for me, a god, that I cannot breathe the air within, but it is different for you.'

The bubbles floated past in uninterrupted progress, their surfaces reflecting the light from the wall. They squeezed themselves into the entrance to the room and stayed there.

'They block our retreat,' Lysistratus yelled.

'That I can understand,' said Alexander. 'The first line of defence also becomes the last. We are fighting a worthy if slippery adversary.'

'We shall all die this time, so far from home.' Aristander thought longingly of the life he had left, it seemed, forever.

'Nonsense! We have fought the Persians, we have conquered the Chinese, we have waged war in the mountains at Mir Samir, we have fought in the deserts of the Gobi, we have tackled tall men with whirling spears, dwarfs with glancing arrows, wild men with fire in their blood, and all these men we have vanquished. Bubbles and sludge? Ha! We shall soon declare ourselves their victors!'

'If we get out of here.'

'I can find the passage out. Have I not led you to the stars? I did not bring my men here to fall before mere froth.'

But two men fell, two of the best, Tamaris and Theopompus, caught as they jumped the wrong way. Trapped in a bubble, they drew their swords, but before they could break the film that surrounded them, they fell, choking, to the floor, gasping in the escaping hiss of poisoned air.

There, with the rats and the snakes, two brave men died, and Alexander wiped his eyes. Yet what was this? The bodies lay still on the floor, the light shone on them, and quickly, quickly, their flesh dissolved and their bones settled into tidy piles.

It was then that they noticed the other bones.

'Truly, this is the city of the dead,' said Lysimachus.

'The bones,' Marissia had said to Alexander. 'You know about the bones?'

'Yes,' he had told her. Then he had lied. Now, he knew.

In the city the bones stirred and raised themselves from the ground. They took to the air, and feebly tried to beat back the intruders, as if a trace of memory remained from a past war-like life.

'The bones,' cried Alexander. 'They mark the second line of defence.'

The bones of a hand, loosely jointed together, struck against Alexander's shield, but carelessly, as if there was little spirit left for fighting.

Alexander declared himself impressed if not subdued

by the defences of the city. 'They may not speak to us, but by Hammon I can understand what they are doing. The tactics of battle are the same in the stars as they are in Macedon.'

Before Alexander's eyes the bones of a hand came together, 'click-click' in the air, then 'click-click' on the console of a large desk commanding the room. 'Click' went the bones, then 'click', they threw switches.

The wall that glowed with light sprang into life. Large figures appeared on the screen. 'Giants! Magic! Will we ever leave this cursed place?' The shrieks flowed round Alexander. He stood back, amazed, but because he was immortal, unafraid.

Two men, twice as large as was natural, peered from the screen into the darkness of the room. 'It's men in armour!' one of the people on the screen said, incredulously. 'Bloody Romans!' They pointed out to each other the sights of the scene to which the bones had summoned them.

'Romans?' roared Alexander. 'Never! We are good men from Macedon.' He moved towards that wall of light to investigate further. 'Aha! These men are not real men!' He turned to his cowering troops. 'It is merely a trick they are playing, with images. See?' He strode to the screen and the men saw the images play upon their leader while he remained unharmed.

The voices spoke accusingly from the screen. 'What are you doing so far inside the zone?'

'I have captured your city, and claim it for my own. This is the first Alexandria in the Stars, the first, I hope, of many.'

'Inside the zone? You must be crazy. Crazy men in armour!' One of the faces on the screen made looping motions to his head with one of his hands.

'Your bones do not frighten us, nor your poisons which you place so cunningly into these bubbles.'

'The bubbles are still there? I thought we got rid of them years ago.'

'Why would you want to rid yourself of your defences?'

'Defences? The bubbles are the problem, you dumbwit. If the bubbles have come back, you'd better get out quickly. The whole place is likely to go up, at any minute.'

'I must confess, the flares have quite gone out.'

'Flares? You took fire with you into the zone?'

'How else could we see our way? We did not know before we came about the ground which glows with light, which has directed our feet to this place.'

'Sludge, Jerczy, it's leaking radioactive sludge again!'

'Listen, you, get out of there! The place will explode at any minute!'

'What does it mean, explode?'

One of the faces loomed larger on the screen. 'Very big bang. Boom boom!' it said, loudly and clearly.

'Aha,' said Aristander. 'Big Bang! When all the atoms fell through the void and met together at the other end.'

'So all our atoms will soon be falling through the void?'

'That is his message.'

'We will be blown to atoms?'

'It seems so.'

'Is this a trick?'

'Look at is this way, Alexander. Say it is a trick, and we leave, what have we lost? We can always come back and fight another day. But if it is not a trick . . .'

'You are right as ever, Aristander,' said Alexander. 'Sound the retreat!'

'But Alexander, there are poison bubbles in our way.'

'I shall conquer them,' said Alexander. 'Follow me, and try not to breathe.'

Alexander cut a swathe through the bubbles, and his men admired him all the better for it, saying, 'He is a god, and a great leader. He took us from the abode of the dead, and he led us back into the land of the living.'

As they ran out of the city and away, back to their camp, the city exploded behind them and the cloud reached to the skies. Alexander said, 'I think I may not count that city as one of my conquests.'

Later many of the soldiers who went into the city fell sick. Their skin blistered and their strength went from them. Some died, some lived, and of their children, some died young, while others grew to be giants. The city bequeathed a legacy to Alexander, though it was not the gift he sought.

Later Aristander sought out Marissia. 'Why was it you said to me, that we were all captive to the city?'

'No longer,' said Marissia. 'You have released the spirits of the dead, of my brothers, and now they dwell among us, as they should. We are no longer captive, nor are you. You can go now, to continue your voyage to the stars. The bones will rest, now we can bury them, my father, my brothers. Though the young people will not return to this place, not in my time.'

Alexander called the people together, and made a speech. 'I came to conquer this strange city, so unlike other cities I have known, Tyre, or Damascus, or Baghdad. The city of Sher is truly the city of the dead. Some of my men are dead, yet still their spirit lives. I have performed the task. I shall leave behind, outside the city, it is true, the seed of a new army. One day a new city will rise here, open to the world, a new Alexandria in the Stars to rival those I left behind, but its time is the time to come.'

Alexander led most of his men off into the night and onto the surface of another world.

Chapter 8

Freda played the message from Eva on her answering machine. 'It was true,' she told Sergio. 'Everything she told us, when we were small. Even though it's impossible, it's true!'

'Another mad dream. She can't have gone off with Darius I, or II or III. They're all well and truly dead,' Sergio said.

'Mum was alright when I saw her. Last week.'

'She's never been alright, Freda, you've just got to face it. There's always been a few screws loose.' Sergio left for work. Freda sighed. Baby Mickie waved a royal farewell to Sergio's back, first one hand in a circular motion in the air, then the other, while the first hand took a rest. Chubby hands, small fingers, but already practiced and assured.

The cat jumped in the window and grovelled before Mickie, slinking along, scraping its belly on the floor.

The more Freda thought about it, the more she thought her family was really rather strange, and not like other families she knew. Mickie was strange, the way the animals grovelled before her, and the way she seemed to expect it of them. Her father had definitely been strange, and her mother's acceptance of her father's strangeness was peculiar. Sergio was half-right about that. Here she was, alone in a house with a child who commanded animals to her bidding, worried about her mother, who had always been firm in her belief that her husband Darius had not only fallen from the skies, but also had been wearing a full set of armour at the time.

Nothing for it. She would have to go round to Eva's house and check.

Freda changed Mickie's nappy, marvelling at the royal composure of her baby daughter even at these moments of mother-child intimacy. Mickie smiled regally and clapped her hands with royal approbation, and was especially appreciative of the rub with baby powder.

When Freda tried to talk to her friends about her intimations of royal blood in her baby, they only laughed at her. Where could she turn for knowledge? Her claims were always trivialised, her anxieties disregarded by her unfeeling confidantes. But when Freda saw Mickie ruling her small kitchen kingdom, she knew that the cat knew more than it could tell.

Once, at the baby health centre, Freda bravely ventured the notion that a mother always knew when something was wrong. What could she say, though? Is it possible to have delusions of grandeur, at one year old? The nurse told her, firmly, brooking no nonsense, 'Nothing is wrong. You have a perfectly lovely baby.' Freda watched, helplessly, as Mickie smiled her most regal smile and bestowed her royal blessings on the infant welfare sister.

Freda must keep her suspicions to herself, while Mickie practised her benificent rule on the animals and her toys. For her benificence, Freda was grateful. Mickie could have proved herself a tyrant from birth, like Olympias, Queen of Macedon.

Freda let herself into Eva's house. No-one was there. She searched for clues. The windows were all locked and intact, and there was no sign that anyone had broken into the house. Vonnie's homework was spread out on the kitchen table. The beds were disturbed, as if both Eva and Vonnie had first been asleep, then woken. Eva's nightgown was on the floor. As Freda picked it up, a handful of sand fell from it. Sand? Freda was more puzzled than ever. Then she noticed that there was more sand, all over Eva's bedroom floor, as if a whole lot of people had walked into the house from the beach.

Freda walked out of the house, puzzled by its mysteries. There was no sign of any kind of struggle, no feeling that here an act of violence had ocurred. Eva's voice on the phone message had been excited and happy. Freda worried about what she should do. She should, she supposed, ring the police, and report them missing. What could she say? That her mother had gone off with her father? Hardly ground for a full investigation. And if she attempted to tell what she thought might be the truth, she would never be believed.

Freda walked into the back yard, her baby on her hip.

She placed Mickie down in the small paved courtyard and looked back at the house. All seemed normal and as it should be. 'Except it isn't,' said Freda to herself. 'It isn't normal, not at all.' She watched as a small green snake slithered across the brick paving of the courtyard. 'Look,' said Freda, 'Nice snake. This snake won't hurt you. Some will, the black ones, and the brown ones, but this one is just a harmless green tree snake.'

Of course this snake won't hurt you, thought Freda, as the snake, in Mickie's presence, flattened itself on the warm bricks and grovelled before her. Snakes won't hurt Mickie, thought Freda, because, like all other animal life on this planet, they go into attitudes of humble worship in her presence.

Eva bent down and picked up the snake, holding it expertly, the way her mother had shown her. As long as she could remember they'd always had snakes in their garden. It was a brick-walled courtyard garden, with plenty of sunny crannies, and snakes and geckos and lizards liked it there. 'They probably eat each other when we're not looking,' Eva had said, but she liked them, and kept them. 'They're no trouble, and green snakes, they're harmless. And so beautiful to look at. Your father always liked to have a few snakes about him.'

Keeping snakes, though. Now Freda thought about it, she could add that to the list of rather odd things about her family. The only reason she'd never thought it odd was because she had grown up with it, thinking it was normal.

Thoughtfully, Freda draped the snake around her neck, and paraded round her daughter, showing her the small green head, the lithe green body. 'My mother is strange, my daughter is strange, my father was strange, but I am definitely normal.'

The snake wriggled and lay still. Mickie smiled, and reached to touch it. Freda sighed. She supposed Mickie would accept the snakes in her grandmother's garden, just as she, as a child, had accepted them, and the practice of keeping snakes would no doubt go on, handed down the generations.

Slowly Freda paraded with the snake, in the garden of her mother's house. The sun was warm. Mickie was happy, exploring the courtyard on her hands and knees, picking the flowers. Freda fell into a slow dance, her feet stepping lightly from one brick to another, her arms moving in a vaguely Indian fashion, the snake coiled around her neck. 'I am dancing with snakes,' she said, and Mickie looked at her and smiled a happy smile. 'I am dancing with snakes, the way they dance with wolves elsewhere. But here, in this garden, there are no wolves to dance with, and indeed, I much prefer it that way.' The sun shone, the air was warm, the dance slowed as Freda felt a heavy languour in her slow-moving limbs. She shut her eyes, and thought of what had happened, to her mother, to her sister Vonnie, here, in this house just next to the garden, where they had been the night before, from which they had disappeared. Before, she had been worried about them. Perhaps they had been kidnapped, murdered even, but now she knew that whatever had happened it was not quite like that, and the thoughts in her mind floated free, trying to find an answer. 'Where are they, where have they gone? Where is my mother, my sister and my father? What is the truth of it, not only of their going, but of his coming here in the first place, coming here to have three daughters, to bring them into the world, and then to leave them, so casually?'

The sun shone, the breeze was warm.

The answer came to her. 'This is where they have gone. This is the place. They are here, with your mother, your father, your sister. Open your eyes, and you will know something of what has happened to them.' Freda could hear Mickie, still making her happy sounds. She could feel the snake cool upon her neck, the sun warm on her back. She could smell the sweet smell of sandalwood burning, she could feel the sand under her feet. Her eyes were shut, her breathing was slow and regular, the sun was hot.

Freda opened her eyes, jolted into awareness. She saw the golden leaves of the pomegranate, its boughs hung heavy with ripe red fruit. She saw a walled mud-brick courtyard. She saw a woman reclining, asleep, under the pomegranate. The woman was dark in her complexion, her lips were full and bright red, her gown was the colour of blood.

Freda saw her daughter Mickie, at home in her new kingdom.

Except this wasn't home. It wasn't Melbourne. It was another courtyard, in another time, another place.

The woman woke. 'At last,' she said. 'I thought you would never come.' She clapped her hands, and two women entered the courtyard. 'Take her away and swaddle her,' she commanded, pointing to the baby. Then, to Freda, 'You can go now.'

The two women bowed low to Mickie, who waved her hand most royally, and smiled with the full glory of her benificence.

'Hey! That's my baby!' Freda rushed to Mickie. 'What's going on here? Where am I?'

'Does it matter? You can go home now.'

'I'm not going anywhere without her!'

'Are you her wet-nurse?'

'I'm her mother.'

'On your way.'

'But she needs a mother!'

'What a quaint idea!'

'Who are you?'

'I am Olympias, Queen of Macedon.'

Mickie started to cry, and held her arms out to Freda.

'She really wants you.'

'Yes! I told you.' Freda bent down and lifted the baby to her arms. Mickie cuddled in and smirked at Olympias.

'Alright, you can stay. You can help out with my snakes.'

'I want to go home.'

'If you want to go home, then why did you come? You can go, she stays.' Olympias pointed to Mickie, who gave a start, and began crying again.

'She's only a baby! Look! She needs me!'

'She's a royal baby, and they have to be brought up properly. By handpicked slaves.'

'But slavery is wrong!'

'We're very nice to our slaves. What's wrong about that? We let them learn geometry.' Olympias waved them away. 'Take them to their chamber, and get them some decent clothes. And swaddle that child, before it comes over faint from over-exertion.'

'Swaddling a poor defenceless baby is wrong,' Freda explained to the slaves, as they led her away to start her new life in ancient Macedon. 'It restricts their freedom of movement. They can't express themselves, they can't explore their new world.'

Chapter 9

Eva sighed and said, 'I suppose you want to take up again, where we left off?'

'Come,' said Darius. He led the way to a door set in a wall, and through it into a walled garden. 'I have found us a new home.'

As they entered the house women paused in their activities and made their obeisance to Darius, while keeping sharp eyes on Eva.

'Let's stay here awhile,' said Darius, and smiled, and Eva heard herself say, faintly, 'Just for a short time. I have to get back. Vonnie will be worried. She won't know where I am. Where am I?'

The room was large and comfortable, with rugs of the kind she had at home, and scattered cushions, and small tables with brass lamps softly glowing in the gloom. There was a smell of incense in the air.

A woman entered, carrying a large bowl of water on her head. She moved gracefully towards Eva and motioned her to sit down. Eva sat, puzzled. The woman placed the bowl of water on the rug, and bent over to remove Eva's runners, fumbling with the laces, puzzled by the unknown. 'Oh, no,' said Eva, when she realised what was happening, 'No, you don't have to do that, I can take my own shoes off.'

'She wants to wash your feet.' This was from Darius, his voice muffled by the various items of warrior apparel which he was busy unbuckling and pulling over his head.

'Oh, no, I think I really prefer to wash my own feet. You don't have to do that. Darius, please, tell your servant she doesn't have to do that.'

Darius waved the woman away. 'She is not my servant.'

'Who is she then?'

'Um . . . ,'

'One of them?'

'Er . . .'

'Darius, Darius. This is quite impossible. You have changed, and I have not. Not quite as much.'

'Eva, you are right, you are just as I remember you, in the full flush of youth, glorious as the day I first met you.'

'Really?'

'You must understand, I have changed, I have had to change. Here I have to be an emperor. It is expected of me.'

A second woman entered, bearing coffee and Turkish Delight. Darius motioned for the tray to be left, and waved her out.

'What is this place? They act as if it is theirs.'

'They think they can come and go as they please, because that is the way things are, here.'

'Is this a harem?' Eva hissed.

'Certainly not!' said Darius. 'No, this is more a place that these women inhabit. Together. Sometimes. And sometimes I visit.'

'It is a harem.'

'It is, and it isn't. Look, try to see things from my point of view. I'm having this perfectly frightful time with Alexander . . .'

'What about me?'

'What about you? Ah, Eva, you are magnificent when you are angry.'

'Why can't we go back to the way we were, the time when we were happy?'

'Anything is possible, here, at the place where time-paths cross. If only I could stop this endless coming and going of Alexander, which happens here, at this place. This place holds the secret.' Darius flung himself down beside her, and began to renew old acquaintances.

Eva sighed. She was in the grip of forces far stronger than herself. He was an emperor, and she was, at this moment, the first among his wives. There was one thing she must not forget, however unequal the power relationship, however much she was willing to let herself be carried along by the inspiration of the moment. It would be up to her to broach the delicate matter of contraception, something with which they had never bothered, when she was young and helplessly enraptured, and hence, inevitably, a teenage mother. Not that she ever regretted it, then, but now . . . no. Definitely. Three daughters was it. Enough. Her family was finished.

Darius took her face in his hands, and gazed deep into her eyes. 'War, this war without end,' he said, abstractedly. 'Once I thought I could win. That was my big mistake. But now, I know it. I can't win that way, not by fighting hand to hand. For a while I appear to win, but then, Alexander just takes what's left of his army off to the stars, stays there a while, replenishes his men by natural increase, and all too quickly he comes back again.'

Eva leaned back among the cushions. Darius followed. 'Natural increase,' she said. 'Now, I've got just the thing to prevent it.'

'You have? With Alexander and his army?'

'With us. Surely we have enough children?'

Darius agreed. 'They are the gift of the gods.'

'There is something you can do about it.'

'There is?' Darius listened with interest to what Eva had to say, as she groped in her handbag for the packet of condoms she was carrying. Darius looked, uncomprehending, at the oblong silver packet which Eva showed him, with the same air of distraction that Eva knew she might feel if Darius presented her with an ancient image of a fertility goddess.

Eva tried her best to explain. 'It's the 2,000 wives, you see, and too many children, and there's also another factor, what we call VD. I know you couldn't help it. I can see that there were forces beyond your control, immortality and all, but you can catch some pretty nasty diseases that way, and I've got my health to consider.'

'I don't know,' said Darius, doubtfully. 'I don't see how I can persuade the whole of Alexander's army to adopt as unusual a practice as you describe, they barely stand still to allow me to fight them, let alone to carry your message to them. Though I do see your point, Eva, I take your concern deep into my heart.' Darius took Eva's hand, and pressed it to his chest. She could feel the strong beat of his heart, the warmth of his skin.

They were interrupted by a woman who entered without knocking, bearing a silver tray on which were arranged small pieces of melon and sweet smelling herbs.

'I need to stop the cycle, with Alexander,' said Darius, waving the latest intruder away, getting up after her to place the bar across the door. 'Get him off the path of endless repetition.'

Under his breastplate Darius wore the same style of rough shirt that Eva remembered from the first day she had seen him, so long ago, that day on the beach at Sandringham. Her heart went pitter patter. As his armour fell from him, his sword, and chain mail underpants, so did his imperious ways.

Darius paused. 'There is one thing,' he said. 'Roxane. I have to talk to you about her.'

'Roxane?'

'What I have to say may come as a surprise to you, but I want you to try to see things my way. Suspend your disbelief. Suspend your true beliefs, too. All these women . . .'

'All your wives,' Eva prompted.

'They were, in a manner of speaking. Once. No more. What I have done, is this. I have gathered together here, in this place, all the women by whom I have had three daughters. That is why Roxane is coming.'

Eva thought about it. 'So all these people are here because they want to be here?'

'They can always leave,' said Darius airily, waving in the direction of the desert. 'They don't have to stay.'

'Can I leave?'

'No.'

'Neither can they.'

'I need you. I need Roxane.'

'Why?'

'They said of Alexander, that he was fired with the love of boys sometimes to madness, but I never saw any of that, myself, personally. This Roxane, she's of marriageable age?'

'You should know.'

'How old is she? Her date of birth, for the astrologer. Such a small thing, for a husband to ask of his wife. Whom he adores. About his daughter. Her age?'

'Again, why?'

'Alexander is coming back. I know the signs. The ground is shaking, the wind is blowing, the sand blows in from the desert and down into the Lake of the Crescent Moon. It's all a question of the date, the time, the place. And the entrails of a goat.'

'Don't go slaughtering a goat on Roxane's account. She won't thank you for it.'

Darius moved closer to Eva. In spite of herself, Eva felt the old fondness return, and the warmth of his presence flooded through her. Languour stole upon her. She was reunited with her lost love. For the moment, she would forget the 2,001 wives. This moment was hers. She seized it.

Eva woke. Darius was struggling into his armour, cursing. A messenger stood at the door. Darius turned, saw that Eva was awake, and said, 'I must leave now.' He blew her a kiss, holding his sword to his lips. 'I shall return.'

'Bugger it,' said Eva. 'You've said that before.'

'I mean it this time,' said Darius, walking briskly through the door.

'Oh, what a mug am I,' muttered Eva, sitting up. She looked around for something to put on. A white robe was draped over some cushions. Eva picked it up, admiring the fineness of the material, the glory of the gold embroidery. 'If he's the Emperor round here, then I shall be Empress. Or one of them.' She struggled into the white robe, half-regretting, half-careless of her mad moment of careless rapture.

Eva opened the door and looked out. The room opened into a larger room, furnished, like the other, with rugs and cushions. The women were waiting for her. They greeted her warmly. They motioned to her to join them, and offered her slices of melon, and orange segments, coffee and Turkish Delight. Eva was bemused. It looked like a harem, to her. Eva sat in the room with her sisters, her friends, the women with whom she must share Darius, and she entered into this new life as if it was the most natural thing in the world.

A girl, about eight years of age, approached and smiled shyly at Eva.

'What is your name?' Eva asked, hesitantly. She spoke slowly, in the language she had learned in her dreams. The child understood, and replied, 'My name is Roxana.'

'Oh, I have a daughter called Roxane,' said Eva, delighted. Roxana received the news with laughter and spoke to her mother, translating what Eva had said into another tongue. One by one, as the message went round with the children, the translators, the same word, Roxane, was repeated, again and again, always accompanied by the same soft laughter.

'You too!' Roxana said to Eva. 'They say, to tell you, that each of them has a daughter called Roxane. Or Roxwitha, or Rosanthe, or whatever . . .'

'Extraordinary!'

The child shrugged.

That was how Eva met Isabella, from the time of the Crusaders, and her daughters Henrietta, Roxanna, and Maria; Uncumber, and her daughters Urith, Roxwitha and Thoroth, and Dorina and so many children called Roxane who took delight in the confusion their names called, and forever responded to the wrong call, to someone else's mother.

'What do we do about Darius?' Eva asked anxiously.

'They have to share him round,' said the first Roxana.

'Of course,' said Eva, weakly. 'But how? Do we take turns in his bed?'

Roxana smirked and translated for Isabella, who glared at Eva.

I need to think about this, thought Eva. I am a woman of the late twentieth century, and I find myself in a harem. 'It is a harem?' she gestured round her.

Variations on the word 'No,' greeted Eva, ranging from the indignant to the pitying. 'This is not a harem,' the agreement was. It was more (this was where Eva found her sociology most helpful) a locus at which the separate partners of a rather special kind of serial monogamy were gathered, through temporal dislocation, and through, they agreed, no fault of anybody's, at one time and place, instead of being in their normal states of being apart, and ignorant of each other's existence.

'Normally, I suppose, we would never have met, never have got to know each other,' said Eva. They were rather a nice bunch of women, thought Eva, helpful, when you got to know them, concerned for Darius, and worried for the future of their children, in a strange place in the desert, where, it was generally agreed, the children were running wild, learning a wide variety of ancient and modern languages, it was true, but little else of any practical use to them when they all returned home again, as they all agreed, Darius had promised them, each and every one, would be the case.

'What about Alexander?' Eva asked.

The name of Alexander provoked an intense response. Eva could see that, though the women were prepared to take Darius more or less as they found him, they were united in blaming Alexander for their plight. It was Alexander, there was general agreement, who was the cause of their trouble. Without him, each woman seemed to believe, things would have been alright. Each would have had their version of their life with Darius.

'I find that very hard to believe,' said Eva, weakly. Heads shook vigorously, as Eva's scepticism was translated round the circle.

'No, don't you see?' said Isabella, waving her perfumed posy of dried flowers. 'That's why Darius has summoned all the Roxanes.'

'Why? That's what I'm trying to find out,' said Eva.

'Only one Roxane is important.'

'Please tell me!'

They told her. Eva grew thoughtful.

Why one particular Roxane is important, the Roxane whom Alexander will choose as his bride.

'It is written that Alexander defeated Darius, and wed his daughter, Roxane.'

'I don't remember it that way,' Eva argued. 'That wasn't what I learned in ancient history at university.'

'If it is written, then it must be true.'

'It depends on where it is written,' Eva insisted.

The women looked at her as if she was odd. 'Alexander defeated Darius, and wed his daughter, Roxane. When that happens again, we believe that these endless cycles of comings and goings will come to an end, and Alexander will return to the Macedon of his youth, and there die a drunkard's death.'

'How does Darius feel about that? His defeat, at the hands of Alexander? The marriage of his daughter, to the victor?'

'Darius has a plan. He wants to organise things this time without the defeat. He's a good man. He doesn't like his soldiers getting killed. He's sick of it.'

Eva nodded her head. She now knew that she was here for a purpose greater than herself, for the cause of peace. It made the confusion easier to manage.

Chapter 10

'I'm not really his acolyte,' Jerome explained to Vonnie, as they walked along the path beside the Flaming Cliffs. 'I'm his son.'

'Why do you put up with it? The way he bosses you round?'

Jerome looked puzzled. 'He'll beat me, if I don't do what he tells me. It's what fathers do.'

'Mine doesn't. Darius.'

'Fathers beat you, until you're bigger than them, then you beat them, that's the way of it,' said Jerome.

'You don't have to put up with it. I wouldn't. Then, I never had a father until two days ago, and I can't say I missed him, when he wasn't there. And look where he's got us.'

'I don't care if he does beat me,' said Jerome. 'I just have to say it. It's not true. What my father said about Jonah.'

'I didn't think it was.'

'Jonah wasn't real. It was just a story about a wicked city. It was the city that was the monster, the city that swallowed him up.'

'Tell me, have you ever seen a whale?' Jerome blushed as Vonnie pulled out her shirt, and pointed to the picture of the whale.

'No. But I know it is just a story. The sea, a place where water stretches for so many miles, that is true, I know it from *Robinson Crusoe*. But Robinson does not talk of sea-monsters, the way we talk of desert demons.'

Vonnie looked sideways at her companion. 'You know my father?'

'Of course.'

'Then where is he?'

'He comes, he goes.'

'I give up,' said Vonnie. 'My father. He never was any good, when he wasn't there, and now he's gone and disappeared again, except we're worse off than before. He's left us in this dump.'

'My father has it wrong. He believes the wrong book, the wrong word. The Bible. It's got him all mixed up.'

'I suppose that's only to be expected. He is a missionary, isn't he?'

'He brought with him another book, the story of Robinson. Now, that book is the true book. The other book, the Bible, that is just a book of stories. That is so, you know it, too?'

'Stories. I'll tell you what's a story. The Time Gate.'

'You have heard of it, though?'

'On TV. You go in one door, and out another. The Time Gate.'

'No, that's not it,' said Jerome decisively. 'There are no doors. The Time Gate is a rift, a shimmer, a haze. Step through the haze, and you emerge who knows when.'

'Why don't you go then? Step through, and leave this place? Get away from your father?'

'No, I can't. None of us can leave that way.'

'Of course you can't. It's only a story the way *Robinson Crusoe* is only a story.'

'If it's only a story, how did you get here?'

'It's all rather strange. We just climbed out the window.'

'Aha, a Time Gate.'

'No, a window ledge.'

'Where did it get you?'

'The other side of the window.'

'No. The other side of the Gate. Here. Now.'

'Then we can get back?'

'Not through this Gate,' said Jerome, leading her through a wide opening into a large cave.

'Why not?'

'Because it leads to the Land of the Giants.'

Vonnie rolled her eyes impatiently, but, she had to admit, as her eyes grew accustomed to the gloom, there was, in the corner of the cave, a faint haze, a shimmer, just as Jerome had said. 'That's a Time Gate?' she asked, not believing the evidence of her eyes.

'Yes. Look.'

Vonnie watched as the largest egg she had ever seen in her life rolled out of the haze and into the cave.

'See? That's an egg of one of the Giants.'

'Giants don't lay eggs,' said Vonnie.

'What is it then?'

'It's a giant egg, yes, but Giants are giant people.'

'Not if they're giant lizards.'

A large crack appeared in the top of the egg. 'Quick,' said Jerome, 'Help me put it back!' He picked up a pole with a large net on the end, and scooped the egg into it. Then he extended the scoop into the haze, where, much to Vonnie's surprise, both the egg and the end of the scoop disappeared. Jerome pulled the scoop back, looking pleased with himself. 'They have very careless ways with their eggs, Giants. They lay them any old how and leave their young to fend for themselves.'

'Oh,' said Vonnie. 'What happens if there's no-one here to catch the egg and put it back?'

'Roast lizard for dinner,' said Jerome. 'Delicious.'

Half an empty egg shell rolled back into the cave, and a baby lizard with an extremely long neck poked its head through the haze.

Jerome picked up a large rock to hurl at it, and the lizard, a powerful inborn sense of self-preservation stirring in its young brain located somewhere at the end of its tail, quickly withdrew its head to the other side of the Gate.

Vonnie stood, shaking.

'Don't be frightened,' said Jerome. 'I sent it back to where it came from.'

'That is not a lizard.'

'A baby Giant.'

'That's *Tyrannosaurus Rex*.'

'King of the lizards?'

'It grows up to be a monstrous fierce flesh-eater the size of a very large tree.'

'That's why we eat it when it's small.'

'You eat a member of an extinct species?'

'What else can we do? We can't let it live to eat us. It's the best thing to do, hit it on the head with a rock, and have it for dinner.'

'That is the most awful thing I have ever heard in my life.' Vonnie stamped her foot, cross and confused.

Chapter 11

Roxane knew she was dreaming. She was with some strange people who seemed to be arranging her marriage. She heard as if from a great distance the voice of her mother Eva. 'Roxane! I'm so pleased you could come! There's so much I have to tell you.'

'Where am I?' asked Roxane. She felt dazed. She seemed to be in a tent, reclining on a very familiar carpet in a room full of women chattering in strange languages.

And what Eva was telling her could not possibly be true. 'Roxane! Your father, Darius! I've found him again!'

'Where am I?'

Eva talked on, excited. 'What I've got to say may surprise you. Remember, when I did sociology?'

'You want to talk to me about your sociology assignment? Here? Now?'

'There's this very important idea in sociology, the idea of the family.'

'Who are all those people?' Roxane gestured weakly at the other women milling round the tent, crowding over her, anxious to bid her welcome.

'Them? Stand back!' Eva commanded, imperiously. 'Roxane needs time to adjust.'

'Well, who are they?'

'Wives,' said Eva, summoning some tea from a shrouded figure.

Roxane looked abstractedly at the tea-cup in Eva's hands. She closed her eyes and opened them again.

'Darius. It seems he's had a number of wives. Quite a number, really, when you think of it.'

Roxane took the tea-cup from Eva. 'That's what you want to tell me? We always told you, Mum, there was something wrong about the way he got up and left.'

'What I want to say to you is this. In my sociology days . . .'

'Eva, is this a harem?'

'Kind of. Well, yes.'

'I'm in a harem with you, and you want to talk to me about your sociology lectures?'

'What I have to say may come as a surprise. Are you quite comfortable?'

'No. How can I be? And what's all this about my wedding?'

'In sociology, we talk about the family. There's the nuclear family . . .'

'That's not us.'

'Well, no, that's Mum and Dad and two point five kids.'

'Dad, where's he been all my life?'

'In our case, the nuclear family broke down.'

'Dad blew through.'

'In a manner of speaking, he blew through, but Roxane, I don't think he could help it. I think he was blown through, really I do.'

'Ha.'

'I believe he was in the grip of forces far greater than himself.'

'What did he know about sticking around, watching his kids grow?'

'The point is, there is also the concept of the extended family, and that is what we now have to consider. Look around you.'

Roxane looked around her, with vision still blurred with the fatigue of travel. 'I don't know.'

'The family, Roxane, the really very greatly extended family. I have reason to believe, Roxane, that Darius is not only your very own father, but the father of all the children in this village.'

'What village?'

'This is Bazaklik.'

'I was dreaming of this place, and here I am. What happened?'

'It's hard to explain.'

'And they're all my relations? Brothers and sisters?'

'Sisters. Mainly.'

'How many?'

'A thousand? No, it's, let me see, 2,001 wives, three daughters each, that comes out at 6,000. Or thereabouts.'

Roxane felt the tea-cup shake in her hand. She lay back among the cushions. The women of the harem crowded round, solicitous.

'Half-sisters,' Eva amended her statement. 'Your new family.' Eva summoned some water, and pressed moist muslin to Roxane's brow.

Roxane tried to speak, but only a squeak emerged from her lips.

'Megapatriarchy,' said Eva, helpfully. 'That's the best word I've found to explain it.'

'What's all this about my wedding?'

'You see all these people?' Roxane nodded. 'They're in my dream.'

'This is a place where dream worlds intersect.'

'What's that supposed to mean?'

'Soon. You'll know soon. You'll meet them soon, your sisters. They'll all be there, waiting for you. And your aunts. They've all come for your wedding.'

Roxane struggled to get up. 'I'm not going to my wedding.'

The voices of strangers buzzed around her head. 'Nonsense, nonsense,' came in a variety of tongues, which Roxane somehow understood.

'They're saying that you can't not go to your wedding.'

'Who am I getting married to?'

'Alexander,' said Eva.

'Who is Alexander?'

The voices buzzed, 'Alexander the Great, King of the World.'

'Why should he want to marry me?'

'Why not? He married you before.'

'I am not married. I have never been married. I'm not old enough to be married.'

'How old are you?'

'Twenty.'

'There you are. You've come here, a young girl travelling in a strange land. Why did you come, a virgin, if you're not looking for a husband?'

'I'm not!'

'You're not a virgin?'

'What business is that of yours?'

'Alexander won't like it!'

'But if I'm married to him already . . .'

'No, not now. But you were, back then.'

'It wasn't me.'

'You are Roxane?'

'Yes.'

'There you are!'

'It was a different Roxane.'

'As he will be a different Alexander! He has seen the error of his ways. He wants to end the round of ceaseless conquest, non-violently.'

'How do you know?' asked Roxane.

'Darius said so.'

'Darius, your father,' Eva explained, helpfully. 'Oh, Roxane, I've found him again, and he's explained it all to me. I can see it all makes sense.'

'So you've been busy here, arranging my marriage? Behind my back?'

Eva turned to the other women. 'I told you Roxane wouldn't see it your way.' She faced their blank incomprehension. 'I told you I didn't think Roxane would agree.'

A murmur ran round. 'She doesn't have to agree.'

'It's just marriage, after all.'

'I didn't agree.'

'Nobody here agreed to their marriages.'

'Did you?'

'No.'

'And you?'

'Of course not!'

'And you?' To Eva.

Eva paused for a moment. 'I'm not sure I ever did get married. There was always some reason or other, some problems he had, with birth certificates, and passports, that kind of thing. Having to prove you're born, you know, it can be a problem, especially in his case.'

'Surely he told you that you were married to him?'

'Oh, yes,' said Eva. 'Lots of times.' Well, good as married, she added, to herself.

'That's it. Marriage.'

'It is?' Eva.

'You'll like it here, in the desert.' This to Roxane.

Roxane's thoughts grappled wildly with the idea. 'For the rest of my life?' she asked, incredulous.

'You are Alexander's destiny.'

'No, I'm not, not really. Where I come from, we don't do this kind of thing. Mum, how come you're not helping me?'

'Alexander is coming. We need you to save us.'

'Are you really sure?' Roxane lay back, feeling giddy.

'You will marry Alexander.'

'I won't. It's all quite impossible.'

'Nothing is impossible here. This city stands at a crossroads in time. It is a rather unusual place. It is where Alexander will come again, and where we must get him to listen to reason.'

'You must get Alexander to listen to reason. It's nothing to do with me.'

'In another life he married you.'

'But this is my life, and I'm just not ready for marriage.' Roxane's voice started to break. Her eyes clouded with tears.

'Just a simple ceremony, just for the sake of what you might call citizenship, a bit of a farce, isn't it? You meet for the first time, you marry, then you go your separate ways back to wherever it was you both came from. Look on it as something small, something you can do for us. Do for the world.'

'Why does it have to be marriage? Why can't we just be friends?'

'No. Destiny must be fulfilled. Alexander must defeat Darius, and we have chosen this path of non-violence.'

'It will be violence against my person.'

'Oh, you don't have to consummate the marriage. Not really.'

'Is that what Alexander says?'

'It's kind of written,' Eva explained. 'Alexander takes Roxane, the daughter of Darius, and marries her.'

'If it's just an arranged form of marriage, what happens after?'

'Oh, the usual thing. The women of the village dress you for your wedding night, in fine lace and satins, silks and embroidered what-nots.'

'I thought you said this marriage would not be consummated.'

'Did someone say that?'

'Yes, you said it was a marriage of convenience.'

'So it is.'

'Whose convenience? Look, I'm just not going to be fucked by some mad dictator, even if he is the King of the World.'

'That's a bit hard, Roxane. Look at it another way. You will be doing your best for your family. Family, doesn't that mean anything to you? And you will be part, not only of our family history, but also of the whole history of the world. You will save the world from all these wars, all these pointless activities of conquest.'

'It's not fair,' said Roxane, but her arms and legs felt too heavy to move, and soon she gave up the struggle against a great weariness, and she fell deeply asleep.

Chapter 12

The voice of Alexander summoned his men through the mist. 'Aristander, where are you?'

'Here, Alexander.'

'Costys, where are you?'

'Here, Alexander.'

The voices drifted to where Alexander stood, ankle deep in water. 'Here we are,' he said, in a tone of booming jollity. 'Here we are. We have arrived at another world in the stars, a new world for us to conquer.'

'It seems to be a world full of water,' said Costys, glumly. His sandals squelched in the mud. Small black leeches clung to his ankles.

Loud noises of threshing in the swamp came from all directions.

'That must be my men,' said Alexander. The noises grew closer, until Alexander was surrounded once more by his good and faithful army. The men stood there in the water, looking at their leader. Men, the men with whom he had travelled, and they stood there, in the water, thinking.

'Where is the edge of this swamp?' asked Alexander, brightly.

'Not that way,' said the men who came from that way.

'Nor that way either,' said the men who had come from the other direction.

'Then we must start marching at once, or we'll never get out of the swamp.' So they marched, and sometimes the water grew deeper, and sometimes it seemed to rise to high ground, only to plunge them more deeply into the swamp. Where reeds grew and gave promise of higher ground, there the sharp edges of the grasses cut them about the legs. Unknown reptiles slithered under their feet. The mist swirled round their heads. Strange sounds of large animals lumbering around in the swamp came from the directions they tried to avoid.

Together they marched and marched until the ground gave a small spring under their feet, and the mud gave way to dry land, and the sun started to shine through the mist, forcing it to rise in the air and disperse.

'We must find another city and conquer it,' said Alexander.

Three burly soldiers pushed Aristander forward before his king. 'Go on,' one of them hissed in the philosopher's ear.

Aristander sneezed. His eyes were streaming with tears. His nose ran. He felt awful. 'What if, my king, it might be as I have been thinking, what if we come to a place in the stars, where there are no people?'

'Why would we be here, if there were no city to conquer? There would be no point to the exercise.'

'My point, exactly.'

'No people, no women.'

'That's a real problem. How can I found another Alexandria, if there are no local women to take my surplus men, men too old and weary for war, yet ripe for settlement, and fatherhood, breeding the new race of Macedonians among the stars, colonists of the new worlds. Men who have founded Alexandria on the Sher, Alexandria on the Oxus, Alexandria on the . . .'

'Alexandria at the bottom of the Swamp,' muttered Costys.

'Ha, you are my jester, Costys. Why don't you don the jester's habit which we found on the Star of Avignon among the Popes? You can be my jester, with ringing of bells, and merry quips, and prancing around. Bring on the jester's new clothes!'

'They're somewhere back in the swamp. With the slaves.'

'Pity,' said Alexander,' I could do with a fool. Instead of a philosopher.'

Aristander groaned.

'Well, philosopher, if this is a star without people, how can I conquer it, tell me that? It is written, that I shall go on in eternal conquest.'

'Ah, but where is it written, Alexander? Have you ever seen where it is written?'

'No, but my soothsayers tell me so. In the entrails of a goat. Where are my soothsayers?'

'Somewhere back in the swamp.'

'Soothsayers, what can you say? See how bad they are,' said Aristander. 'They couldn't even predict their own end.'

'I hear stirrings in the swamp. The men who are lost will find us.'

'We could go home,' muttered Costys.

'You could say, here you are lord of all the creatures in the swamp,' Aristander continued, in diplomatic vein.

'I know that.'

'That being so,' Aristander continued, 'there is no need to stay here longer.'

Small strange reptiles scurried from the ferns under their feet, and dashed across the open spaces. Fish slithered from the water and walked clumsily on their fins across the mud before climbing into the high foliage of the tree-ferns. Mosquitoes the size of dragon-flies buzzed in the air.

'Dinner,' said Alexander, pointing to the lizards and the fish. His men drew their swords, and began the chase.

'Fish that walk on water? Fish that climb up trees?' Aristander stood, stunned. 'Where are we?' From the distance came noises of other, possibly much larger, swamp residents thrashing about in the water.

'I name this place Alexandria,' said Alexander, and bade his followers make what camp they could. His weary men put down their damp bundles, and started to make a new home.

As the day wore on the mist over the swamp lifted, and the sun shone through the clouds. To the east the ground seemed higher and the vegetation changed to large trees of some strange species. Lunch of a rough and ready kind was served, and after it men felt themselves slide in the languour of the afternoon. Aristander lay back on the thick stem of a large fern, and felt his eyes grow heavy. He closed them, but behind his closed lids, he saw the trees on the horizon walking, and nodding their heads.

'The trees are walking,' he cried, opening his eyes, and glancing towards the line of trees on the horizon. 'One of those trees has a head!'

The creature dipped its head to drink.

'You are dreaming,' said Alexander, glancing towards the trees, where for the moment of his glance, nothing stirred.

Feeling foolish, Aristander started to close his eyes. Through half-open lids, he saw a large head emerge from the distant swamp, and swivel around in the tree-tops.

'There!'

The soldiers looked again at where he pointed. A giant lizard the size of a tree lopped off the tops of the trees and munched on them.

'It is the Land of Giants!'

'Ah,' said Alexander.

The dinosaur sunk its head back into the swamp and took a long drink.

'If it comes this way . . .'

'There must be more out there. Behind us. In front of us.'

'If it comes this way, we could run,' said Alexander, upon reflection. 'Retreat.'

Alexander called for his men. 'We should aim for the highest ground we can reach before nightfall. Sound a retreat.'

Aristander sighed, and packed again for another march. What was there about human nature, he reflected, that drove men like Alexander on to conquer? Some essential inner core of his being that cried, 'For-ever onwards!' And what was there about his followers, that they too replied when he called, a resounding, 'Yes!' And up they would rise, so obediently, and take up their swords and follow, into the unknown, into dreadful danger, and here, into the swamp.

It was the weird lizards that flew through the air, the giant mosquitoes that he must fend off with his sword, the leeches that clung to his knees, they gave him food for thought. These creatures had no urge to wander in ever expanding circles of conquest. They find the swamp congenial, it is their home, and there they stay. Walk onto dry land (at least, as was the case in Macedon) and the fish do not follow. They stay in their natural place, the element of water assigned to them by a bounteous nature.

So, he was starting to believe, should man.

'There is a place in nature, and each thing to its own place,' said Aristander to Alexander as they walked.

'So you have told me before. You talk of the scale of nature, with each creature assigned a place, in ascending order of complexity, until at the top, there is the kingdom of men.'

'And ruling over all men, there is the great Alexander.'

'Yes, that I can accept. Carry on.'

'I need say only this, that in our travels, we have seen other places, and have learned that there, nature and human nature bear a different relationship to each other. I am beginning to develop a theory of natural place.'

'My tutor, Aristotle, explained to me, that there are elements of air, water, fire and earth, and each has its natural place one on top of the other.'

'Yes, and more. All things that are composed of a mixture of these elements have their natural place, and the nature of all things is to find the true centre of their being, and there to stay. To move beyond that still, calm centre is to plunge into turmoil, and chaos. Following you, my leader, we have taken the passage out, to see where it would lead us, and that is part of our nature, a restlessness to go on, and on in eternal quest. But the end of the quest, ah, that is where the great leader must be wise enough to know when to stop.'

'Simple,' said Alexander. 'We stop when the goal has been reached, when the object of the quest has been attained and that will be the conquest of the world, and the bringing of all the stars under the rule of Macedon.'

'How to know when to stop . . . tell me, how is Macedon, and how is it presently ruled?'

'My mother rules,' said Alexander. 'She is an extension of myself, as a right arm. She rules as I would have her rule, as caretaker, waiting for my return.'

'How do you know for sure?'

'It is a natural thing, for a mother to do.'

'Yes, true, for the generality of women, but in the particular case, sometimes the general rule does not apply. Queen Olympias, it seems to me, has always been her own person. She has never done what others expect her to do, as befitting a woman.'

'If she transgresses her true nature, according to your story, then she too will fall into chaos.'

'As will your rule in Macedon.'

'Hum,' said Alexander. 'I do not like what you are saying, but why keep a philosopher, if I do not want to learn something new each day? You may be right.'

'Perhaps it would be a good idea,' said Aristander, 'to make a quick trip home and check up on things. I believe it is possible. Costys, your messenger, always could find the path home.'

'It was different,' said Costys, when Alexander summoned him to march beside him. 'When I went before, it was because the Queen sent for me.'

'Or I sent you with a gift of snakes.'

'Which she knew you had collected.'

'And news of glorious exploits of her son.'

'News to which she did not respond as a fond mother

might,' Aristander prompted. 'She did not send her congratulations in return.'

'True,' Alexander mused.

'Perhaps you should go back, and see for yourself.'

'Or she can come here. To my marriage. Here in this new place I shall take a new bride. My astrologer told me so.'

'In the swamp?'

'Why not? My mother might enjoy it. Plenty of unusual snakes. Tell Olympias, the Queen, that I plan to marry, and that a mother's place is by her son at such a time.'

Costys bowed and reminded his leader, 'She has not come, in the past.'

'She may not want to come, but she will. Tell her I am looking forward to returning to Macedon soon.'

'So are we all,' murmured Aristander.

'I shall make her a present of a small island somewhere in the Mediterranean, and there she can end her days. The burdens of care of my empire shall fall from her, and she will die in peace. Aristander, you agree with me?'

'Eminently.'

'Arrange it.'

'The Queen may send me back,' said Costys.

'It was my mother that did that? I thought it was the force of destiny.'

'She has the power. First she appears in my waking thoughts, and issues a summons. Then, when I sleep, I find I wake in Macedon, and there I see my family again, my dear children, my old parents, my sweet wife . . .'

'Yes, yes, yes,' said Alexander, 'But I've given you all that on your travels. A new wife on each new world, new children. I myself shall set the example. I feel the urge about to come upon me, to take a new wife once more. Tell me, though, how does it happen? Your voyage to the other world?'

'In my dreams I see a mist, and I walk through the mist, and there I am, at the other place. Home. Where I most desire to be.'

'My mother Olympias, is she ruling well?'

'As well as you would be, were you there.'

'Then there's nothing to worry about.' Something, though, about the way Costys shifted his gaze and looked thoughtfully at the distant horizon just behind Alexander's left ear made him uneasy. 'A short visit home, just to check for myself, might be a good idea.'

'Then we must look for the mist,' said Aristander briskly. 'There was quite a lot of it around this morning.'

'It's not that kind of mist,' said Costys. 'It is a mist with a halo of light, a mist with a roseate glow, a mist which beckons with hope, a mist which calls of home.'

Alexander was impressed. 'Go off, Costys, and as you march, compose a poem on the subject, and recite it to me as we sit around the camp fire tonight. Guards, keep your eyes open for a roseate mist of hope and joy. Philosopher, pray continue.'

'What are men, in their natures?'

Aristander settled into his stride, and began. 'Once there was a place where all men were equal, and women too, and slaves, and no-one any higher than the other, in the esteem of their countryfellows, in their place in the city, in the manner of their trades, in their walks of life.'

'It sounds like a place that cannot be. We have never found a place like that in all our travels,' said Alexander.

'Yet it was there,' said Aristander. 'Once. If not in our world, then in another we have yet to visit.'

'That is a question into which I, as a god, feel I may be able to offer a privileged insight. Philosopher, listen to me. It is a world which exists in my thoughts. It is the world which will come at the end of my conquests.'

'But what of you? You will be here, no higher than the rest.'

'No. I shall be higher, for I shall don my true raiment, as a god.'

'What if, though, the gods were all equal, too, to each

other, and to the rest of us? To the men, the women, and the slaves.'

'I had not allowed for that,' said Alexander. 'But why employ a philosopher, unless he tells you things you'd never have thought of all by yourself? You tell me.'

'Gods, men and slaves,' said Aristander. 'All equal, and in their natural place, their place where the spirit finds its best repose. Centred. Together.'

'Tell me, in this ideal world, what would people do each day?'

'They will rise, and go about their business. At each social encounter, they will be polite, and nice, and never think themselves as either above, or below, the other. All men will work harmoniously together, to bring in the harvest, to write the book of the good life, and none will say, how he worked harder than the others, how he worked while others rested, while they stole the results of his labour from him. There will be no quarrels, no arguments. The women will debate geometry with the men.'

'All day?'

'There will be other pursuits. "What is truth?" the people will be asked, and that is how they will spend their lives, each day getting a little closer to the answer, but never, never, quite finding it. That will be their happiness.'

'Happiness, for a philosopher. But for a warrior? Look at my men. Is that their desire in life? Their purpose, their true end? Men of action, they require more than you can give them.'

'Men of action, what to do about them,' sighed Aristander. 'It is an eternal problem in philosophy. Perhaps there is a way to use up their boundless energy, harness it to, if not good ends, then to harmless ones.'

'They are men of action, men for who joy lies in the swirl of the sword, the clash of spear against shield, the vigour of the chase, the thrill of the kill. That is the good life, for them. What can you offer them, that will take their minds off conquest?'

'What if,' said Aristander, 'and this is just a wild idea, pure speculation for its own sake, what if they learn to channel their energies inward, on themselves? So, instead of contemplating the perfection of geometry, they contemplate the perfection of their own bodies? They will work hard on shaping their muscles, work on looking their best in a loincloth. I too, have had a great vision of the future.'

'What kind of vision is that? When the man of action does not go out, each day, to kill?'

'It is a vision of the quite impossible,' sighed Aristander.

'What of the women? If they all do geometry, they will run out of geometry to do, sooner or later. All the geometry in the world will be done. And what if geometry is not to their taste? My mother, the Queen, for example.'

'As I see it, it can still be a world in which everyone is equal, but different. Some women will be good at geometry, others will specialise in keeping snakes.'

'But that will mean that one will be better at geometry than the other. Or be able to breed more snakes.'

'Ah, there you have me, Alexander, your thought is far swifter than mine, and you have beaten me in argument.'

Alexander smiled.

'That is the problem. The trick of it is to have a world in which this difference does not matter. And the secret of that, in all my reading of human nature, I have never been able to discover.'

'Do you expect men to give birth, and suckle their young? That, dear Aristander, that is where your vision embraces the absolutely ridiculous. Men will be like women? That will be against all nature.'

'Only against nature as it now is. What if nature changes? Look around you, at this place. Is this not a kind of nature, which is different from ours in Macedon?'

In the distance, dinosaurs waved their heads.

'Might this not mean,' Aristander continued, 'that nature changes?'

'Agreed, but this is on another world. This is not our nature. This is not our home.'

'That is why we must go home,' said Aristander. 'That is the inexorable conclusion to which our conversation is leading.'

'Look!'

They came to a sheltered place on the high ground where, in a roseate shimmering haze, a clutch of large dinosaur eggs lay, hatching.

Avoiding the nipping jaws of the hatchlings, Costys slipped through the haze, and tumbled into the cave. Vonnie and Jerome leaped back, alarmed. Costys leaned back, the top half of his body disappearing from the sight of the two in the cave, as with the top half of his body visible to Alexander and his men, he waved the soldiers to follow.

'Who are you?' asked Vonnie, when Costys stepped more properly into the cave, as an entire person.

'Out of the way,' said Costys. 'There's an army coming this way. Or what's left of it. Desert,' he sighed, looking out of the mouth of the cave. 'I love it.' He sat down, and started pulling leeches off his knees.

'He's not Robinson, either,' said Jerome.

'Alexander's coming,' Costys explained.

'Oh, they said it would happen,' said Jerome, 'Everyone's been talking about it. The bundles of snakes that kept arriving, the portents . . .'

'It is written that we should come, that we voyage among the stars.'

'This is not a star. This is planet Earth,' said Vonnie. 'People can't live on the stars. They're too hot, like our sun.'

'You are wrong. We've been there,' said Costys. 'Make way there, for the rest of the army!'

A baby dinosaur ran, squawking, through the haze into the cave, pursued by half a spear. A sandalled foot appeared, tentatively testing the other side of the haze. The toes wriggled, the ankle jerked, and the foot was rapidly withdrawn, as if its owner had taken a sudden fright. The dinosaur ran out of the cave and into the desert, where it stood, stunned, in the full heat of the desert day.

'That's not a star where that comes from,' said Vonnie. 'That is our own planet, in another time. The time of the dinosaurs. That is a member of an extinct species, poor little thing.'

'Dinner,' said Jerome abstractedly. 'Look, Vonnie, we'd better run and find the Emperor Darius.'

'Darius,' yelped Costys. 'Wouldn't you know it.' He sat down disconsolately on a rock. 'Where am I?'

'You are at the city of Bazaklik in the Desert of Lob, beside the Flaming Cliffs.'

'Aha,' said Alexander, as he led his men through the haze. 'I know it well. We have returned to our place of departure. It must be written, that I return to Macedon, my kingdom, and announce my triumph in the stars, and meet my dear mother once more.'

Vonnie and Jerome turned, and ran as fast as they could back the way they had come.

Chapter 13

Meanwhile, back in Macedon, Olympias sat, stunned. 'Alexander will come back here? To rule my kingdom?'

'That is why he has sent for you, to come with me. He is planning to take a new wife, and he wants his mother with him, to walk ten steps behind when he makes his triumphal return with his new bride.'

Costys stood, a glum messenger, waiting for a cross answer.

'Why now? Why doesn't he stay a while, in his new kingdom? He's at Bazaklik, you say? If I could stay there fifteen years, why can't he?'

Olympias called for Mickie. 'If I go, she goes,' she said, nodding curtly to the baby in her servant's arms.

Freda came running up. 'If she goes, I go!' she insisted, indignantly.

Costys counted silently. 'You three all want to come? It's a desert, in the middle of nowhere.' Alexander had not mentioned a baby. And whose baby was it? Not the child of Olympias, and a usurper to Alexander?

The young usurper waved regally at Costys. On the other hand, thought Costys, if the child is a usurper, possibly it was best for Alexander to deal with the problem himself as soon as possible.

Olympias took charge of Mickie. Mickie cried and held her arms out to her mother. Freda swept across to comfort her child. Olympias looked down at the cross and crying Mickie in her arms, and handed her to Freda. Freda clutched Mickie to her. Mickie cuddled in to Freda, and stopped crying, with a smirk at Olympias. Olympias called for her gold cloak.

'And who is Alexander marrying, this time?'

'Roxane, the daughter of Darius.'

Freda looked at Costys in amazement.

Costys continued. 'Darius has called for peace, and has offered his daughter as a surety of it.'

'Hasn't he married her once already?' asked Olympias.

'It's a long story,' Costys began.

'You mean, Roxane, the daughter of Darius, my sister Roxane?'

Costys peered at Freda. 'Roxane, the daughter of Darius. It is written. In the stars.'

'Roxane is getting married because it's written in the stars? Roxane will never agree to that.'

'Agree to it? My son Alexander, the King of the World? Of course she will marry him if that is what he wants!' Olympias glared at Freda.

Freda stood her ground. 'Do I get an invitation to the wedding? She is my sister.'

'Come,' said Olympias. 'Help prepare your sister for her wedding night. Darius will see his grandchild, will see that in her veins the royal blood is flowing. Matriarchy moves in mysterious ways. What's so great about direct blood connections? What matters is the spirit, and the royal spirit lives in this small child, this queen to be, the granddaughter of Darius, the niece, though not by blood, of Alexander.'

'She's just Mickie. We call her Mickie,' Freda babbled, in a state of shock. 'Though her real name is Michaela. Queen Michaela. Of course, if I'd known she was going to be queen, I'd have called her something different, like Elizabeth or Margaret Rose . . . Let me see, the granddaughter of Darius inherits the kingdom of Alexander?'

'That's it,' said Olympias.

'Does Alexander know?'

'I haven't told him.'

'But Mickie is just a baby! She's not old enough to decide if she wants to be Queen. She is my daughter, and she belongs in the twentieth century.'

A cat slithered along on its belly and nodded its head at Mickie. Mickie nodded back, in return.

'It's not a question of her deciding anything for herself,' said Olympias. 'It is a question of one's station in life, one's calling, one's destiny.'

'Then, before we go, I'll just change her nappy,' said Freda. 'She's got a bit unswaddled, for a Queen.'

Chapter 14

'Where am I? I was told this would be the city of Bazaklik.' Alexander marched his remaining men into the city, and made his inquiries. His eyes closed to a slit as he squinted into the sun

'So it is,' replied the envoy.

'Then where is Great Sea at the Edge of the World?'

'The sea has retreated, the land has become desert, and water no longer crashes at the foot of the Flaming Cliffs.'

'Times have changed?'

'As they must. This is, after all, the city that stands at the crossroads of time.' The envoy spoke as he had been instructed.

'Block up that cave,' Alexander ordered, pointing back the way he had come. 'Seal the entrance. Stand some men on watch. The monsters will escape and eat us.'

'You came through the swamp?' the envoy asked, incredulous. Then he noticed how water steamed from the slime-covered armour of Alexander's men, how their sandals were caked with mud. 'There are other ways,' murmured the envoy. 'Easier ways. I take it, Alexander, because the swamp is the hardest way, the toughest way, that is why you chose that path to come to us?'

'Naturally,' replied Alexander shortly. His men shuffled and looked mutinous. 'We have travelled from the stars this very day.'

'Through the swamp?'

'The stars, too, have their swamps.'

'As you say.'

Aristander whispered a note of quiet caution. 'On that point, Alexander, you are best advised to keep your peace. People will not believe you. They will say that you have not really been living on the stars, for they are too hot to stand upon. They will say that you have been travelling, not to the stars, but travelling upon this earth, in time.'

Alexander nodded. 'My story is true, but we are far from home, and I accept your caution.'

'I come to announce the preparations for your wedding,' said the envoy.

'All is in hand? The feast, the dowry?'

'And the bride. You wish to meet her?'

'Later. I have my men to see to, and their provisions, and the shields and the spears and their swords. Spit and polish, spit and polish, a soldier's work is never done. Then there'll be the tents to mend, and the reprovisioning for the next stage of our journey, and the new recruiting drive.'

'The wedding is tomorrow.'

'When better?'

Alexander stretched, called for some wine, drank, watched while his men prepared his camp, then slept.

Eva was upset. 'Darius! I can't find him. He's gone again, hasn't he? Left us, stranded, miles from home.'

There were nods all round the harem.

Eva sighed. 'I knew it. I knew he wouldn't stay, not even for his own daughter's wedding. I know,' she continued, looking at the sad faces around her, 'that you, too, feel sad. And I can see why he's gone, this time. It's hardly diplomatic for him to stay, under the circumstances. So he just dropped in to Bazaklik, arranged a marriage, and left, as quickly and as effortlessly as he came.'

Her new friends, Isabella and Uncumber, comforted Eva, Isabella with a hug, Uncumber with a tray of salted melon seeds. 'Companionship, and good food, that's what life is all about here, in the harem,' Uncumber soothed. 'Comfort, that's something we can always offer. Men, they come and go as they will. You too, like us, have loved Darius, and lost him.'

Eva wiped her eyes and went to find her daughters.

'He's gone,' said Eva to Vonnie. 'Darius. I'll never see him again. I fell asleep, and he was by my side. I woke in the morning and he was gone. It was just like before, when I woke, and thought, he's stepped outside to bring in the milk, and then I remembered, here there is no milk to fetch. He stepped outside, and now he's gone.'

'Don't come crying to me for sympathy,' said Vonnie.

Eva sniffed. 'One day you'll understand.'

'Never. Now listen. What I think is this. I've been asking

round, and everyone seems to think that this wedding marks the beginning of the end of the Great Circle of Eternal Return, got it?'

Eva nodded, drying her eyes. 'Alexander, when he weds, will go back to Macedon, and there die the death of a mortal man. That's what I've been told.'

'The thing I can't work out, is, why bother coming here, and getting married?'

'His astrologer told him to. Besides, he doesn't know that bit. About going back. About dying mortal. For him, it's nothing special. Only another wedding. Darius knew this all along.' Eva's eyes filled with tears.

'I told you he was no good.'

'He planned this.'

'It's Roxane who's getting married. It's Roxane you should be sorry for. Poor Roxane. She's the sacrifice.' Together they peeped in on the sleeping Roxane. 'She's slept well,' said Vonnie. 'For a blood sacrifice.'

'Not blood, dear. Nothing to do with blood.'

'Just a sacrifice, then.'

'In a manner of speaking. Though, I think we can speak of these things differently, Vonnie, if we adopt a larger, more generous perspective.'

Roxane stirred in her sleep. Then, as if recoiling from some vile nightmare, she sat upright, wide awake, in bed. She looked at her mother, and her sister, then at the strange surroundings of the harem. Then she screamed.

'This is a form of marriage that is not recognised in Melbourne, Australia. Where I come from, this wedding is not legal.' Roxane draped the wedding finery around her, quite liking, in spite of herself, the swish of the silk, the richness of the embroidery, the swirl of the long robes.

'You are doing it for all our sakes.'

'None of this nonsense about a wedding night.'

'No no no no no.'

'Alright. What's he look like?'

'Rather nice. I've only seen him in the distance. Rugged. Handsome. The outdoor type.'

'A sensitive man, would you say?'

'Bit too far away to tell.'

'He's a god, too. Will that make me a goddess? Except, of course, I'm not staying.'

'You must convert him,' said Vonnie. 'Tell him that war is very, very wrong.'

'Everyone seems to expect it of me, that I sacrifice myself for the good of the world. Why me? That's what I ask.'

'Why not you?' said Vonnie. 'The ultimate pacifist act, Roxane. It would be ecological, and feminist, and a really nice thing to do.'

'OK, Vonnie, you marry him then.'

'I'm too young.'

'What, fifteen? That's positively old for marriage in this part of the world.'

'Mu-um, Roxane is picking on me.'

'Roxane, how could you think such a thing!'

'It's just pretend, Roxane. They say that afterward Alexander will return home.'

'But he might want to take his new wife with him.'

'You could do something absolutely vile, and he will divorce you on the spot.'

'Like what? What absolutely vile thing can I do to a mad dictator that he hasn't already done himself?'

'You could insist on safe sex.'

'Sex! You said it. What do you know about safe sex? Mu-um, you said I didn't have to do anything, just get married and go back home.'

'Of course, dear.'

'Are you absolutely certain that is what will happen? How do you know?'

'This is destiny, the full force of, this is fate, the finger of it. This is karmit. Kermit? Karma.'

'Uh, oh, Mum, you're off with the birds and the butterflies again.'

'VD!'

'VD?'

'Oops, sorry! It just slipped out. I don't think they had VD, certainly they didn't have AIDS in ancient Macedon,' said Eva, 'I've just remembered, if that's any help.'

'I just keep thinking,' said Roxane, 'that all these plans of yours could come unstuck. What if it isn't true? What if this marriage is not recognised by the powers that are guiding our lives, just as this marriage will not be recognised in Australia? What if I get married, and then, that's it? Nothing happens? I stay married, the way people usually do?'

'That won't happen,' said Vonnie. 'Jerome says so.'

'Who is Jerome?'

'He's nice. He's the son of Wolff.'

'Vonnie! You've got a boyfriend!'

'Jerome says, its the end of one cycle, and the beginning of another.'

'The new cycle might be worse.'

'He dies quite young, Alexander, I remember that from ancient history,' said Eva. 'So it won't last all that long. Your marriage.'

'You said I wouldn't be going back with him.'

'Of course, of course.'

'How do you know, then, Mum?'

'It's written.'

'Where? Let me see it.'

'In the entrails of a goat. It is the local custom. It's the way they do things here. That way, there's plenty of goat left for the wedding feast. It combines the getting of food with information about life choices.'

'Great. I'm the goat. I'm the sacrifice,' said Roxane, gloomily. 'You are selling me off.'

'In the cause of the peace of the world. Look at it my way,' said Eva. 'Here we are, all together again, like the family we used to be, and we're helping and supporting each other. And I now think I've finally got Darius out of my system. Our relationship has come to an end. There's no going back in life. I just have to treasure the memories, and there were some great times, some good times together. I have had to acknowledge, this last time I met him, that our paths have gone very different ways, and we could never really get together again the way it once was.'

'That's all very well for you, to feel you've come to some great life resolution. What about me?' Roxane threw a veil over her eyes. She stood, resplendent, a bride fit for a king.

The women of the harem crowded round in admiration. Isabella whispered some final works of advice. 'Remember, whatever you do, don't let a drop of *qumiz* past your lips.'

Olympias walked crossly along the path beside the Flaming Cliffs. 'Don't they know Alexander can't just get keep getting married like this? He's got wives scattered all over the place.'

'I divorced them,' said Alexander, when he was asked.

'Olympias, it is Olympias, she is coming!' The women of Macria crowded round in welcome. 'We have met you, at last! Look, we wear your image.' They bowed and made her welcome.

Olympias was flattered. 'You know my life and work?'

'We know that Alexander wears the crown, but that you do all the work. For that we honour you, and look, in this likeness of you we wear upon our headdresses, here is the crown of Alexander, but it sits in its rightful place, on the brow of the great Olympias!'

'Of course,' Olympias agreed. 'What exactly do you know about me? What have you heard, and how did it come to you?'

'Come with us,' said the Macrians. 'We'll make you welcome, treat you like a god.'

'That's better than being a goddess any day,' said Olympias, as she was led away, a queen among her true people.

'What about me?' cried Freda as she picked Mickie up from the desert floor, and ran after Olympias and her entourage. 'Where do I fit in? And Mickie?'

Olympias looked critically at Mickie. 'I made a mistake,' she told Freda. 'She is not the Queen to be. I am.' With an imperious wave, Olympias dismissed them both, and went off with her courtiers. 'Now, what I have planned,' she confided, 'I have asked two of my ex-lovers, Jupiter and Dionysius, to drop in at the wedding feast, and that's not all . . .'

'Great,' said Freda, standing in the middle of the city, and at the crossroads of time, with a wet and hungry baby in her arms. 'What about me? I'll have to go and get something for Mickie to eat, even if she's not going to be the future queen.' Freda looked around for a familiar face.

'I need to find my sister, Roxane, and my mother Eva, and some proper food for my baby,' said Freda. 'She's been eating all kinds of odd things lately. Sesame seeds and dates. Do you have any milk?' Freda caught up with a young girl of about eight years of age, who seemed to be able to understand her.

'Milk?' The young girl looked surprised, but led Freda to a large open space in the centre of the village. '*Qumiz*,' she said, pointing to where jugs of milk were being poured into a large cast iron pot.

'Pasteurisation, primitive, but it will do,' said Freda. 'What kind of milk is it?'

The child pointed at the various animals gathered round.

'Ah,' said Freda. 'Camel's milk, I see. Sheep's milk, how interesting. Mare's milk. Oh, my. All in together?'

'*Qumiz*,' the child repeated.

'*Qumiz*,' repeated Freda.

The young girl smiled happily. Then she pointed to another cast iron pot, linked to the first by a tube, which ran from one taut sheepskin cover to the other. '*Buzah*,' she explained.

'That's all very interesting,' said Freda, 'but is it baby food? I think I'll stick to dates.'

The *buzah* was a pale milky-white fluid with pale green scum floating on the surface. 'Oh, I couldn't,' said Freda. 'Not really. Thank you for offering. It's too generous of you. Tell me, how is it made?'

Qumiz must first be prepared from the milk of forty mares placed in sheepskin bags, the cook explained, and it must be rocked gently until it ferments. Then place the *qumiz* in a cast-iron pot, boil it, collect the condensation in the second vat, and there you have it, a fine vat of *buzah*, fit for a wedding, Alexander's wedding.

'Alexander's wedding!' said Freda, in consternation. 'I'd almost forgotten why I was here! Excuse me,' she babbled to the cook, 'I must hurry to my sister. She is getting married to Alexander,' she explained. 'I'm sorry,' said Freda, 'I really am, but I must rush.'

'I see Dionysius has arrived,' said Olympias, as Alexander took another long draught of *qumiz*. 'Dionysius, I asked him to drop by. And Jupiter, your father, he said he'd send a message.' A thunderbolt rent the clear blue sky. Lightning flashed. No rain fell.

'Mother,' said Alexander. 'How nice to meet you again. You may be seated in my presence.'

'My dear son,' said Olympias, seating herself with a glare, and dismissing to a distance her Macrian entourage. 'You have called me at an extremely inconvenient time.'

'It is my wedding day, Mother. I thought you'd like it.'

'I am delighted, pleased and overwhelmed that you should want me by your side on such a day, but I really must get back as soon as possible. You must excuse me if I rush away, straight away, after the ceremony.'

'Mother, I've been thinking of making you a small gift.'

'Oh?'

'A small island, somewhere in the Mediterranean. An island of your own.'

'I don't know when I'd get the time to visit, but thank you so much for the thought.'

'You misunderstand, Mother. I was planning to give it to you, on my return, so that you can have a kingdom of your own.'

'On your return? But that will not be for a good long time. Don't bother yourself with me. I'm just an old woman now, getting on in years. Look how frail these old wrists are. I don't want to be bothered with gifts for which I can't find a good use.'

'Yes, Mother, it's because of you I think I shall come back, and rule my own kingdom for a while. I thought you'd like it, retiring to a small and peaceful island all your own, far from the hurly burly of rule and conquer, conquer and rule.'

'When?'

'As soon as I am married.'

Olympias sat, thoughtful, for a few moments. Alexander smiled genially. Then Olympias rose, summoned her entourage, and moved off with only the faintest of faint farewells.

Roxane appeared in the city square, resplendent in her wedding dress.

'Roxane,' said Freda. 'At last I've found you!'

'How nice of you to come,' said Roxane. 'I really didn't expect it.'

'Roxane, marriage, have you really thought long and deep about it? Look at Sergio and me, we've got Mickie, but we still haven't taken the big plunge. This is all so sudden. You've got to give it time. When did you first meet him?'

'I haven't met him yet. I'll see him at the wedding.'

'Roxane, do you think that's wise?'

'He is the King of the World, Freda. Come, there is going to be some entertainment at the edge of the city.

Men have come from the mountains and they shall be riding for me.'

Roxane sat on a high throne, and watched the sports. Freda and Mickie sat at her feet. Men rode furiously round and round chasing an inflated goatskin bladder, falling off their horses, calling for *qumiz*, getting on again, the blood flowing from gashes in their skin, their bodies black with bruises.

'It's the way they do things here,' Roxane explained. 'It's called a *baiha*.'

'Isn't it all a little bit dull?' asked Freda. 'Drinking themselves stupid, climbing on their horses, chasing that thing, falling off and climbing up again?'

'Oh, Freda, if I wanted a society wedding, I never would have come here.'

'Roxane, try to remember. When you left, you weren't planning to get married then.'

'How long ago and far away all that seems!'

'Two days,' Freda prompted.

'Listen! Songs! Music!' Raucous male voices were joined by the one-stringed harp and the two-note flute and the three-pronged zither.

'Loud,' said Freda.

An official motioned for the music to stop. 'It is time,' he announced. 'The hour has come when the bride price must be paid. Call forth Eva, the mother of Roxane.'

'Me?' said Eva. 'What do I have to do?'

'Where is the bride price that I must pay?' Alexander clapped his hands and called out. 'Ah, there it is!'

Alexander bowed towards Eva, 'Madame, allow me to bestow upon you, as is the marriage custom in these wild parts, a fair and fitting bride price for your daughter, Roxane.'

Alexander waved his servants forth, and forth they came to Eva, leading two camels and two yaks. 'These two fine camels and these lovely yaks, one male, one female, are for you, in exchange for the hand of your daughter in marriage.'

'They're very nice yaks,' said Eva. 'I'm quite overwhelmed. I wasn't expecting . . .'

'It is my custom, when I travel,' announced Alexander, 'to marry in the local tradition. More *qumiz*!' Alexander drank deeply and staggered to his seat. He leaned across and took Roxane's hand in his. 'At last!' he said, 'We are married at last!'

'Was that it?' asked Roxane, 'Is this all?'

Alexander nodded.

'That's it, horse riding, and music, and *qumiz*, and camels, and yaks, you sit down beside me, I meet you for the first time, and we're married?'

Alexander rose to his feet and motioned to Roxane to do likewise. Roxane stood. She turned to Eva and beckoned her closer. 'He's supposed to disappear,' she hissed. 'Why hasn't he?' Eva shrugged helplessly.

A figure burst from the crowd in a swirl of black and red. It was Wolff, in full canonicals.

'Wait,' he cried. 'The bride is from another time, and though, great Alexander, you have fully met the local requirements for marriage, I think your bride expects something a little different, am I not mistaken?'

'I do?'

'You feel there is something wrong?'

'Yes!' said Roxane, heartfelt.

'You want a proper wedding?'

'I don't know,' said Roxane, doubtfully. 'Who are you?'

'I am a traveller, as are we all, a traveller in time.'

'He's alright,' said Eva. 'I met him earlier.'

'He's a proper priest?'

'He says he is.'

'Are you a proper priest?'

'Of course I am.'

'If you marry me, then it will be a proper wedding.'

'Naturally.'

'But I don't want to get married.'

'You already are married, to Alexander, according to the local rite.'

'But if you marry me, then I shall be really married.'

'One moment,' said Wolff to Alexander. He took Roxane aside, and whispered in her ear. 'Don't you see? The fact that he is still here, drinking *qumiz*, and has not returned to his own time means that this marriage was not a proper marriage, according to the powers that are shaping our lives here, at this place at the crossroads of time.'

'So I have to get married again?'

'It seems so.'

Roxane stood, rueful, at the crossroads of time, in front of a priest from the eighteenth century, listening to a marriage service in Latin.

'What,' roared Alexander a few minutes into the ceremony. 'What barbarous tongue is that? Latin? I refuse to get married in that language.' He raised his sword high, and waved it after Wolff, who took to his heels and ran off, his canonicals flapping red and black in the breeze.

Roxane passed a moist hand over her faint brow. 'I think I'll retire for a few moments,' she murmured faintly. 'It's all been a bit too much.'

'Go with your sisters, and your mother. Go, and prepare for my coming.'

Chapter 15

'Quick,' Vonnie called to Roxane. 'Quick, stop mooning around. It's in one side of the tent and out the other, remember?'

'That was the most amazing wedding I've ever been to in my life,' said Eva. 'What on earth am I going to do with those yaks?'

'You can give them back, and liberate me,' said Roxane.

'We must escape,' said Vonnie. 'Jerome has promised to show us the way.'

'Let's get out fast,' said Roxane. Then to Jerome, indignantly, she said, 'Alexander didn't disappear. You said he would.'

'He will. It will happen when he falls asleep. We just didn't wait long enough.'

'Great,' said Roxane. 'Nobody told me that. And what do you think was going to happen to me before he fell asleep? Did any of you think of that?' Roxane glared around her. She pushed back her veil and rolled up her sleeves.

'Where are we going?' said Freda, panting to keep up. 'Wait for me. This milk for Mickie. It keeps slopping all over the place. I wish I'd brought a bottle. And it's so hard, doing all this running round with a baby.'

'Look at those village women,' said Roxane, without sympathy for Freda. 'They just sling the baby over their shoulder in a blanket and think nothing of it.'

'Alright, Roxane, you do it. Be big Earth Mother. You sling her on your shoulder. Here she is. She weighs a ton.'

'I can't. It's hard enough keeping going with all this wedding gear.'

'I'm going to do my back,' Freda grumbled.

'Jerome, where are you taking us?'

'There is a passage out,' said Jerome.

'The swamp sounds good to me,' said Roxanne. 'Take me to it.'

'Why didn't I bring the pusher?'

'Shut up, Freda. Vonnie, can't you help?'

'Mum, Roxane's picking on me.'

'Give Mickie to me,' said Eva. Mickie was sleepy and drooped heavily in her arms. Eva trudged on.

'Mickie pongs, Freda. You should change her more often.'

'You change her, Vonnie. It's not my fault I came on this expedition with just one nappy. I know, Jerome, the women of the village have been most generous with their swaddling bands, but it's just not the same as terry towelling. And swaddling, unswaddling, here they only do it once a month. I'm just not used to it.'

'Pooh,' said Vonnie.

'Vonnie,' said Eva, 'you have to look at it their way. It's a social necessity of their life. It's a way of surviving in a land without washing machines.'

'Always looking for the nearest pond to rinse the nappy in, I tell you, it's getting to me,' said Freda. 'Then I ask myself, what is it that we're drinking when we have a drink of water?'

'Yuk. Mum, Freda's making me feel sick.'

'Freda, we all have our problems.'

'Look at you, you got us into this.'

'I was called,' said Eva.

'So was I,' said Roxane. 'And you followed,' said Roxane to Freda. 'So there.'

'I won't bother next time.'

'There won't be a next time,' said Eva sadly. 'Darius has gone for ever.'

'Here we are,' said Jerome. He led them through a narrow opening in the rock and into a large dim cavern. As their eyes grew used to the gloom, the daughters of Darius fell silent as the magic of the caves cast its spell. 'It's so beautiful, Jerome,' whispered Vonnie. 'I can see why you feel as you do about it.' Rays of light shone through the gloom from the upper clerestory levels, highlighting here a lotus flower, there an event from the life of Robinson.

'What is this place?' asked Roxane. 'This is weird, this is really weird.'

'It is the story of a great traveller,' said Jerome. 'It is the story of Robinson Crusoe. Like all of you, he travelled to strange places, and yet, he returned, as you will with his help.'

'Let me get this straight,' said Roxane. 'We are going to be helped to go home by one Robinson Crusoe?'

Jerome nodded proudly.

'But he's only a story,' Roxane wailed. 'At least Alexander the Great was a real person. I'm beginning to regret this.' She looked around her suspiciously.

Light fell on patterns of leaves and flowers, on delicate intertwined arabesques, the colours vibrant and glowing, delicate blue-greens, soft pinks.

'They are the colours of the bloom which lies on the surface of the young lotus,' Eva explained to Roxane, as Darius had explained it to her.

A narrow passage at the end of the cave gave way to a larger space, then other passages, other rooms, each lit a little from each other. 'We'll never be able to find our way back,' said Roxane, nervously.

'You are not going back,' said Jerome. 'You don't need to know. You are going to take the passage out.'

Half-glimpsed through openings half-obscured, beads of light danced like distant fireflies. Jerome hurried them on. The light rose from a large brass saucer-lamp tended by shadowy figures. A gong was beaten three times, and the sound reverberated softly though the echoing chambers. Then a slow drum beat commenced, soon joined by the sweet sounds of a harp and a flute. The smell of incense wafted from the lamp.

'This cave is special,' Jerome announced.

They saw a map of an island set in a golden sea, and on the island was painted a thick grove of luxuriant green trees. Robinsonian acolytes hurried to meet them.

'Quickly,' said Jerome. 'Prepare the outward passage.' The acolytes nodded. They stood in a circle behind the four women and the baby, chanting softly. Jerome took five long pieces of cloth. 'Now close your eyes,' Jerome commanded. He quickly tied a blindfold round the eyes of Eva, Vonnie, Freda and Roxane. Gently he tipped Mickie's sun hat down over her eyes. Mickie stirred in her sleep, and squirmed, before settling back, her eyes still firmly closed, in Eva's arms.

'Jerome, what is this all about?' asked Eva.

'Shhh, it is the passage out. You want to go home, don't you?'

There were nods all round.

'Good,' said Jerome, before he tied the folded cloth around his own eyes, and motioned the acolytes forward, with his arm.

The acolytes advanced, their chanting increasing in volume. They gathered round the blindfolded ones, and gently propelled them round and round, as in a game of blind-man's buff.

'I feel very silly,' Roxane muttered.

'Shhh,' said Eva.

'You've still got Mickie?' asked Freda.

'Yes,' said Eva.

'Shhh,' said Jerome, 'Silence. Concentrate. Hear the music. Feel the beat.' The pace of the music increased, and the dance grew wilder.

'Hey!' shouted Roxane.

'Wow!' said Vonnie.

'I think I'm getting too old for this,' said Eva. 'And Mickie is so heavy.'

Together, unknowing, they faced the grove of trees on the map of the island.

'Forward,' cried Jerome, and together they stumbled into the trees. Birds sang above their heads. A warm wind ruffled their hair.

Roxane took off her blindfold. She stood, resplendent in her wedding gown, and looked around her. 'Hurrah! Jerome! You did it! I've escaped! He can't come and get me here!'

'Where is here?' asked Freda, removing her blindfold, and gently taking Mickie from Eva's arms.

'Look!' said Vonnie. A wild bearded man was looking at them from the trees. He started at the noise of Vonnie's voice, paused, then darted off into the forest. A herd of goats ran after him, crashing through the undergrowth.

'Look, Mickie, goats!' said Freda, 'Milk, lovely milk!'

'This isn't home,' said Eva suspiciously.

'This is Robinson's island,' said Jerome proudly. 'This is the passage out. I have rescued you. I feel I've known this place all my life. These are the trees and shrubs, and over there, I'm sure we'll find the food crops, the shelter, the castle, the enclosures for the animals, the beach of bones, evidence of the richness of the life of Robinson.'

The women turned on Jerome and glared at him.

Jerome did not notice. He was too excited and pleased with everything.

Vonnie sat down and wailed, 'Mum!'

'Right,' said Roxane. 'Here we are with Robinson Crusoe on his island. It seems to me, Jerome, that we are as far from home as ever we were.'

'We've got goats,' said Eva. 'And there are two men, at least, Jerome here, and Robinson. Civilisation can survive. The sexes have some kind of balance.'

'Mum!'

'Speaking purely from an anthropological point of view, a theoretical point of view, of course,' said Eva, hastily.

'You can have him, then,' said Roxane. 'The wild man of the woods. I'm not taking on anyone else. One wedding in one day is quite enough.'

'It was always a mystery,' said Jerome, his face radiant with the joy of discovery, 'how Robinson managed, without women. But now I know. He didn't! He had women on the island. You! He just didn't write about them, in his book. And this small child,' he said, ruffling Mickie's sleeping head, 'she may well be the daughter of Robinson!'

'Hey, hang on, no!' said Freda. 'I've never seen him before in my life!'

'Here we all are,' said Jerome. 'We can establish the new kingdom of Robinson, and you, Vonnie, you can be my bride!'

'I'm only fifteen!' wailed Vonnie.

'Old,' said Jerome. 'But it will have to do.'

'Piss off,' said Vonnie.

'Vonnie, you told me I had to marry Alexander,' said Roxane.

'Let's not rush into things,' Eva soothed. 'I think we'd better get moving. Try to find out if we can get help. I'm not as sure as you are, Jerome, that this is Robinson's island. Where we come from, *Robinson Crusoe* is only a story.'

'Robinson will be gracious, and choose one of the rest of you to be his bride.'

'You can draw straws,' suggested Vonnie.

'Loser wins,' said Freda.

'Winner wins,' said Jerome, somewhat affronted. 'To be the bride of Robinson Crusoe, it's better than being the bride of Alexander.'

'Count me out,' said Roxane. 'I've done enough for the human race.'

'I'm married still,' said Eva. 'Good as, to Darius. It can't be me.'

'I'm married, too,' said Freda. 'Nearly. *De facto*. To Sergio. That counts me out.'

'Besides, Robinson, if that's him, doesn't want to marry anyone. He took one look at us and ran away.'

'Jerome,' said Eva, 'did I ever mention it? We are cannibals. That's why Robinson ran away. He is scared of us. And you are very, very plump.'

Vonnie nodded. 'Yum, yum.'

Jerome started in horror. Then he relaxed. 'You're joking. Cannibals are black, and they don't wear any clothes. I know that.'

'That is a racist remark,' said Eva indignantly. 'Cannibals are black? How do you know? Have you seen any, I mean, before now?'

Jerome looked very worried.

'It's a stereotype,' said Eva. 'I learned that in sociology.'

Freda asked, 'Where's the sacrificial knife? Did you bring it with you from Melbourne, Mum?'

'It's in here somewhere,' said Eva, rummaging in her handbag.

'You're having me on,' said Jerome. 'Stereotypes don't eat people.'

'There's always what we cannibals call the kernel of truth in the stereotype, Jerome. Hey, though, see that cave over there? Do you think that might be the way back for you? There's a certain haze over the entrance.'

Jerome looked back over his shoulder.

'Go on, go and see,' Vonnie prompted. 'Check it out.'

'I might just go and have a look,' said Jerome. Then he walked over and out of their lives forever.

'Nice guy, Vonnie,' said Roxane. 'But the obsessive type. You've got to watch that sort.'

'Marriage!' said Vonnie. 'I've got far better things to do with my life than get married at fifteen!'

'That's the spirit!' said Eva. 'Come, let's explore this place where we now find ourselves. I'm sure there's a perfectly rational explanation for everything. This is, after all, the twentieth century, and we are inhabitants of Melbourne, Australia, and you know, I don't really believe, in my heart of hearts, that we are on an island near the mouth of the river Oronoco, inhabited by Robinson Crusoe and his man Friday, sometime in the late seventeenth century. I believe that we are in the Dandenongs, east of Melbourne, and that the elderly gentleman we saw tending his goats is far from being Robinson Crusoe, but more a crazed local who is a few bob short of the full quid. Let us keep marching downhill in this direction, following this stream, and we shall shortly arrive at a place of settlement, and, if I am not mistaken, find ourselves at the Upwey railway station on the Belgrave line. Come, follow me.'

As they walked down the hill, Mickie woke up, and smiled a benificent smile on those of her family gracious enough to carry her. She waved royally at the trees, and at the birds which swooped in welcome.

'I wonder,' said Freda, looking at her baby. 'Would it have been worth it, for Mickie to have stayed in Macedon, and become its queen? Have I deprived her of her rightful heritage, by insisting that I, as a mother, must stay with her, through thick and thin? Through insisting, through everything that has happened, that her true family is Australian, and resides in Melbourne?'

'Queens get deposed,' said Eva, with conviction. 'I learned that in my study of ancient history. If Mickie comes back with us, she is in no danger of court insurrections, or external conquests.'

'I love her so much,' said Freda. 'And Sergio does, too, and he wouldn't like it, if I came back without her, and said I left her behind, to become a queen, to fulfil her proper destiny. She will never fulfil her proper destiny now.'

'It is woman's lot,' said Eva. 'That's what I learned in Women's Studies. Most of us feel we were born to greatness, but circumstances have conspired against us. Women have to make their own greatness for themselves.'

'Which we have,' said Roxane, with feeling.

'It is now our duty to raise Mickie to be a loving and nurturant ruler of the world. There's a lovely diddums,' said Eva, tickling Mickie under the chin.

Mickie smiled, serene, radiant, and knowing.

Freda was aghast. 'I'm not worthy. I don't know how to raise a future Queen of the World.'

'You just have to train her to be powerful, but nice.'

'Never mind, darling, we'll all help out,' said Eva.

They continued down the hill, until they came, as Eva had predicted, to the Upwey railway station, and there they waited two hours for the train, and made their way slowly home again, stopping at all stations.